ROSS NEWBURY. /A GI

CHAPTER 1.

Following surprise orders from his superiors in army intelligence only yesterday, **Jack Rogers** carried on along the street which formed the South side of **Windsor Square London SW11**, looking for number No.47, glancing at notes he had made from a card displayed in the window of the local post office, (after telephoning as requested) .

The postcard was written in copperplate handwriting announcing that 'Accommodation is offered by a lady of this parish, please telephone 0207-39562 to arrange a viewing.' He thought it to be a bit flowery in that day and age, but presumed the writer was trying to set an image for the sort of person they were looking for as a lodger.

He was not sure if he fitted the criteria as he knew his general appearance was not exactly that of a gentleman, but felt he was able to project a reasonable image to satisfy the lady of the house, he had always seemed to be able to please the female acquaintances of his varied past. Especially with the more mature ladies, as he had presumed his possible future land-lady to be.

Having located the house, he noted that No 47 was a tall, imposing four floor Georgian property, with steps leading up to an imposing columned portal and solid Oak front door.

On approaching that front portal, and before he could knock the door was suddenly thrown open by a busy looking lady of indeterminate age, obviously rushing out somewhere, calling back to the inner house area in a loud, strident voice, "you have a handsome young man on your doorstep Anne, better come out to see to him." Jack all but doffing his cap said "good morning madam, I phoned earlier" but was cut short by the lady in a hurry, saying, "it's not me you need to speak to, it's **Mrs. Eden-Smythe**, she's just coming!" she then rushed off down the steps to street level.

The lady of the house was answering the phone in her study and placing a hand over the mouthpiece, called out "I will be there in just a minute." and now continued her conversation over the phone. "Yes Director, I understand, I will be ready for collection when you need me; I think that must be the gentleman you referred to at the door now, goodbye", replacing the handset, she headed for the front hallway.

As she appeared, Jack noted she was a tall, upright, elegant looking, with an air of breeding and authority, probably in her mid, seventies, he estimated. He repeated his former greeting of "good morning madam, I phoned earlier from the post office regarding your display card offering accommodation."

In a precise, English Public School, accent, she replied, "oh yes! Please do come in, I have been expecting you," closing the door behind him as he entered, saying "please follow me, if you would."

Jack followed into a high ceilinged entrance hall decorated in the style of another decade, with much Maroon and gold leaf trim against a Cream background. Which Jack guessed would prove to be the general theme throughout the house.

Into a cosy living room of indeterminate furnishing style, originally of good quality, if a little out of date by modern standards, yet containing a rather large and up-to date television set beside the Adam-style fireplace.

"Please sit down Mr...?" She stopped in mid-sentence awaiting his clarification of surname, to which he replied "Rogers, Jack Rogers madam" hoping he was using the correct amount of deference and politeness to strike the right note.

Seating herself in an overstuffed armchair and indicating another one opposite for him to sit, she said "Yes; Mr. Rogers. Would you mind if I asked you to tell me a little about yourself so that I may assess your suitability for the kind of tenant I am looking for?"

Jack thought to himself, 'I must be careful to say just enough to create a right impression' so began; "As my previous employer recently decided to re-locate his business back to New York, for family reasons, I was unfortunately redundant, and as my apartment is located within a commercial property owned by my firm, I am required to move on, hence my need for other accommodation, until such time as I can be sure of my future movements. But that should be at least several months."

As the lady made notes on a small pad at her side he continued, "I'm considering new business opportunities, or employment of some kind at present. But my previous employer was most generous with my compensation package, due to our long acquaintance, and his very good deal on the sale of his U.K. holdings. I am therefore quite able to pay my way during that period.

Prior to that employment, over 16 years, I was for some time in the Army, with the Royal Signals Regiment, as a motor engineer and dispatch rider, due to previous experience within those fields. of that Regiment.

(Not able to mention his connection with the Intelligence side.)

He continued, "at one time, married, but then divorced. However, my ex-wife has re-married and moved to Canada with her new husband, and my son, so that I have little contact with them now".

Mrs. Eden-Smythe OBE, was still busy making notes on a little pad of pale blue paper with a gold plated propelling pencil, she finished and said "thank you Mr. Rogers that was most frank, may I ask if you are in any way a D.I.Y. person, bearing in mind your past engineering experience? I am asking this as it may help with my decision and the question of rent."

Jack had always been quite handy with most facets of D.I.Y. and realized why the question was being put to him, so replied; "as a matter of fact I can paint reasonably well, enjoy solving and correcting technical problems, quite competent as a woodworker, understand electrics to some degree, but would not attempt major installations. I hope this helps?"

Again the lady of the house completed her notes before replying, "That sounds most satisfactory, shall I show you the rooms? Then if acceptable, we can discuss rent etc; Over a cup of tea."

With that, she rose to lead the way up two flights of stairs to a small landing leading to a bathroom and sizable bedroom/sitting room, again dated, but clean and comfortable. Then a further small staircase, leading perhaps to a further box room or roof access, he guessed.

Jack was more than satisfied with this accommodation and the general ambiance of the old house, although he was aware of committing himself to a certain amount of work in the near future, due to the rather worn-out state of the property.

To his future land-lady he said "yes; I think the rooms would suit me very well thank you, providing we can agree mutual terms."

"The bathroom facilities are of course for your use only" replied Mrs. Eden-Smythe, shall we go back to the sitting room for that tea and discussion."

On reaching the ground floor she said, "I will just be in the kitchen preparing the tea, perhaps you would like to sit there instead, and you would need to know your way around there anyway."

"Yes, thank you, I'd like that", said Jack thinking, 'she seems to have her mind made up already' which pleased him.

He followed her through to the rear of the house, emerging into large old fashioned kitchen, the centre piece being a huge brick-built fireplace with built-in Aga cooker.

"Please take a seat "she said, pointing to a large wooden table surrounded by several wheel back kitchen chairs, all in keeping with country- style comfort.

He sat at the table imagining the days of old when this would have been the domain of the cook and other servants of the time.

He could see that the lady had gone to some trouble to prepare in advance for his visit, as a matching set of Royal Dalton crockery was neatly laid out on a tray, with a selection of small sandwiches and homemade cakes on a tall stand, which reminded him that he had not eaten since breakfast, then only coffee and toast at home. He would not be able call that home for very much longer of course, having notice to quit by the end of next month

"Do help yourself Mr. Rogers, the kettle has just boiled, how do you take your tea? I prefer lemon with mine, but it just a matter of taste don't you think?"

Jack had the impression that she was warming to him and had little opportunity to talk to strangers, as she was beginning to babble on a little, but he didn't mind that, as it was to his advantage after all.

He replied "I like Lemon on occasion but with a spoonful of sugar please", whilst helping himself to the scrumptious looking food, realising that he was using his best vocabulary to match this lady.

Mrs. Eden-Smythe sat down opposite and began to pour tea for them both, "Now, we must 'talk turkey' as they say. I have in mind a rent of £500 per. calendar month, including main meals. If you could agree to work for a few hours per week, to do certain maintenance work that you would feel able to carry out.

Although Jack took some time to drink his tea seeming to consider the offer, he knew it was most reasonable and more than within his capabilities.

"That seems to be most satisfactory, but may I ask, what if I should consider some jobs to be beyond my competence to carry out safely. I would not like you to feel that I was avoiding the work."

She had obviously expected this to come up as she readily replied "I feel sure that in time we should learn to trust and respect each other's opinion, and if we both consider that a specialist should be brought in, you could supervise that work for me, could you not?"

It suited Jack very well so he replied "in that case my only question is, when it would be convenient for me to move in?" "I must vacate my present apartment by the end of next month, but could move to a Hotel if that is too soon."

"I wouldn't hear of it, I will have **Mrs. Tilson** prepare the rooms for you in the next few days, after which, with my legal adviser's approval, you can make the move as suites you."

Jack had wondered who kept the place so clean apart from Mrs. Eden-Smythe, who was obviously an organised person and he suspected, much more intelligent than she liked to portray to the outside world. "Mrs. Tilson? Is she perhaps a part time housekeeper then?"

"Oh! Much more than that, she is a godsend to us, with cleaning, cooking and organising our domestic requirements. She and her Husband rent the basement flat from me on a mutual arrangement similar to the one we have just discussed. Her husband is a Black Cab owner/driver, whose passion luckily is gardening; he has access to the rear garden directly from their flat, so keeps it in good condition all year round."

Jack was relieved to hear that there was a gardener, it was one job he was loath to tackle and had been concerned that it may have become one of his duties, saying, "that sounds like an ideal arrangement all round, and it would certainly suit me, as I am not the most enthusiastic of gardeners, to put it mildly, but would be happy to assist in any heavy work of course."

"I am sure Mr.Tilson will be relieved to know you are here also, as he tends to get stuck with many jobs he would rather not do, being the only man in the house", agreed Mrs. Eden-Smythe.

"You mentioned 'us!'Would that be the lady I met going out as I arrived?" Jack asked.

"Yes, that is my companion, **Miss. Nora Aston**, she used to work for my husband as headmistress of his Prep-school, but when the school started to fail financially, and as he was taken ill with a stroke; Being a trained nurse, she moved in with us and after he died, just sort of stayed on, but she has her own life and being financially self sufficient, is no burden to me and is a great friend."

He wondered at this arrangement but considered it to be none of his business, so simply said, "I see, thank you, I understand the house occupants now and will conduct myself accordingly."

His future landlady laughed and said "Oh please don't concern yourself Mr. Rogers, we are all quite relaxed it this household and as we both live on the different floors, not likely to clash at all, and do feel free to use the kitchen etc. as you wish."

One more thing had occurred to Jack as they talked about room usage and asked, "Would there be a space available for storage of a few personal items I may wish bring with me. I have already arranged for the disposal and storage of my present furniture, but would like to decide just what to leave or hang onto."

The lady thought for while then said "of course, did you notice the little staircase leading from your landing area? That leads to a small box room with access to the roof, you could certainly use that."

"Many thanks, that would do very well and if that is all, perhaps I should leave you now to consider what we've said, as I'm sure you would like to clarify things with your advisor and perhaps check my references." With that he passed over several documents covering his personal details saying, "Should I pay you a deposit and advance rental now, or when we sign the agreement? All my details and telephone numbers are here, including my solicitor's.

Mrs. Eden-Smythe then became businesslike again, as she realised that she had allowed herself to be carried away by the presence of this personable young man and had forgotten to ask such details. "That would be most satisfactory Mr. Rogers, I will contact my solicitor today and give him all the details, would you mind if he needs to telephone you at all?"

"That would be fine, the number I have left is a mobile phone, as I shall be out quite a lot looking for business opportunities, I can be in touch at anytime," said Jack, pointing to his card and other notes of reference on the table.

Mrs. Eden-Smythe stood up and offered her hand, saying "thank you for coming Mr. Rogers, I have enjoyed our meeting and feel sure all will be in order and that we shall get on well together, should you decide to go ahead with our arrangement."

Jack also stood up to take her proffered hand and said "my mind is quite made up and baring complications, I look forward to moving in very soon."

With that he made his way to the kitchen door saying, "Shall I see myself out?" As he already felt quite at home there.

"Please do, I shall look forward to meeting you again in the near future." She then began to bustle about clearing the tea things as he left. Suddenly realising that she felt a little flushed at his leaving, which was quite silly of course.

On closing the front door, Jack looked up at the facade of that lovely old house, feeling that he had found a comfortable new home and somehow, although with little evidence, a new future !!

Little did he know just how true that was to be? Although he had been told by his superiors that he would be welcomed at the house, he did not expect it to be quite so easy and convenient to his situation.

After the departure of her visitor, Mrs. Anne Eden-Smythe had spent some time considering the meeting to be sure that she had not been carried away by the occasion, as she had so few visitors these days. Being fully aware that she had taken to this man, his manner was that of someone used to meeting people and knowing how to behave in accordance with the situation, in this case wishing to impress upon her that he would be a trustworthy person to have in the house.

Apart from the recommendation by the Director, her boss at the Ministry of Defence that this man should be an asset to the household.

He appeared to be happy with the accommodation offered and the terms she had suggested, being aware that it would be quite possible to ask for more rent in that location, but more concerned with having a man around the house with some knowledge and work skills that she badly needed, instead of having to put her trust in local builders.

She sorely missed old Albert who had maintained the property since her husband's day, but had unfortunately had to retire through ill health a couple of years ago and the tradesmen used since seemed unreliable, erratic and expensive.

Nora had always been helpful around the house and still would if asked, but did not used to need to be asked. She had been someone to sit down with to enjoy afternoon tea and other meals for a conversation. But nowadays much more was happening in Nora's life away from the house.

Especially with one particular lady in her new group of friends, from the way Nora spoke of this 'Jocelyn' and her house, which seemed to be the regular meeting place for that group, so that she now spent more time there than at Windsor Square.

Anne was pleased for her, as she had little to occupy her after the closure of the school, which had been her whole life prior to the death of Anne's husband, when the school was thriving as an education centre, if not financially! Nora's friends were obviously of a certain gender orientation as was she.

Although she and her husband John had always been aware, it was hardly ever discussed, they did not consider such a personal matter to be their business and it had no impact upon the school activities, being a boy's only establishment.

Anne hoped that having another person to consider and in particular a man would give her a new interest in life, if only to get the house back into some sort of improved condition, as she had been only too aware of its deterioration. It was not so much the cost (though she hated to waste money) as the fact that she had no one to trust in these matters anymore.

Yet for some unknown reason she already felt that she could put her trust in Mr. Rogers having only met him for the first time today and only then for approximately an hour.

That disturbed her a little, as she was not sure just why, perhaps after not being close to a man for so long, she had been flattered by his manner, yet that was silly, as he must be at least 20 years her junior. Then she thought, 'Oh! What did it matter, it was only in her imagination after all, why shouldn't she have a little excitement'? The main thing was that she now had something new to occupy her days, at least for a while, as she was unsure how long Mr. Rogers would decide to stay. He had explained that he was planning for a new future; hence he could move at any time.

Unaware at this time, that she was about to be called upon again by her old boss in the near future, to help to resolve a possible National Crisis, even though she had been officially retired for some time.

She then busied herself with phoning her solicitor **(Mr.Wetherall),** to set things rolling, knowing that he would start by cautioning her on being certain of her facts before committing to this new venture, as he always did, having been the family legal advisor for many years.

Back to her list; first she must settle the legal and financial details with Mr.Wetherall in the morning; her appointment was for 9.15 and as it was a good 20 minutes walk, she must set off by 8.45. So that was noted.

Then she must advise Mrs.Tilson of the situation tomorrow, so that she can start to prepare the rooms for occupation and let Anne have a list of requirements, although that had been mostly seen to prior to the advertisement being placed in the Post Office window.

Next, a note must be made to ask Mr. Rogers what his food preferences might be, although Anne knew she was getting somewhat ahead of herself, she was quite looking forward to preparing meals for a man again, with the help of Mrs.Tilson of course, something else to plan for on a daily basis. She had stopped trying to plan meals for her and Nora, as it was impossible to know when she would be there and it was not the same just for herself.

Then to a plan of campaign for house improvements once he had settled in of course, she must not frighten him away again.

She continued with her work around the house, as Mrs.Tilson was away today, taking her son to the dentist. This occupied the rest of her afternoon, apart from a snack in the mid-afternoon, and some letter writing.

She could then think of nothing more at the moment, so returning her notebook to the bureau, decided to go to bed to read for a while, she had a busy day tomorrow.

Just as she settled herself into bed and started to read, the front door banged, as it always did when Nora came home and as Anne heard her come up the stairs and near her bedroom door, called out "Nora could you spare a minute, I need to talk to you?" "Certainly dear, be back in a minute." Nora called.

A few minutes later, Nora bustled into Anne's bedroom to say brightly "right now dear, what's the news is it to do with that young man on the doorstep this morning?" Anne laughed saying, "I'm sure Mr. Rogers would love to hear you say that, he is probably approaching 50 years old for your information, although very personable." Nora grimaced and said, "Yes but to you and I he is still a young man, isn't he?"

Again Anne chuckled at her friend's enthusiasm saying, "anyway, he had replied to the advertisement about the rooms and I had a long chat with him, showed him the accommodation and to cut a long story short, we got on very well together and he seems to be just the gentleman we were looking for, so I am meeting my solicitor in the morning to set things in motion."

"My goodness, he must have been personable! You made up your mind very quickly didn't you, normally you would need to see many more and then chew over your many notes before deciding." Anne replied, "Well I feel he is the right person and providing his references stand up to scrutiny, I shall offer the rooms to him, so there!"

For once Nora managed to look serious and a little concerned saying, "just so long as you are absolutely sure, I would love to think you could find other interests, I know I have not been around much lately for companionship, but I have found another life since the school closed and it makes me happy, do you understand Anne?" "Of course I understand, I'm so happy for you, you have been such a help since John died, I am always pleased to have you as a close friend and companion, but you are not tied to me in any way."

Nora stood up, leaned over to give Anne a peck on the cheek and said "well goodnight darling, let's hope your right and all works out for the best, I'll see you in the morning!"

As Nora walked back to her bedroom she had a guilty feeling of relief, as it had been on her mind for some time that she may soon decide to move in with her friend Jocelyn, but she did not wish to let Anne down, when she had been happy to live in this house for several years.

Therefore if this new chap turned out to be trustworthy and decided to stay for a while, it would be just right for Anne and at the same time, convenient for Nora.

However, there was no immediate rush, she would not mention it for the time being, it could wait until she saw how things worked out with the new lodger and it did not interfere with her present lifestyle at all.

Selfishly, she hoped it would all go well for Anne, if simply to assuage her own guilty feelings and give her the opportunity to plan for a new life, which she found quite exciting.

Thinking back on her life, Nora had always known that she was not attracted to men in the way that other women were, but still found them good company just in a different way, as friends. Her life had always been a busy one, being trained in nursing, when she had moved on to teaching in the profession, after graduating from University.

Then moved into academic teaching proper, this had kept her constantly occupied and taken up her whole life, (apart from a couple of flings with colleagues on the way). She loved being involved with children and watching their achievements as they grew up. Hoping she had made a difference to their young lives. Above all, she had enjoyed the responsibility and kudos of being headmistress at St. Stephens School, alongside John Eden-Smythe and other dedicated colleagues.

On moving into the house with him and Anne on the occasion of his illness, she had again found fulfilment, after the disappointment of the school's failure.

But after his death and being a friend to Anne in her bereavement for a while, was then at a loss what to do. Being of an age when schools were no longer interested in her expertise.

She was financially provided for by a secure pension supplied at the start of her nursing career, continually added to by her over the years, and Maturing at the Civil Service age of 55.

Now here she was, on the verge of a new life where she felt comfortable with like friends, who were also enjoying the un-encumbered bachelor type lifestyle.

But Anne's news had relieved her of what she had perceived her duty to her friend and would not feel so bad about moving on. That was always providing that this new fellow turned out to be as reliable as Anne seemed to think, of course. So climbing into her bed she settled into a dreamless sleep, with a clear conscience.

CHAPTER 2.

Windsor Square was typical of many such areas in central London dating back to Victorian and Georgian periods, when these developments were in demand by the wealthy gentry of that time, who were looking for town houses from which to do the necessary business and shopping transactions in a capital city, required to run their country estates, with travel by horse being so long and arduous at that time.

Many of the professions required to service this trade, doctors, lawyers, dressmakers, bankers and so on proved most lucrative, therefore some could afford to purchase and live in these desirable properties, As did many of the more senior members of Parliament and the military services.

This kind of clientele were used to, and expected the best, therefore the houses and facilities when built, reflected this, including walled gardens to each property, where staff could deal with many of the chores required to run such a household at that time, including the production of fresh food.

Also a central park area was created where the gentry could exercise, walk their pets and parade in style for all to see, usually on a Sunday after church when the latest creations were shown off.

In the modern, busy environment of today these squares provided an air of quiet sanctuary, even though they are often quite close to a noisy major artery into the city centre. This tranquillity was jealously guarded by the older residents in particular, occasionally causing some strife with certain of the ‘newcomers’ as they didn’t see the peace to be quite so important.

Therefore Windsor Square had a residents association for the purpose of maintaining the standards set many years before, the leader of this was a **Colonel Batesby-Fortesque**, who revelled in the position, as it allowed him to bring to bear his military training.

But often tried to press matters a little too far and was generally thought of as a bit of pain by other residents, but as no one else relished the position and realising the job had to be done, they left him to his various rules and regulations, providing it didn't intrude too much.

Some leading lights of the association were: **Lord Swinburne of Malwana**; as he liked to be known, having once been High Commissioner of that area of West Africa.

Sir Clive Simpson, ex –government Minister of Arts and Culture, covering Opera, Ballet etc. which he constantly attended and sometimes wrote about for the local newspapers as a critic, being in his opinion an expert, he liked nothing more than to try to educate anyone who would listen.

Gloria Coltrane; retired actress of the old school, constantly reliving her days in Hollywood, where she claims to have once appeared opposite the great Charles Laughton, although no one could remember having seen such a film. Yet she did seem to have many theatrical type visitors who all seemed to be rather overdressed and overloud, but harmless.

Jim Parker, A young, self made millionaire in the advertising industry, somewhat out of touch with those aims of the resident's association. Considering them to be old fashioned and stuffy.

From time to time there tended to be a clash of egos between some residents of the square, as many were retired from careers in which they had been a figure of authority and it did not sit well with certain of them to be considered to be "pompous old twits" among other less flattering phrases.

On these occasions a meeting would be held in the old school, where personal views were aired and if it was felt that the leader had perhaps exceeded his authority, they would vote the Colonel down, when he had the good sense to accept rather than lose his privileged position, even though it was a voluntary one, he cherished the authority he thought he held.

One of the biggest problems he faced was un-authorised car parking perpetrated by visitors to the square and other 'outsiders'. Each property had allocated spaces, but as there were never enough, it was the colonel's given duty (or so he thought) to stick large labels across the windscreen of such an errant vehicle, which tended to cause some upset among the drivers, to say the least!

Some of the properties had been converted into apartments, creating an even bigger problem, for the association and its leader in particular.

Many had tried the gates of a locked private school which occupied almost half of the park area, most were put off by a large Green sign attached to the tall rusting gates stating in bold Gold lettering :-

SAINT STEPHENS PREPARATORY SCHOOL

FOR BOYS 4 YRS. TO 11 YRS.

'PLEASE KEEP GATES CLEAR AT ALL TIMES'

Principal: Mr. J .Eden-Smythe. **Head: Miss N. Aston.**

Although the school had closed some years ago, the colonel would still protect the official wording with zeal, stating to those drivers, "Can't you read? Please move on!" Alternatively he would stick one of his labels across the windscreen, with a similar notation added.There were now few of the original long term residents left, as age and the economics of present day running costs began to encroach, but Mrs. Eden-Smythe was still a respected member of this group, as her husband's family had been living there since the time of the first world war;

When, on his return from service in Naval Intelligence, her husband's grandfather had re-established the private school there, which had been in existence since earlier decades.

Previously under the auspices of an obscure religious faith, (this later fell out of favour after fraud allegations) had been granted permission under an old land governance in the original plans, allowing for the;-

'Establishment of an Education Facility for the children of entitled residents of that estate, with accommodation consisting solely of low roofed buildings, and secure recreation areas for use as seen fit and by agreement with those residents'.

The above document will prove to be of great importance, as will be seen later in this storey.

CHAPTER 3.

Mrs. Eden-Smythe arrived at the offices of Ainsworth, Smith and Wetherall, at 10 minutes past nine, punctual as ever for her appointment at 9.15am. On recognising the lady as an old client, the receptionist asked her to take a seat, whilst pressing the intercom button and informing the listener that his client had arrived.

The inner door was opened almost immediately by Mr. Robert Wetherall, who appeared to be the epitome of the old time lawyer, in his late sixties, wearing an immaculate white shirt but rather gaudy blue, pink and green tie, (a gift from his Grandson) under the usual pinstriped dark blue suit.

He greeted his old established client who he had known most of his adult life, since the days when his father had acted for Anne's family over many years. Indeed they had met on several occasions when younger; at parties given by mutual friends, she had even attended his wedding.

He showed her in to his office and to the comfortable looking, leather elbow chair across his desk, both of which had seen better days. Asking "how are you these days Anne haven't seen you since John's funeral and the will reading?" (He was aware that she was well taken care of financially, via an endowment, life assurance and pensions).

"I am quite well in myself Robert, but do miss having old Albert around since he retired, hence the house is ailing somewhat. That is the main reason for my decision to let out the upper rooms to a suitable man, who can help with the work needed and costs, taking some of the responsibility away from me.

She handed him the various sheets of paper containing his details given to her by Mr. Rogers, plus her own notes on the agreed arrangement.

Mr.Wetherall perused the notes for a while, then commented "it seems to be a reasonable arrangement, I take it you are entirely satisfied with this gentleman Anne?"

"Yes, I spent some time chatting to him and we seemed to get on well, but most of all I feel that I could trust him to carry out his side of the deal" she affirmed. "Also he has been vetted by my old boss." (the lawyer was aware of her past employment) "He has just taken redundancy with a good compensation package and is looking to set up a business in the future, but assures me that he is in no hurry, so that he currently has time available to help me." Mr.Wetherall made a note on his pad saying "did you have an initial period of tenancy in mind?" Anne was ashamed to not have thought of a time period and said so. "In that case, may I suggest 6 months to start with, until you are sure? We can always extend it later if required, as we of course hope it will be. But it is now a matter of law to set some time limit on a lease."

"Oh dear!" she said, "when I first considered it, I thought I just placed the card in the Post Office window and that was that, I didn't think of leases and so on. I don't think Mr. & Mrs.Tilson have one do they?" He replied. "That is because their flat is under a tied arrangement with Mrs.Tilson being your employee. Should she leave your employ, she would be required to vacate it. That was arranged by your husband when they first came to you." He continued, "Anytime accommodation is rented nowadays there must be a legal arrangement, in order to protect both parties if a dispute ensues."

"Well, do you know that in all this time, I have never known that, but it is why we employed your services after all, so I will follow your advice of course; what happens next then?"

Her solicitor had known all about her husband's long illness and Anne's devotion to him and that when he eventually passed away, she had been at a loss for some time on how to manage the house.

He replied, "after all you did have other things on your mind, after John's passing, and prior to that, he dealt with all of the business and legal requirements, so there was no reason for you to be aware of such things. Also you had your own career to deal with."

"Now I have to check these reference contacts given by Mr. Rogers, to confirm his suitability for your tenancy agreement, including his financial stability. I see that he has given his legal advisors name, it so happens that I know the partners quite well, so that there should not be any delays in settling matters.

I shall prepare a lease for both parties to sign and an invoice for a holding deposit and two month's rent in advance, once these are dealt with to our satisfaction, he can move in when convenient to you and Mr. Rogers."

"My goodness!" said Anne, "I would never have thought to do all that and could not have asked for so much money in advance; thank goodness you are dealing with such matters for me, do we need to ask for so much though, it seems quite a lot?"

He smiled, saying "I can assure you that it is quite normal, and Mr. Rogers would expect it to be so, as from what you have told me about his past employment, he would be used to dealing with such property matters in his job. The deposit would of course be returnable at the end of his tenancy providing there was no damage to your property, furnishings etc." "By the way, as you are letting furnished, you will need to provide me with a inventory of the fixtures, fittings and furnishings, to form part of the contract, or I can arrange for someone from this office to come along to do it for you, although there would be an added cost on top of the preparation of the lease." "Something else I wouldn't have thought of," said Anne, "but don't bother your staff, it will give me a job to do, after all I am always making lists, I'll get it to you in the next couple of days." Then she added, "I take it that I will pay for this lease then?" Her lawyer chuckled, as he knew she could be a careful spender "Oh yes! You are a landlord now and these are your new responsibilities.

But just think, you will be able to claim it as legitimate expenses on your tax return." Standing up, Anne grumbled "I suppose I should be thankful for small mercies. Well goodbye Robert, I shall wait to hear from you in the near future."

He saw her to the door with a wry smile, as he knew he had hit a raw spot with Anne, she didn't like to spend on what she considered to be unnecessary items. 'At least, he thought, it was a sign that she was back to her old self again.'

Anne made her way back onto the street, then heading for home she considered Mr. Wetherall's humour about her care over money and thought, 'right, I'll show him, if I am a property tycoon now I will treat myself." With that she quickened her step and headed for Kensington High Street, one of her favourite 'window shopping' areas, to look for a nice new day dress ready for her perceived change of direction in life. After all she was quite comfortable financially and all being well that should soon improve even further with an extra income.

But in her own mind she was sure it was more to do with this un-explained excitement she felt since the visit by Mr. Rogers.

CHAPTER 4.

As Jack travelled home on the underground he contemplated the possible new future, and found himself reviewing his past life up to his current forty ninth year.

At the age of 31, he truly thought that he was at last settled on a solid career with the New York Auto Storage Company. Being at a dead end in life (with a few indiscretions on the way), and having tried differing careers after his years in the army, from, motor engineer, to selling various commodities including, door to door brushes etc. (which he hated) and Television in its infancy where he did very well for a few years, through to bad debt collection, (which he also hated).

In all this time he was still being held under a reserve contract to his old Regiment in Army Intelligence, receiving a small annual remuneration as a sleeping agent, with his mundane lifestyle as a cover.

But then he had read an advertisement for a trainee manager in a car parking organisation, which seemed to be a useful skill for the future, and having family and a mortgage to consider, thought it to be worth a try.

In the event, It proved to be a good move, enabling him to enter a long term career, moving through the ranks to become general manager in charge of some 56 sites all over the U.K. including many prestigious hotels and real estate. (*Allowing him to travel around the country unobtrusively).*

In all some 16 years, until fate decided that the company would be sold to a competitor as the principal moved back to New York.

Although he was offered a position of sorts by the new owners, he had no desire to become a lesser member of a rival nationwide firm with a somewhat shady reputation, so opted to accept a considerable compensation package from his old boss, hence his current position.

He felt sure that the expertise and contacts gained over past years would be most useful, with current local authority parking restrictions and the premiums being asked for any available space.

Also he felt that here was opportunity within his field of knowledge to be found; particularly in central London, but he needed to find that niche somewhere.

At least he now had only himself to consider, since his family life had failed some years ago, when he had moved into town, and luckily into his current address.

He was loathe to give up his present living quarters, located as they were close to Vauxhall bridge with views across the Thames, but he had been compensated fairly after the firm's sale, and understood his moving out to be part of the deal, after all, he had been living in their property free of rent for some years now.

Admittedly it suited the company's' requirements, located as it was above the London area operations offices where one of the major sites housed not only extensive auto storage facilities, but also London's first fully automatic drive-through car washing facility, instigated and overseen by Jack, and proving to be very successful, as the constant queue of cars daily could testify.

But that was all due to be relocated now and the buildings demolished in order that a new residential development could take place, these properties would of course be of the more expensive price range, in such a prime position in central London and overlooking the river.

Even so, Jack wondered if fate had stepped into his life again for a reason, not that he was a fatalist by nature, just that he felt comfortable after finding what seemed to be an ideal solution today, even if only of a temporary nature, until he found what he was looking for.

Yet somehow he had a feeling that it could prove to be a good move. If for no other reason than it would be nice to be pampered now and then, after such a long time living alone since his wife moved on.

As the train stopped at Vauxhall Station, he alighted and made his way to the apartment he had called home for several years now, to continue with his packing; at least he could now select what was to go with him or be left in the storage facility which he had arranged with a removal firm. Providing of course all went well with regard to the solicitor's enquiries,

This reminded him to contact his own solicitor to explain the details of the transaction and to expect contact from a Mrs. Eden-Smythe. He dialled the well known number and a familiar young lady's voice answered "Chapman Younger and Associates, may I assist you?" He grinned to himself, as he had always thought this greeting to be a little 'over the top'. "Hello Maisy, its Jack Rogers," "Oh! Mr. Rogers! "She exclaimed, "I keep telling you that is not my name, it's Barbara", he chuckled, "sorry but you will always be Maisey to me, it's in your voice, is **James** available?" A short wait, then James came on, "hello there, I thought you had retired with all your money in the bank."

They had become good friends over the years, as his firm dealt with most of the past transactions in the U.K. on behalf of New York Auto Storage Incorporated and it had been Jack's responsibility to deal with the various site negotiations and transactions involved. Hence a bond of trust had built between them.

Jack laughed and then said, "I'm Just ringing to warn you to expect a call from a firm of solicitors acting for a Mrs. Eden-Smythe, of 47.Windsor Square, W11. It's in connection with my renting rooms from her."

"So you've decided to take temporary lodgings after all, I thought you'd be buying a fancy property somewhere, how long do you want commit to in the first instance "Make it six months for now with an option for a year until I know where I shall be operating from, but it will certainly be in central London anyway."

"O.K. then, I'll call your mobile number as soon as I have the arrangements sorted, by the way, hate to mention it again, but you are aware of when you will be kicked out of your current place aren't you?" Jack laughed and said "Yes, and thanks for your sympathy, I might have known you'd be enjoying my plight."
"Right, see you for a drink sometime then, bye."

It had not occurred to Jack previously that a residential term should considered when discussing the tenancy with Mrs. Eden-Smythe, for some unknown reason he had presumed he would be there for some time, perhaps he had simply felt too comfortable immediately, but that was not very businesslike. After all, he was not even sure what direction his career was heading yet, never mind where he would be. But, that's why one employed professionals, so he could now leave them to carry out the various enquiries and settle the details.

No worries on that score due to the fine references provided by his ex. employer through Jack's own solicitor, and his latest financial situation could be proved beyond doubt at last.

Perhaps he should have made more positive moves towards buying a property, but as his future plans were so fluid, there seemed little point in that kind of commitment yet.

After working hard for a couple of hours sorting and packing furnishings, personal items, business documents etc. and marking the destinations, he decided to get out and about for a while and thought it a good opportunity to look at possible usable sites he had spotted earlier.

Jack thought he could use the time taken by the legal parties to sort out the details of his new accommodation, to continue looking around for the right opportunity to turn up, by perusing local newspapers, agent's property details etc. plus just plain foot slogging around the right areas of the central metropolis.

On leaving his apartment, he passed the busy office where had spent so much time over the years, when not at head office, which was located in the City business development of London Wall. It seemed unreal to him not to be called to solve some problem as soon as he appeared, and pleased to see the drive through car wash as busy as ever.

He could see **Berty Blacksmith** the manager busy as usual, then spotting Jack he waved, they had always got on well together from the time that he had been selected for training by Jack and the German manufacturers at the initial setting up of the system. By now, they were possibly the foremost authority in the U.K. on problem solving in that operation, he had seen it all, from water systems and rotary brushes freezing solid on a winters morning to cars being totally jammed within the machinery, with an irate driver screaming abuse inside the car. Hence the new owners had seen the good sense to make sure they re-employed Berty on favourable terms. Even so he had first asked Jack if he could work with him on any future projects, which was not yet possible due to the uncertainty. However, the new owners were made aware by Jack that he may be tempted to move on, unless well looked after, hence the good salary and bonus offer.

Waving back, Jack set off to walk the mile or so to look over possible property projects, still feeling that today was a good day for his future in some way.

After his walk and a fruitless search of the suggested properties, which he deemed totally unsuitable, Jack returned to his favourite watering hole, as he called the George Hotel. It was a typical London back street pub, located on a road which was once one of the main approaches to Vauxhall Bridge, but was no longer a major road, which suited the locals well.

The hostelry had been in a poor state when ex-Sergeant Jim Smith and his wife had invested most of their savings in its purchase and refurbishment some nine years ago, after both had retired from the Metropolitan Police within a few years of each other. (About the same time that Jack had moved into his present accommodation)

They had turned the trade around and it was now a most comfortable pub/restaurant and small hotel with six bed and breakfast type, letting rooms.

In fact it was on their opening night that Jack had first discovered the place.

He had already arranged that should the need arise; he had temporary accommodation available there as needed.

On entering and greeting the proprietors, a voice at his elbow said "what will it be then, I've been waiting to spot you", it was Berty Blacksmith. It seems he had taken the earlier suggestion literally about having a drink sometime. But it seemed there was another reason, as he was soon to find out, meantime the drinks were decided and food was ordered.

These were then carried to a corner table, once seated, Berty said, "since seeing you earlier, it occurred to me that you may just be able to help my brother." Knowing his rather obscure way of approaching a conversation, Jack simply responded with "Oh yes! How would that be then?" "Well he phoned me over the weekend from Swindon where he lives, to say that he and all of his mates had just received redundancy notices to say that the company they worked for, you know! Blake's was goin' bust. Although they knew it was on the cards for some time."

Jack considered this for a while; With the National Financial restrictions as they presently were; Blake's being suppliers of body parts to the motor trade, this was an obvious blow to all those ancillary companies dotted around the country, but how did that affect him? He allowed Berty to continue in his own way to get to the point.

Seeing that he was not making himself clear he continued; "The point is that he's been thinking of moving nearer to me and my missus as we all get on well together, they're sisters you know, and he will be lookin' for work in this area."

Jack was first of all surprised to hear about the close relationships but did remember that in conversation, Berty had often referred to visits back and forth to Swindon , which although in Wiltshire, was only a matter of around one and a half hour's drive, down the M4 motorway. It had become a major motor manufacturing town since Honda Motors decided to invest there some years before; by taking over the old Vickers aircraft works, including an airfield.

He replied "now I see what you are getting at and if he is half the worker that I know you to be, he would be a good man to have, but as I just don't know where I am heading at the moment, I can't offer anything, but will of course keep him in mind when I do." Providing it is in this area of course, but it could be some time into the future." Berty was unperturbed replying, "yeh! I understand that and it's O.K. because it's going to take him some time to sell up and find a place near me, I just thought it might be somethin' to consider in the future, I know he'd be good for you to work with."

"That's fine by me, let's leave it at that then, I've got your home and mobile phone numbers so will contact you if anything develops." "Anyway, how's the new company working out, are you getting on with them?"

"O.K., they tend to leave me alone to get on with my job, not that there's anyone there to tell me what to do anyway. Only you and me know how it all works over there eh?" "But what about when the site is developed, they must have plans for it?" Jack had been involved in the original talks between his old boss and the new owners when this was discussed.

As the car wash was such a money spinner and the location so well known, it was at one time being muted that it could perhaps be incorporated within this new development, but the architects involved were unhappy about that, as it was not the most aesthetic looking piece of machinery.

Also at that time the new people were hoping that Jack was likely to stay with them and they needed his expertise.

However, after meeting the current joint managing directors to discuss his future with them, it was obvious that they were more concerned with their own positions and his possible climb through their company ranks, than how useful he would be to their company.

Berty laughed and said "they still can't make up their minds, one day it's going to stay within the new buildings and then it might be moved lock, stock and barrel to one of their other sites, but as I pointed out to um!, it could not be as busy anywhere else, but they're not good at making decisions, too much infighting in the boardroom." He punched Jack on the arm, which was a mannerism of his in order to make a point, "I bet they were hoping you would be there to solve it for em!"

"There you are then, I knew you would, no wonder those wimps didn't really want you to join em!"

Jack chuckled saying, "I shouldn't let your new employers hear that sort of talk, it wouldn't endear you to them." Berty was non-repentant saying, "I wouldn't want 'em to 'ear me, but I've give 'em my opinions before now and as I say, they leave me alone." Having finished his drink and bought Berty another, Jack decided to take his leave saying that he had much to do at home.

Saying his goodbyes, and promising to contact Berty once he had something to offer, he set off for the walk back to his apartment

On the way he was reflecting on Berty's comments regarding the new owners of the business that had been almost his whole life for the last 16.years.

Jack had arrived at a similar impression when meeting the management of that particular group, namely; 'London Parking Limited' he knew the original owner and his methods and that the 'managing directors' he had met were simply employed to follow orders and take the flack. They were certainly not employed to answer back to the self appointed chairman, known within the profession as **'THE MAJOR'**, or his full title of **Major Kingston-Green**, who made sure he had total power in his organization, to which he was entitled after all said and done.

Jack had met him on a few occasions alongside his friend and boss **Ned Kane** to discuss possible co-operation on some projects, but Ned had little or no trust in this gentleman since he had obviously researched the opposition before coming to London and knew there was more than one blot on that man's past.

Indeed, one of the main objections Jack had to the man was when an offer was made for him to change companies after such a meeting, whilst his own boss was still in the building, which to his mind was underhanded.

The Major was of 'the old school' in the car parking profession and had built the business from a time when there were many derelict building plots about from the wartime bombing of London, but to be fair to him he had had the foresight to see the future of car usage, which was much lower in those days.

Becoming very wealthy over the following years yet was well known for not paying bills on time and under paying his employees.

Many of those meetings referred to were held in sumptuous offices and top hotels belonging to some of the best known property men of that time, as were the architectural firms involved. It was a time of re-building on a huge scale and everyone wanted a slice of the monetary cake.

Major Black had made it plain that he should get the first crack at the motor handling in each of the new developments, consisting mainly of large hotels and high grade residential blocks, due to his being there first.

In some ways that may have been true, but there had to be competition, also he had a poor reputation in the business world, so was not favoured.

Jack reflected as he neared his apartment, that attending those meetings had taught him a great deal in speaking skills and confidence for future negotiations within any new business venture he may consider. Indeed he had learned a great deal over the years within his given career of auto storage and organization and now considered himself somewhat of an authority on that particular subject. He had therefore decided to use the knowledge gained to pursue that course in his plans for the future.

A week after his visit to Windsor Square he received a phone call via the phone message service from his friendly lawyer, to say that he had heard from Mrs. Eden-Smythe's solicitor and that they had exchanged details. He asked if Jack could come to his office on the following day to sign the lease and be sure to bring his cheque book along. No time was given, but he presumed it could be fitted in between other appointments as it should not take too long to deal with.

Jack presented himself at his lawyer's offices the next morning, and approaching the reception desk, he spoke to the pleasant looking redhead sitting there saying, "morning Maisy! What a pleasant sight you are on a miserable morning, is your master available?"

"Oh! It's you again Mr. Rogers; I keep telling you my name is not Maisy. Anyway depends which master you mean, I've got several here."

"Now come on, you can let me call you Maisy can't you? Anyway, you are well aware who I mean; I've been coming here long enough."

Just then one of the inner doors to a conference room opened and his friend came out ushering a well dressed man, who Jack recognised as one of the leading property owners in 'The City', as he had met him on several occasions.

The gentleman was well known in the property world, with a reputation for shrewd investment in commercial buildings. Thanking the solicitor, he nodded to Jack and walked off towards the lifts.

"Morning James, I have a complaint to make about your receptionist, she won't let me call her Maisy and is treating me very disrespectfully." Poor Barbara was blushing when James said to him "you just leave her alone, she's the best secretary we have ever had, I'd rather sack you as a client."

He led the way into his office, pointed Jack to the chair across his desk, produced a legal looking document out of a drawer and pushed it towards Jack, saying "you should read that through whilst I finish off these notes from my last client," busying himself with a Dictaphone.

As he read the legalise of the lease, he saw that it contained all of the relevant details discussed with Mrs. Eden-Smythe, noting that it referred to an initial period of six months which suited him at the moment and duly signed it in the places marked for his signature.

James then handed him an invoice detailing the payments previously referred to, for which he duly wrote out a cheque, handing both back to James. Saying "is that it then, can I go now?" James reached for the document saying, "Just a minute, after I have witnessed your signature. Don't you want to know what you are committing yourself to, or are you in too much of a hurry?"

Jack had noticed several other clients seated in the waiting room and felt a little guilty at pushing in, so answered "I thought you had other clients waiting before me."

James laughed saying "don't flatter yourself, I wouldn't keep my important clients waiting just for you, my next appointment is not for 10 minutes yet." "Oh Charming!" said Jack, "so that's how you treat your old established clients, I'll remember that when I'm a millionaire and your desperate for work sometime."

Enjoying the banter with his friend, James retorted, "first of all it is your ex! Employers who are our clients, you only represented them, but if you promise to behave in our office, we may consider you as a client. As for you being a millionaire, I'll try not to get too excited about that possibility, it is most unlikely." He then stood up saying, "anyway now it's time for my next customer, you know, the paying kind, so clear out and leave our Barbara alone on your way out." Jack stood up, saying "O.K. I can take a hint; wait to hear from you then?"

James opened the door for him affirming as he passed through, "yes, should only take a few more days now, I'll see you for that drink next Friday at the squash club." Then to an attractive and expensively dressed lady sitting beside his office door, "good morning Mrs. Gilano, please come in", holding the door for her to pass through while glancing at Jack, knowing he would have a smirk on his face, then followed the lady in, closing the door behind him.

Heading for the lifts he called over his shoulder, "bye then Maisy, promise I shall be nicer to you next time, your boss tells me I must." She giggled, liking him in spite of his teasing, "Goodbye then Mr. Rogers, I do hope so"!

On reaching the street, he hailed a taxi to take him to the **Royal Gardens Hotel**, in Kensington High Street, to keep another appointment, with a past contact he had within his old profession.

He had received a telephone call from **Tom Clancy of Canada Parking Inc.** Whom he had met on occasion at various conferences and seminars to do with the transport controlling authorities, who were all trying to solve the same problem, that of a growing vehicle population on the same old road system. Jack presumed he was about to be offered a job with them, as being much smaller than competitors in the U.K. although big in Canada and USA, lacked local knowledge, which Jack had in abundance.

Arriving on the approach ramp of the five star hotel at the main entrance, the door was opened by Paddy the doorman saying, "good morning Mr. Rogers, how nice to see you again." Alighting from the taxi and paying the driver, Jack said "morning Paddy, a bit formal today aren't we?" He had known all of the door attendants for many years, as the hotel basement parking was controlled by his old company and he had used an office there together with one of his area managers.

Indeed, he had been in at the designing and building of this development with his previous boss and the architects. It had been something of a challenge due to the prime position on the edge of Kensington Gardens, but restricted space, hence a major part of the structure needed to be below ground, with very steep approaches.

Paddy replied with a smile "well, you are a customer now, not just an employee, any way, the assistant day manager is just inside waiting for a V.I.P. to arrive, and so I must be seen to do my job." Jack laughed and said "Oh dear! Does that mean I have to tip you then?" "I should be most upset if you did, I hope you are still a friend" and with that he touched his cap for effect and opened the main entrance door for him.

He crossed the main foyer, nodding to the assistant manager whom he had met a few times in the past when solving the odd internal problem, heading for the lounge and coffee shop to meet Tom.

He was sitting at a booth built into a corner with a pot of coffee on the table, he shook hands with Tom and sitting down was about to get the attention of a waiter, when Wendy appeared at his table with a tray holding a large croissant, black coffee and preserves and saying "

I saw you coming in and brought your usual order Mr. Rogers." "Thanks' Wendy" he said, smiling at her.

As she walked away, Tom remarked "now that's service for you, but I didn't get served like that when I came in." "Oh! Wendy and I are old pals, I've known her and her husband who also works here, for a long time, I was here on a regular basis, used it as a meeting place quite often" said Jack, we had an office in the basement garage." "Anyway to what do I owe the pleasure of this meeting, you will be paying I presume, I'm sure Canada Parking Inc. Can afford it"?

Tom smiled and said "O.K. if you insist, now we hear that your company has been sold off and your boss is moving back to the 'Big Apple', is that correct"? Nodding, Jack affirmed "correct, I am now un-employed, if that's what you are asking, but it was a voluntary decision I can assure you." "Must say, I couldn't imagine you moving into The Major's outfit, their methods are not yours" said Tom. "So would you be open to a job offer with us? It would be in a senior position of course."

"Sorry, but at the moment my future is a bit fluid as they say, until I decide what opportunities there are for my own enterprises and just where I might operate from, I shall not be making any decisions for some time, but many thanks for the offer, I'll keep it in mind for the future, if that's alright."

Tom smiled and said "I thought that might be your answer, my masters asked me to chat to you as we could do with your local knowledge and expertise as you can imagine."

"So you are intending to grow over here then are you? I thought you may feel that there is little room for more of the same." Jack remarked.

"We have no plans to compete in the same arena, as we don't have the connections over here, our operations in Canada and the U.S. are in a slightly different field, but I won't go into that aspect too much if you don't mind, at least until you decided to join us" said Tom.

Jack was fully aware of the activities of Canada Parking Inc. It had been part of his job to research them when they first decided to move into the U.K.

Their business model is based more on working with local authorities, supermarkets, hospitals and the like as professional operators of car parking facilities. This was a niche market of little interest to the main players, as they would not have sufficient control, with the sites owned totally by their clients.

It then occurred to Jack that another avenue may well be available to him on a part time basis so made the suggestion,."Perhaps we could come to an arrangement on a consultancy basis if you had a specific requirement for information at some time, it's something worth looking at later, but at no time could I jeopardise my compensation package, as there were certain agreements I made to protect the old and new company's privacy."

Tom mused for a while, and then said, "it could certainly be something to consider in the future, I'll put it to my board and get back to you sometime."

They both then stood up to shake hands bidding each other goodbye, as Tom beckoned to Wendy for the account.

Leaving him to pay the bill, Jack waved to her as he turned on his heel to head for the lift to take him down to the basement car park. Where he thought he should visit his old colleagues before leaving, they would know he had been there and as he had become friendly with them over the years, thought it right to call in.

On alighting from the lift into a familiar setting, he walked across to the operations kiosk only find that he knew no one on duty. On asking for them by name he was told that they had been sent elsewhere in London to other sites. So! Thought Jack, they have already started the usual system of disruption of staff. Being far more concerned with security of their profits, from paying very low wages, all prime sites are rotated to avoid establishing fiddles as they saw it instead of paying for decent controls. Instead of considering what the customers might prefer, thereby keeping the hotel happy too.

London,

He made his way back to street level, asked Paddy to call him a taxi, said his goodbyes and headed for home again.

As he sat in the back of the taxi, he mulled over what had been discussed with Tom Clancy. The more he thought of the 'consultancy' idea, the more he liked it.

There would not be that much demand of course as it was a rather specialised field, but as he did not need an immediate income, he could take his time in planning it and getting the word out within the industry. Yes! He thought, it could work with very little outlay and could be operated from wherever he chose to live, by using his lawyer's address as the contact point initially.

Starting to make notes on the miniature Dictaphone which he always carried, he decided to spend the rest of the day at his computer, when he got home, expanding this whole new idea and developing the scope of it.

If nothing else, he could leave his name and availability 'out there' in the right circles.

CHAPTER 5.

It was a week later that Mrs. Eden-Smythe received a package from Mr.Wetherall, her solicitor containing a copy of the lease previously signed by her and now by Mr. Rogers, a letter and a cheque for £500. Being the first month's rent in advance. The letter explained that she should keep the copy lease in a safe place, though the original was held by the solicitor's securities department, as were the deposit funds, 'in a separate client's account of course', she chuckled at this as it was typical of Robert Wetherall to be correct in every detail. The letter went on to say that commencement date for the contract was March 1st. The actual starting date of the tenancy was to be arranged directly between the landlady and lessee at their mutual convenience.

Anne considered this for a while thinking that as she was all set from her side, as with the help of Tilly she had made sure that the rooms were now clean and organised, ready for occupation. As the actual date was some 10 days away there was no rush, even so she was looking forward to starting what she now considered to be a new episode in her life; she would wait for Mr. Rogers to telephone her, as she presumed he would also have been contacted by his solicitor in a similar way. However, if she had not heard from him within a couple of days, she would contact him and made a note in her diary accordingly.

She also made an entry at a later date reminding her to bank the cheque when it became due for presentation.

'It is quite exhilarating to have something different to look forward to', thought Anne, after so many years, with her private life set in a quiet routine after her husband's death, and later, her retirement from the Ministry of Defence.

This reminded her of the days before she met her future husband, John.

She sat musing over the time when, as a young girl just out of University, where she achieved high grade degrees in worldwide languages; excelling in a deep understanding of many differing dialects. In fact she became somewhat obsessed with the subject, especially out of the ordinary, little known obscure languages and the dialects that they encompassed; mainly those from Middle and Far Eastern regions, but including European and even versions of Gaelic. She was also fascinated by the many religious languages of past times.Over the years she had travelled far with her parents, as her father was posted to naval stations in many parts of the world. Here she was able to hone her language skills even further, moving between schools, colleges and later at universities around the world.

On leaving university, she was immediately employed by the Ministry of Defence, de-coding department, having been introduced by her father, who was with naval intelligence at the time.

Beginning as a filing clerk in the first instance, then after her sharp, analytical mind and retentive memory was discovered; as a decoding specialist. This would lead her deeper into the intrigues of wartime defence and code breaking.

Very different for a woman in the days of the 1940's when the Second World War was on every one's mind, and the male population mainly being enlisted for military service, it was suddenly the time to use all of the intelligence and muscle available from all parts of the population.

In those days, her mind was full of problem solving activity and intrigue, far from the everyday problems of survival that existed for many ordinary people, living outside of her very secretive occupation.

There was little time for socialising as she had during her days at university, yet even there she had been a bit of a recluse compared to many of her fellow students, preferring to study, as she had promised her studious parents so to do.

Hence she was an ideal recruit for the rather strict and somewhat stuffy civil service and as her father had a naval background, was considered suitable for the Defence Ministry and its secret intelligence section.

Even so, there were occasions such as inter departmental dances when various military personnel were invited, to give all a brief break from the war.

It was on such an occasion that she met **John** for the first time. He was up from Portsmouth on a 5 day course in London. *(Officially, in connection with his position at the Naval Education Department.)*

Anne was sitting at a small table with a couple of work colleagues and had seen him standing at the bar alone, looking a bit lost she thought. He was not the sort to stand out, looking very average even in his uniform, but pleasant enough if a bit shy, she suspected.

Just at that moment he happened to look over towards her seeing her eyes on him, he smiled, then seemed to make up his mind and headed towards her table. He asked her to dance somewhat nervously, she accepted, and led the way onto the dance floor where after some time they eventually began to relax and talk, a relationship of sorts began, on finding that they had very similar personalities and backgrounds. After the dance he led her back to the bar asking if she would take a drink with him, which was in itself a sign of his shyness; they sat at the bar together for the rest of the evening just chatting.

Until she had to take her leave as she had an early start the following morning and as he was due to travel back to his H.Q. in Portsmouth the next day, they would not be getting together again. *Or so it seemed at the time!*

At the time Anne had not thought a great deal about the meeting, apart from the fact that he was quite a pleasant man and that she could relax and converse with him easily, but was much too engrossed in her work to think about him in any depth.

Anyway, he was back doing his job too, so she was unlikely to be seeing him again and that was that, so far as she was concerned.

During the next few weeks she was deeply involved at the ministry, in language de-coding activities, until being transferred to the now famous **Bletchley Park** de-ciphering establishment, where she was to remain until the latter years of the war.

However, she was pleasantly surprised one day when during lunchtime in the canteen, John suddenly appeared at her elbow as she paid for her food saying, "hello there, its Anne isn't it? Fancy meeting you here, will you join me for lunch?" She was so taken aback that she could only nod, following him to his table, where he held the chair for her to sit. "Sorry, she said, but you've taken me completely by surprise, how did you know I was here, it's supposed to be secret you know!" He laughed and said "I know, I've also signed the Official Secrets Act, but I was just about to sit down to eat, when I saw you in the queue, believe me, I was as surprised as you obviously are."

As they began to eat, he explained himself to her; It seems that he had been transferred there as part of a special Royal Naval Intelligence team to co-ordinate new information to do with ships at sea, but apologised for not going into it as he was forbidden. This she fully understood, as her group were under similar instruction. Instead she asked, "How long may you be here, or will you disappear again as last time." "Not sure" he said, "but at least a few weeks, so unless you have other attachments, perhaps we could meet up now and then?"

For some reason, she was quite pleased to find him there, she had found herself thinking about him occasionally just before dropping off to sleep usually for no apparent reason, and it would be good to have some distraction from the intensive concentration of the job. Although they had been warned to be very careful about contacts and liaisons, she could see no problem with him as he was in the same situation.

So replied, “That would be nice but I’m afraid there is very little spare time here, from early mornings to occasional very late evenings, I need my sleep at the moment, but we could try to arrange the odd break later.”

“Oh! So it’s true then, when we were transferred here they warned us not to expect much leave as it appears that what we have to do has a limited time scale with an important deadline at the end. There goes my love life then!” Anne was a bit shocked at this, as he seemed to have lost a lot of the shyness since their last meeting. But she smiled and said sternly, “just a minute, your jumping the gun a bit aren’t you, who mentioned a love life then?” He smiled in return saying, “it’s only a phrase we use when our leave is cancelled, no harm meant Anne.” “None taken John, but I’m sure we will meet in here from time to time, perhaps we can arrange things then. In the meantime, I must get back to work; my lunch hour is almost finished.”

Standing up he said “that’s a pity, but I too have to be at a lecture in ten minutes; I presume it’s to let us know what we are in for while we are here, so it’s goodbye for now then? Perhaps I’ll see you tomorrow?” She nodded and with that parting shot they headed for separate doors out of the canteen.

Walking back to her office, Anne considered what had just happened; did she want to get into such a relationship at the moment? But then did it matter that much, whatever might happen it could only be a temporary thing in today’s fluid climate, with people of all kinds simply being moved around under orders with little notice.

Therefore she thought, why not have some relaxations from the daily grind in the office (interesting though she found it), so, looking forward to tomorrow's meeting now, she returned to her office.

The current project she was involved in was causing quite a stir within the de-coding department, with the 'Brass' (as the upper echelon personnel were referred to) constantly rushing in and out, it had apparent serious implications.

Indeed there was talk that it could turn the war around, yet no one in the section knew the exact nature of what it was, but the rumour was that the Navy were involved.

She now wondered if that was anything to do with John being here, but any discussion on these things was discouraged in that very secret environment.

The story of the German **Enigma Code Machine** is now very well known, but at that time was not, for obvious reasons, as it really did change the course of the war in the Atlantic at the time, involving German U-boats sinking Britain's merchant ships trying to bring in urgent supplies.

It was also the time when the first ever mechanical computer was invented, known as the **'Bombe'** and a later version as **'The Spider'** conceived by two telephone engineers, **Alan Turing** and **Gordon Welchman**, in order to crunch thousands of numbers and letters to assist in breaking the code of this very clever German coding machine. Previously carried out by hand and brain power and taking many hours of boring repetition.

But the main detailed and painstaking work was done by clever and dedicated people like Anne and her colleagues.

Yet even during all this activity, people still had to enjoy some semblance of normal life, so that the following lunchtime Anne looked forward to meeting John again, surprisingly more than she had thought she would. She queued as usual to collect her food and found a small table in a corner hoping for some privacy between them when he arrived. But after finishing her lunch and waiting for a further, half hour, she was disappointed when he had not appeared but guessed that he was tied up with an important job and un-able to get away. She therefore returned to her office to continue the intense work involved, which concentrated her mind on more important problems.

For the next week she was engrossed in this latest very important project as were the rest of her colleagues, so much so that they were not able to leave the department, in fact arrangements had been made to bring food in, the secrecy was that important, they had never known security to be as tight as it was at that time.

At the end of each day there was only time to sleep; all other considerations were forgotten during that time, so that no further meetings would take place between Anne and John for some days.

Eventually however, (as is now well documented), this major event was resolved and things fell back into a sort of routine, not that the work carried out was ever un-important, just slightly less intense.

Therefore when Anne was able to attend the canteen again at lunch time, she was pleased to see John sitting with other naval colleagues at a larger table. As soon as he saw her enter he stood up and came across to her saying, "I suppose you thought I had let you down and gone off when I didn't turn up to meet you?" She laughed and said "I was thinking the same thing as I haven't been here for a week either." "Oh no don't tell me!" Exclaimed John, "so we've both been involved in the same project from different sides I suppose, were you held incommunicado as well?" Anne was relieved; she smiled and said, "Yes, we were, that explains a lot." He picked up her tray and headed for a small, private table.

As they sat down he said "right then, before we have anymore disruptions, don't you think we should arrange a proper meeting sometime Anne?" I have some leave due now that the panic's over, what about you, can you get off?" She had been told that morning that she would now be back on normal shifts and providing she could arrange cover with others in the office, she could take a few hours off from time to time. She told John this and said "where did you have in mind then, the London Ritz perhaps?" Arching her eyebrows! She was surprised at her own rather cheeky attitude, it was not her normal demeanour with men, but was finding it easy to relax with this one.

He laughed once more as he also felt unusually relaxed in her presence and said "you are definitely joking I hope, first of all my pay wouldn't even pay the train fare, also have you forgotten that neither of us would be allowed to stray that far from the fold? But I have heard that the hotel in the local village has a reasonable restaurant, and Security allows us to use it, as they have it covered." Anne liked the sound of that as it had been such a long time since being able to socialise and said, "O.K. then, let me know when you have arranged it and I'll get someone to cover for me. Here is my extension number; they should let your call through as you are on the premises."

She pushed the notation she had just made on a small piece of paper across to him, then had to wolf her food down as time had gone much too quickly and she had to rush back.

He stood up with her and walked to the door and down to her department then turned on his heel and called back, "I'll call you within the next couple of days then, bye!"

The next morning she received a note via her supervisor, (who raised her eyebrows somewhat), to say that he had arranged things for the following Friday evening at 8.00p.m., also he had been able to borrow a car, so would pick her up at her quarters at 7.30.p.m. 'In her posh frock!' But he would not be around for the next few days, being involved in something away from the camp.

She was a little disappointed not to be able to see him before hand, but realised no one could predict their own movements these days, especially in the services, but at least it gave her some time to prepare herself.

For a start, she would need to dig out her 'posh frock' as he called it, the one and only evening dress she had with her was still in a suitcase, as she had not considered needing it here. Also a visit to the camp hairdresser would be called for, which had been un-necessary before, she tended to look after that herself normally.

That Friday night, John duly pulled up in a small, Naval Austin 8 car at the prefixed time, to the entrance hall of Anne's accommodation block, where she had been waiting in the foyer. He climbed out of the car walking around to open the passenger door as she stepped through the foyer doors and into the car. "You look lovely Anne, so you did have a posh frock then?"

She laughed and said, as he got back into the driving seat, "thank you very much, you say that as if you didn't think I would have." "Well, I did wonder after I had left the message" he said. "It's not the sort of thing you expect to need at a place like this. I've only got uniforms with me, not that I'm allowed to wear anything else anyway."

He went on to say, "sorry about not being around for a few days, it all happened suddenly, but then it usually does." "Anyway, we can now relax for a while and I can enjoy the pleasant company of a very attractive lady, can't I?" Anne chuckled at this thinking, 'so much for his past shyness', but enjoying the attention and saying; "Flatterer! Is that the line you use to all the ladies you take out then?"

John seemed to get a little more serious then and said, "You may not believe me Anne, but this is the first time I've taken a girl out on a proper date since my University days, before joining up. You always seem to make me relax when we're together; having always been a bit shy, but the Navy has knocked that out of me."

In spite of herself, Anne was flattered by this and believed him, as she had always felt a similar dilemma herself, preferring the serious side of life to the flippant; with a reluctance to meet new people unless it was necessary. She said "well I'm looking forward to this evening, so as you say, let's enjoy it, we may not have another chance for some time."

She was not to know how true that would turn out to be, as events were to develop against the pair of them.

The hotel restaurant was reasonably well stocked with food and drink within the context of Wartime Briton, as the population had long since come to terms with rationing in all walks of life. So that Anne and John had a very pleasant evening, enjoying each other's company and consequently growing closer. Although not necessarily romantically so, it was much too soon for them both and neither were able to drink as they may have wished to, due to the nature of their jobs and the contemporary project they were involved in.

Eventually they reluctantly had to head for home and as John drew up to the door of Anne's building, he walked around to her door, and as she alighted, he lightly kissed her once on the mouth saying, "Goodnight Anne, I've had a wonderful evening."

To which she replied, " have I, thank you so much, I'll probably see you tomorrow then shall I?" "You can bet on it, providing my masters don't have other ideas" said John.

But he was not to know what new orders were in store for him early the next morning and that it would be several months before he and Anne would meet again.

The only information Anne received, was a short message through her supervisor the next day, saying, that 'Petty Officer Smythe had returned to his unit with immediate effect'. She presumed that this simply meant he would be back in Portsmouth for a while. Ah well! She thought, so much for my love-life, which was over only too quickly.

Yet with the whole population being involved in the war effort in one form or another and being moved around at very short notice. It made for many short term relationships, sometimes whirlwind romances and others just short and sweet, as in this case. *Or so it seemed at the time!*

Many of the things that were happening to people then would seem strange to today's population. Almost everyone within a certain age range was conscripted into some form of service, from the main military services, to farming, mining, and factories. There was no dissention permitted, under threat of imprisonment, although that was rarely used, as people generally wanted to help their country against the common enemy.

People simply went where you were told to go and when. With an odd chance of leave from time to time, hence the short relationships referred to.

People learned to accept, and live with these restrictions, realising that it was necessary for our survival in wartime.

Children were evacuated from Town and City centres to rural areas for safety, which caused much upset within those families, but changed many lives for the better in the long run.

Yet, safe from the constant bombing in certain areas by enemy aircraft.

Even their teachers were conscripted into the armed forces, with retired ones being brought back into the teaching profession.

In fact, many retired, able men and women were brought into service in some form or other. From the Police and Fire services, aircraft and fire spotting duties, canteen kitchens, and other 'voluntary' services.

Even to forming a home defence army, 'Dads Army' as it became known in later years, we were fully expecting to be invaded by the German war machine that had been terrorising the rest of Europe.

So that life had been changed forever in Great Britain, we all had to learn new skills, and narrow the class system to work together against a common enemy.

In fact many of the manor houses and country estates of the richer members of our society were confiscated to be used as military hospitals, barracks and other more important requirements, than simply comfortable homes.

CHAPTER 6.

Jack received the call on his messaging system from his lawyer friend James, to visit his office a.s.a.p. saying documents were ready for signature and there was no need for an appointment, to just drop in.

He decided to make the trip that morning as he wished to get the move going as soon as possible. Time was running out on his current position and he would like to make just the one move if possible, he therefore set off to walk to the offices of Chapman, Younger and Associates taking him no more than half an hour.

On arrival and making his way up to their office, he walked up to the reception desk only to find it occupied by a stern looking lady whom he did not know, so that the usual banter with 'Maisey' was out. He announced himself, explaining the message from James, he was asked to sit and wait, as she buzzed through on the office intercom.

After some 20 minutes, James came out of the office to see him sitting there, "thanks for waiting, you can come in now, I have some time free." As they entered his office he said, "By the way, I'll bet you didn't know that your lady was bit of a celebrity in her younger days, it was all a bit hush-hush, but she was a high flyer in the secret services at the end of hostilities. Got some sort of honour for her work in the war, an O.B.E. I think, she is a very brainy lady."

"Her solicitor is one of the old school and would not normally reveal much, but his father and mine were friends and he has known me since childhood, he's obviously proud of knowing her. Perhaps he was warning me not to let you try to take advantage of her."

Jack was not surprised, saying "no I wasn't aware of that, but might have guessed, although she likes to portray a different image it seems."

Following him into the office and seating himself Jack said "do I take this to mean all is settled then?" "Yes that's right" said his friend, "I just need your signature on this copy of the lease previously signed by Mrs. Eden-Smythe, which I will witness, and your cheque for the amount on this invoice. The document was dealt with and the formalities completed. James then added, "As you will see, the tenancy begins on March first; you can take a copy with you and make arrangements with the land-lady to move in at your mutual convenience."

"Good, the sooner the better now as I need to clear things up at my place, as you know, time is running out there and I would prefer not to make two moves if possible." Said Jack and standing up he leaned over to shake hands with James saying, "Thanks for dealing with this quickly, see you Friday then?" James answered; "Certainly, I intend to win my money back, can you see yourself out? I had better get on with this," pointing to huge file on his desk.

"Don't worry; I can take a hint, not being one of your important clients of course." He smiled, waved a hand and walked out through the door, nodding to the formidable looking lady at reception on the way to the lifts.

On arrival at home he telephoned Mrs. Eden-Smythe to arrange convenient dates for the move in. She sounded pleased to hear from him saying, "Oh good morning Mr. Rogers! I've been expecting your call as I have signed the lease and understand we can go ahead now."

"Yes I've just left my solicitor's office after completing things and would like to move as soon as possible, I am now pressed for time, but as the lease start date is a few days away, I would be happy to pay for the extra days rent, if that's alright with you?"

"I won't hear of such a thing Mr. Rogers," adding, "we have prepared the rooms for you, so you can come along anytime you wish."

Jack was relieved to hear that, saying "That's most helpful, may I come along tomorrow morning then?"

"By all means" she said, "come anytime you like. I look forward to seeing you then, good bye Mr. Rogers." He replied in a similar vein and put the telephone down.

That was a relief he thought, now he could clear the rest of his belongings. Consequently, he began to phone around, arranging various appointments for the collection of his furniture etc. Over the next two days, he also contacted agents dealing with the property he was in, to arrange for keys to be handed over in two days time after he had cleared out the apartment.

Next he began to finalize his personal packing apart from overnight requirements, which he would deal with first thing in the morning. This took the rest of the day to complete, then after a snack meal, he went to bed, more contented to be almost at the end of this phase of his life and looking forward to the next.

Although still somewhat confused by the sudden contact from his Intelligence superiors after such a long time, it seemed too much of a coincidence that he should be contacted just as he was about to look for accommodation and Mr. Eden-Smythe was advertising such. But he had learned over the years not to question his orders, there must be a good reason.

He awoke early the following morning and completed the preparation for his move, carrying boxes and other items down to his car and having finished that, realized he was still much too early. So decided to stroll over to the other side of the site in order to speak to Berty and tell him what was happening.

On arriving at the car wash and seeing that Berty was tied up with a technical problem, he waited for a while chatting to some of the other staff he knew, and catching up on what was new since the takeover. Then Berty came over saying, "what's this then, decided to slum it with the workers again?" Jack laughed replying, "Just this once, I'm moving out tomorrow, thought you ought to know."

Berty grimaced and said "sorry to hear that, but I knew you would be going soon, I take it we will still meet down the pub for a drink now and then though?" "You can be sure of that and I haven't forgotten about your brother, once I know what I'm doing, I'll get in touch, I promise."

They shook hands and he waved a hand to the other workers as he walked away towards his car. Thinking of all the work they had put in when originally developing this installation from scratch some three years ago. But now was the time to move on and with that he climbed into his car and drove off.

On arrival at 47.Windsor Square, he was able to park directly in front, as Mrs. Eden-Smythe had made sure her reserved space was clear for him, which was most thoughtful. As he climbed the approach steps to the front porch lugging two heavy suitcases, the door was opened by that lady, she had obviously been watching for him, said, "We have been expecting you and I didn't want your parking space to be taken. Mrs. Tilson will help with some of the lighter items." "That's most helpful", said Jack "I certainly didn't expect to park right in front having seen the lack of parking in the square."

Another lady (who he estimated to be in her thirties) came bustling up to the doorway and was introduced to him by the lady of the house. "Mrs. Tilson, meet Mr. Rogers, our new gentleman lodger." He shook hands with her nodding and thinking this is all very formal, but not wishing to upset the status-quos, he said "very nice to meet you, I hope we will get on together." She also nodded, smiled and rushed off down the steps to his car obviously eager to help. He would learn that she always moved quickly as if she had little time to waste, which in truth she hadn't, looking after a husband, a child, a home, and working for her mistress,

He put the suitcases down inside the house and between them, he and Mrs. Tilson emptied the car in no time, while the landlady moved into the kitchen.

Mrs. Tilson now went into the kitchen to join her mistress, apparently to busy her-self with the coffee which had been prepared in readiness, while he carried the rest of his belongings upstairs. After which he had been told to join them, thinking 'I could certainly get used to this kind of fuss, but how long will it last'?

Walking into the cosy kitchen, where the two women were seated at the table, he sat down to help himself to coffee and home-made scones with of course home-made preserves, as he already had the feeling of belonging there. Having been made to feel so welcome, saying, "the room's looking very clean and organized, I suspect someone has been busy, looking directly at Mrs. Tilson. She blushed slightly saying "thank you, but we both did it."

She then stood up saying I must get on now if you will excuse me, I'll wash these things later," pointing at the table crockery and bustled out of the kitchen.

Mrs. Eden-Smythe spoke, "Tilly is such a treasure, never stops finding things to do during her working hours here, then starts again down in her flat, before going off to pick up their child from school;" She then continued, "now that you're here you must feel at home and able to move freely around the house, apart from the first floor containing the bedrooms and bathroom of myself and Nora of course." "We have two resident parking spaces allocated where your car is at present and as neither Nora nor I use a car, you and Mr.Tilson are entitled to use them; here is your resident's pass to place in the windscreen." She pushed a Blue printed, square piece of card across and said "but I'm afraid you will need to pay the annual fee to the local authority." Jack picked up the pass saying, "That's most helpful, thanks, I'll be happy to pay that to be able to park right outside the house in central London." She then pushed a pair of keys towards him and said, "These are for the front door and the key for your room is already in that door, so you can keep your own privacy."

"Could you tell me what time you prefer to eat in the evening, we are very flexible these days as I never know when to expect Nora, if at all, as she is so often out with her friends now, so whenever it suits you best." Jack replied "to be honest I have been eating out much of the time, as my job entailed unusual hours and I had many business meetings over meals at various times of the day. So that I've got out of the habit of regular meals, but until I decide what I'm going to do, it would be nice to eat regularly again. Should we say between 6-7pm.?"

"That would be fine, but we will probably drop into some sort of pattern anyway, as we get to know each other" she said.

He replied "I'm sure we will, but for now I had better get a move on, I must go back to my place to load up again. I also have to meet the removal men taking my furniture in to storage, and then I can return to unpack upstairs."

Mrs. Eden-Smythe rose to her feet saying, "That's fine, I shall prepare a meal for us this evening and Nora will be here so that you can meet her too."

With that, he rose saying "thank you, I'll look forward to that, once I've settled things back at my place, I can return and relax over a nice meal with you both. So I'll get on with that now"; realising that he had fallen into the formal manner of his new landlady when speaking to her.

On returning to No.47.Windsor Square later, he again unloaded the car, carrying his belongings up to his new home and started to clear things away. When he heard a call from Mrs. Eden-Smythe to say that dinner was ready in the kitchen.

As he arrived in the kitchen both ladies were at the stove spooning food into serving dishes, placing them on the table, Anne said "Mr. Rogers, this is my very good friend Nora Aston."

"I wanted you to meet her properly." Jack nodded to the lady and smiled saying "at least I know who you are this time, very nice to meet you Miss Aston."

She replied saying, "nice to meet you too at last", then turning to Anne she arched her eyebrows and said "yes he is very personable as you say Anne, now let's sit down and eat the food before it gets cold shall we" pointing to a chair for him to sit at. "You must be hungry after all the hard work today Mr. Rogers."

He was more than ready to tuck in to the delicious looking home cooked fare, it had been a long day and so sat down as invited, wondering if he should ask them to call him by his first name, or if that might by presumptuous with these ladies, so decided to let it go for now.

The meal was not only delicious and satisfying, but the company was good too. He found that they were relaxed with him, as he was with them and the conversation was wide reaching, although they were obviously curious about him and he was as frank as possible about his past.

He could see why his new landlady had wanted Nora to be there apart from introducing them, as she was a real chatterbox and unlikely to allow the conversation to flag. She could also be a little cheeky at times, where Mrs. Eden-Smythe was more reserved but still friendly, but all in all there was a happy atmosphere, so that it achieved the object of getting to know each other on his first night there.

After almost two hours, Nora suddenly stood up and said "well if you will excuse me I have somewhere to go, so you sit there and chat, I'll clear these things away." Jack asked if he could help, but was firmly told no, by both ladies at the same time. They both laughed at that and Anne said "it's just a matter of putting things away and you won't know where at the moment, but don't worry we will take you up on the offer at a later date."

Busying herself at the sink, Nora said, "Oh yes! You can be sure of that, we're not too proud to let you clear up sometimes."

She soon finished the dishes leaving them to drain and saying, right then, I'm off now, see you in the morning. It's been a pleasure to meet you Mr. Rogers, I'm sure we will all get on swimmingly."

Jack stood up saying "I feel sure we will, goodnight", as Nora bustled out. Sitting down again, he turned to Anne, "she certainly moves quickly I must say." Anne laughed saying, "Nora has always been that way, when she was Headmistress at my husband's school she was just the same, always busy at some project or other with the children and a great help to him in running the school, it's just her way, she can't keep still for very long. That's why she was such a help during my husband's illness, nothing was too much trouble for her."

Anne then stood and started to clear the last remnants of coffee cups etc. "would you like to move to the sitting room now, or perhaps settle yourself into your rooms, you must feel free to do whatever you wish." As Jack also rose to his feet he replied "if you don't mind I would like to get on upstairs, I have a lot to clear up, but many thanks for the meal, it was most enjoyable."

"You are most welcome; Nora and I enjoyed it too, please remember, a meal will be available every evening if you wish, but if you could just let me know when you won't be available, it would help. Goodnight then!"

The following morning, after a restful sleep and completing his ablutions, Jack felt that he was ready to make his new start. There were no messages on his phone, so he was free to do as he wished today. This reminded him that he must arrange for a phone line in his room sometime.

He went downstairs to the kitchen to find Mrs.Tilson busy cleaning from the previous night and a delicious smell of fresh coffee brewing; saying, "good morning Mrs.Tilson, what a lovely smell."

She began to pour some of the fresh liquor into ready prepared cups for him, replying, "good morning Mr. Rogers, please call me Tilly, it's much easier, could I cook you some breakfast?" "No thank you Tilly, can I just help myself to toast, you mustn't spoil me, I'm not used to it, and please call me Jack then." She gave a little giggle saying I'm not sure if Mrs.Smythe would like me to use your first name yet, you are a guest in the house, would you mind if I don't, just for now." Jack was busy putting bread in to the toaster and said "whatever makes you comfortable, where would the preserves be please?" She frowned at him and pointed to the table, saying "as if I would be that careless."

He apologised, "sorry, I told you I'm not used to being waited on." Sitting at the table to see to his breakfast, to put her at her ease he began by asking after her family, "has your son gone to school already then, although it's a bit early yet, isn't it?"

"Not really she replied, my husband takes him on his way to work and they have a little breakfast club he attends before school." "What a good idea" said Jack, "I hear your husband is a keen gardener too?" "Oh he would live out there given the chance and Toby enjoys being with him, as they play football too", she said, pointing through the window to the garden.

"I understand you have a son too, but not here?" Jack grimaced, the thought of not being able to play football with his son was hurtful, but replying "yes, but he is growing up now, he's attending college in Canada on a sports scholarship."

He was relieved as the lady of the house came in saying "good morning Mr. Rogers, did you sleep well?" "Yes very well thank you, it seems to be a very quiet house, considering the busy position." "Good, yes we are lucky here as the other buildings seem to block sound from the main road." "Now has Tilly been looking after you?" Jack laughed and said, "She certainly has, I told her, she is spoiling me, I'm not used to it, I normally look after myself." At this Tilly reddened a little saying "I did offer him cooked breakfast, but he preferred just toast."

Jack thought he should clarify his future requirements by saying, "I always prefer a light breakfast, and so please don't bother with food for me in the mornings." Anne pouring some coffee for herself, said "well I often have croissants delivered with the milk, would you enjoy those too?" "Yes indeed I would" he said as she re-filled his cup also.

As she sat down opposite him, he asked, "would it be possible for me to arrange for a phone extension to my room, or if you prefer I could arrange a new phone line with a different number." She exclaimed! "There's no need for that, we had another line fitted in connection with the school when John used to use that room as a study. It will just need to be re-activated with a new number." "I'll telephone my contacts today to arrange it; I have a little influence there so it should not take too long."

Jack was a bit surprised at that, but then remembered what James had said about her past and thought it entirely possible, but said "that's good of you, but will you let me know of any costs involved, I will of course pay them." She smiled saying "oh there will not be any cost I can assure you." She seemed very confident on this matter and Jack could only wonder at her influence in certain government circles.

Standing up, he said "will you excuse me now, I must get on with sorting out my future employment, I have various commercial properties to view over the next few days." Anne also stood up, "do you know if you will be back for lunch or not."

"No I shall eat out as I have meetings too, but I will be back this evening, if that's alright?"

"Of course it will be, I'll arrange a meal for the same time as last evening, but don't feel pressed for time." Jack thanked her and picking up a coat and briefcase, left for the day.

His first destination was Windsor Square itself, he thought it was time he surveyed his new living environment to be sure of his bearings, and its proximity to that part of London he knew so well from his previous dealings in the parking field; It was situated within the more wealthy residential and retail shopping areas of London's West End.

As he walked around the central green park area, admiring the attractive old properties overlooking it, he came upon the old school gates with a sign noting the names of Proprietor and Headmistress, namely Mr. J. Eden-Smythe and Nora Aston.

That surprised him, as he had not been aware of her surname before, also he had not connected his landlady's husband to this school, yet should have as it had been mentioned several times, just not the location.

As he looked in through the gates, he was impressed by the extent of the property, automatically judging the value in such a prime position, as came naturally from his past experience. Wondering why it had been allowed to deteriorate to such an extent, but guessed it was something to do with ancient planning requirements. He made a mental note to ask his new landlady this evening. Walking back to collect his car from outside No. 47, he started to mull over ideas for making use of such a valuable site as a future project, all depending upon it's availability, he felt sure that other speculators had spotted it in the past, so there must be a very good reason for being un-used.

He was later on his way to view the various properties to be considered located in North and East London, without a great deal of enthusiasm, as he had viewed so many of these 'Spectacular Opportunities' offered by property managers and estate agents in the past. Although he had always detailed his requirements to them, they would insist on sending out hopeful prospectuses without caring that they often wasted valuable time of company executives and others.

Hence after a long, unsuccessful day of driving and walking around outer areas of London, with only a quick break for a snack, he returned to his new home feeling somewhat deflated and hungry.

Going straight up to his rooms to shower and change clothes, before heading down to the kitchen again for dinner.

There he found the lady of the house busy at the cooker finalising a delicious smelling meal, with the table neatly laid out with crockery and cutlery for two only, so presuming that Nora was out tonight. "Good evening" he said, "something smells good." She looked up from the stove to say "good evening Mr. Rogers, have you had a successful day?" "Not very" he replied, "it was all rather a waste of time, but then it often is when dealing with land agents etc.

She smiled, "Oh! I'm sorry to hear that, anyway please sit down and we will enjoy a nice meal, then you can tell me all about it, or not, as you wish." "Nora is not in tonight, she's off to see some obscure play with her friends."

He helped her to set the prepared food on the table and they both sat down to begin the meal. He then realised just how hungry he felt, thinking it was probably the smell and the fact that he had eaten very little all day, so he tucked in with gusto.

She said "I'll bet you haven't eaten properly all day have you? It's nice to see you enjoying my food." "That's true " he said, "it's a long time since I had homemade food, I've been eating my own cooking, take away and restaurant food for quite a few years now, that's why so enjoy being here.

It's nice to be spoiled again. But, I really didn't expect to be fed like this when I applied for accommodation." Anne smiled and said "in my case it is nice to cook for a man in the house once more and I have always enjoyed cooking, especially with the help of Tilly."

Jack considered this might be a good time to broche the matter of first names saying "by the way, when speaking to her this morning she told me to call her Tilly, but when I suggested that she called me Jack, she seemed reluctant. Do you have any objection to first names, or do you prefer the more formal approach?"

Anne laughed and said "I have no objection, but you will find she prefers it that way, she seems to feel that being an employee she should not be familiar, but don't worry, she may come around as she gets to know you, I know from experience!" "As for me, I had just been leaving the matter for while, but glad you brought it up, I should be most pleased for you call me Anne, if you are happy for me to call you Jack?" He in turn gave a little laugh, "I'm relieved that's sorted out, not wanting to offend you, but it makes life simpler don't you think?" "Indeed it does, and I know Nora would be happy for you to address her by that name, she thinks I'm a bit stuffy at times, but it is just the way I was brought up."

"That's all settled then", Jack said, now wanting to get onto the subject that had been uppermost in his mind all day, "if you don't mind, may ask a question about the old school? I went for a walk around the square this morning and spotted the sign outside with your husband's name on, is it alright to talk about it?" Anne was a bit surprised by the question, but answered, "of course, if you are referring to his death, that happened a long time ago, what do you wish to know?"

He was relieved, "Well, I suppose the story behind its closure and why no one has sought to develop it since; there must be a very good reason, for such a prime position in central London."

Anne stood up to clear the dishes from the table and pour out the previously prepared coffee from a thermos; he guessed she was perhaps covering her emotions a little, as it must be difficult to bring back such memories.

Then sitting down again, she began; “The school was owned and operated by John’s father for many years after returning from the 1st World War; Then when John was released from the navy after the 2nd World War, having been in the naval education department, he joined his father, who eventually retired to the South coast, until his death a few years later.

St. Stephens Prep School was profitable most for the time, until the upgrading costs of new safety regulations and required building work plus, higher salaries, became too much, as there has to be a limit to what parents can pay for their children’s education. Income was tight in those years after the war. At the same time my husband’s health began to deteriorate after suffering a Stroke, and eventually we had to close it.” I was unable to help as I had my own career which was a full time occupation, being in a senior position at the Ministry of Defence. Though Nora did her best and was a great help to us, being a trained nurse. That’s the whole story really.”

Jack hadn’t realised just how much she had been through and understood why she had not spent time considering the school’s future, but now said, “I can see that it must have been painful to bring all of that back to mind and I’m sorry to have brought it up, perhaps we should leave it for some other time.”

Anne smiled at his thoughtfulness and said “oh please don’t worry, I’m happy to have it out in the open, I know I should have dealt with the matter of the school previously, my solicitor has told me so in the past, but when estate agents etc. came knocking at the door, I just didn’t want to be bothered.” “Anyway, the original land grant has many complications; it can’t simply be demolished and developed as homes or something, for obvious reasons being part of the park, apart from it being unfair to my neighbours.” She then added, “why were you asking, do you have some fiendish plan in mind for it then?" looking at him and arching her eyebrows. Jack laughed at this little gesture and realised that she had now come to terms with it, making him feel much better. He said "I don't know about fiendish, but just wondered at the waste I suppose. Would you mind if I looked into what is possible there, it used to be my job to look into such properties in the past?"

"To be perfectly honest Jack, I would be very happy for you take the responsibility from my shoulders. Tomorrow morning you can help me dig out the old papers for the school, they are stored in the box room you are using for storage, unless you have other plans of course."

"As a matter of fact, I had it in mind to start making plans for what needs urgent attention around the house, it's time I started to keep my side of our bargain, but we can certainly do that first." Then standing up, he again offered to help with the dishes and was turned down once more as he had expected, said his goodnights and retired to his rooms upstairs. He was secretly excited at the possibilities that the old property might offer, but much depended on exactly what the restrictions were within the terms of the lease and how much longer it had to run. Even so, he began to lay plans for what he might be able to achieve should things go his way.

Next morning he was up and about early to continue his arrangements before going into breakfast and to take a walk around the square for a more detailed assessment of the school grounds, from outside the gates at this stage, but mainly to clear his mind. On arriving at the school he was even more impressed than the day before by the amount of space available.

It consisted of a large playground surfaced mainly by Tar Macadam, a further grassed sports area and several low buildings, all in need of attention of course. Yet for what he had in mind much of this could be progressive, so that the initial financial outlay could be minimised. He made several notes on the notepad he always carried, including size estimates which was something he gauged automatically after so many years of surveying such properties.

Walking back towards his new home, he spotted Mrs.Tilson coming up from the basement flat and waved to her and called out a greeting, she held the front door open for him and as he arrived exclaimed, “My goodness Mr. Rogers! You’re up very early or just coming home I wonder?” “No such luck Tilly, just up early, been for walk around the estate” he said, waving an arm around the square.

“I’ll put some coffee on straight away for you, if you’re in a hurry, would you like something cooked?” Jack laughed saying “there you go again, worrying about my stomach, no thanks but I would like some coffee and I’ll get myself some toast, O.K.?” “As you wish, but you should eat more in the morning you know,” she looked quite severe and he could imagine that she looked after her family very well, but standing no nonsense. As she prepared things for breakfast, he helped himself to his food and sitting down at the now familiar table started to read the daily paper which he had picked up from the letter box on the way in, leaving Tilly to get on with her work.

Soon afterwards Anne came in saying “good morning to you both, I’m pleased to see you’ve settled in Jack, are you being looked after then?” He looked up from his paper, “good morning Anne, yes thanks, but she worries about my health”, Tilly giggled, she was a little surprised to hear first names being used, but said “he prefers to get his own breakfast, but only eats toast, he should have more though, anyway, I thought he had been out all night, he was up so early.” Jack explained to Anne about going for an early walk and she said, “Well I don’t blame you Tilly, I might think the same, after all he is a single man!”

Jack realised he was being teased and enjoy the fact that they accepted him so readily after just a few days. He spoke to Anne “are we going to start work today then as we discussed, or would you rather leave it for a while?”

She was busy helping herself to cereal, milk and coffee, then sitting opposite said “of course we are going to work today, I’m looking forward to it, immediately after breakfast.”

Tilly excused herself to Anne, saying she was going to be cleaning the living rooms etc. "I'll probably see you later Mr. Rogers, perhaps at lunchtime." "Yes, I'm going to be around the house today, so if you need help with anything heavy, let me know." She nodded and left the room.

Anne smiled and said to Jack "well, she seems to have taken to you alright, you're lucky, she is normally quite shy of strangers." "Good" he said, "I must say how at home I feel already, it's as if I've been here for a very long time."

At that she became businesslike and standing up said "I'm very pleased to hear it, now I think it's time we stopped talking and got on with some work don't you?" Leading the way out of the kitchen and up the stairs to his landing and then to the box room, where she pointed to a large, green metal box saying "could you drag that out for me please, it contains all of the documents relating to my husband's affairs and the school records. It was packed by Nora at the time, so will be well organised, that is one thing she was fastidious about, filing records."

Just at that moment Nora came bustling in to the room in her usual manner asking,

"Excuse me for butting in, but I'm just being nosey, wondered what might be going on." "Oh! Just in time, we could do with your help" said Anne, "you know these records better than anyone, could you select the lease and other property details on the school for us." Nora replied "of course darling, this is most intriguing but simple enough," she bent down to the locker, opened the lid and sure enough, the contents were neatly stacked in box files.

She quickly selected one with a large Red label, handing it to Anne, who said "thank you my dear, I knew you would find it quicker than we could." Then to Jack she said "would you replace the box now, I shouldn't think there will anything else you will need from it at the moment, but you now know where it is when you do." Jack did as was asked and took possession of the box file.

Nora could contain herself no longer and exclaimed! "Anne, will you please tell me what this is all about? It's the first time you have looked at this box since John passed away, what is so important now? But you can tell me to mind my own business if you like."

Anne laughed at her excitement saying, "It's nothing mysterious, just an idea that Jack might have for making use of the school, perhaps you could help him sometime, you know far more about the place than I ever did." As they walked back down the stairs together Nora was saying "it's intriguing though, I would be most interested in anything that could be done with the place and will do all I can to help."

They had all reached the living room by now and sitting around the coffee table, Jack opened the file, taking out the various legal documents and laying them out. He said "I am mainly interested in any restrictions on the use of the property, being an old lease and in such an area." Then looking at Nora said, "Is there anything that you are aware of Nora?" She mused for a while then replied "I seem to remember when John wanted to extend some of the buildings to improve facilities, and for other uses, there was a problem with the planning authorities because of the residential nature of the area; "

"But it seemed that we couldn't afford it anyway, that's all I can remember. But then I was mostly involved in the educational needs of the school, John dealt with the business side."

He nodded "yes, I can understand that, but tell me did anyone bring a car onto the premises, can you remember?" Nora smiled and said "of course I can remember, we had visitors from time to time and the occasional parent came by car to deliver and collect boys."

"There were not as many cars around in those days of course." She looked at him quizzically, then looking at the clock said, "sorry but I must go up and get ready now, we are all off to the countryside for lunch by the river.

Jocelyn has arranged to hire a mini bus for us." She then jumped up and headed for the door, calling over her shoulder "let me know if I can help later; bye!"

Jack also stood saying, "well that will be enough for now, I can study these tonight at my leisure, but I think we should start doing some real work now don't you Anne?" Looking a little shocked, she said "well if you insist, where shall we start do you think?" "Why not show me the areas you are most concerned about first, and I'll start making some notes, then we can decide the priorities." She nodded and led the way out through the kitchen to the garden in order to show him the rear of the house, pointing to various problems on the facade beneath the roof, window frames etc., and he began to make notes.

This continued all around the house, until Tilly called out to say that she had made coffee and they should come and sit for a while, worrying as ever, but most welcome.

They walked into the warm, cosy kitchen with a wonderful smell of coffee and freshly made scones. Jack thought to himself, 'it is all too good to be true, I could certainly get used to being looked after like this', but sitting at the table said "now Tilly I told you I'm not used to being spoiled like this, but it's very nice of you." She replied "it's just my job Mr. Rogers and I enjoy looking after Mrs. Smythe properly, anyway I thought you could both do with a break, it's chilly out there today."

Anne then chimed in with "just make the best of it Jack; we haven't had a man in the house for a long time, apart from when Tilly's husband is home and in the garden." "Oh! I'm not complaining he said, but I had better get on with earning it. So we should now make out a list of jobs and the priorities while we sit and enjoy the banquet, don't you think?"

Anne laughed at his words and agreed "you are right; we had better get you to work before you find other interests to occupy your time."

Tilly smiled listening to this banter; she was pleased for her mistress to sound so happy and relaxed once more.

With that, they settled down to work and decide where he should start and what needed outside professionals, continuing their tour of the house inside and out, which apart from a sandwich at lunchtime, took them the rest of the day.

By which time they were pleased to relax in the kitchen once more to find that Tilly had left a delicious casserole for them.

After the meal was finished and while Anne cleared away, Jack worked on the priority list, deciding where to start. As Anne sat down again, he asked for her approval of his jottings and after studying the papers for a while, she nodded saying, "it seems fine to me, so long as you are not taking on too much, with your other plans to consider." He replied "well at the moment, whilst I am looking around for opportunities, there will be gaps in between when I can spend more of that time here.

Anne said "well, as long as you are sure, now if you don't mind it has been a long day and I am going to relax and watch some television for a while, but I'm very pleased with what we have achieved today." As they both stood up, Jack said "yes, we've managed to get through quite a lot and it's a job that needed doing. I think I'll go to my room to go through the documents we found this morning, so I'll say goodnight Anne." She wished him the same and they both retired.

Jack was eager to study those documents to see if he could consider pursuing his idea concerning the old school premises, but decided to shower and change first in order to relax and clear his mind.

Finding the original lease, he first discovered that it was a perpetual one, with a proviso that the name of Smythe was the lessee and so long as the premises were used for the express purpose of education or otherwise for the express benefit and use as agreed by the residents association.

There were also several caveats about size, height and type of building etc. but the main theme of the terms appeared to be that it must be used for the benefit of the residents of Windsor Square.

He was happy to find among the files a land map to scale, which was his other major requirement, as he could now start to plan his ideas in detail which kept him busy late into the night. But at the end of his studies he was pleased with the result; it was all that he had hoped for.

Retiring to his bed, he started to think of what needed to be done the next day, but dropped off to sleep.

The following morning saw him wide awake and raring to go, he was always the same when a new project was in his mind, but was also aware that he had promised to get on with some practical work around the house and he would need Anne's co-operation to get his plans into action.

Therefore dressing ready for some real work in a pair of overalls and boots to show that he was serious, he headed down to the kitchen for breakfast.

He was surprised to find Anne already there with Tilly, preparing food etc. together. "Good morning ladies, I do love that smell of fresh coffee in the morning."

They both replied to his greeting, and then Anne turned around to see his attire saying, "somebody looks the part this morning all ready for work then?"

"Yes, keen to get started I am, just need some old cleaning tools, I would like to look around if I may, must be some stuff out in the shed?"

Tilly spoke then saying, "Well it so happens that my husband is home today, as his taxi is in for service and he'll know what's available out there."

Jack was pleased at that, as he would not have known where to start to look and did not want to upset anyone; he knew how possessive some chaps could be about their sheds and tools.

Anne spoke up then to say, "I'm afraid I won't be here to help today, I have to be somewhere else and shall be gone all day. Can I collect anything while I'm out, to help? I shall be passing various shops on the way.

" Jack replied "well at this stage it will mostly be cleaning walls etc. so if you pass a hardware shop, perhaps you could pick up some sugar soap and colour charts."

"Yes, I can do that" she replied. Standing up from the table, she said her goodbyes and headed for the front door. Jack followed her into the hallway on his way to the rear garden and the tool shed.

At that moment the door bell sounded and Anne opened it to reveal a tall, well built young man who greeted her with "Good morning Maam, are you ready to go?" She obviously knew him and replied, "All ready Toby, may I introduce Jack Rogers; he is going to stay with us for a while.

Toby nodded making a mental note of his face and scruffy appearance, as he would need to report the new member of the household to his superior. Jack shook hands with him.

Knowing that he was about to be scrutinised in detail by the internal security section of the M.O.D. even though he had been put forward to them as a suitable tenant to the household.

Anne smiled at Toby's look, saying, "He is just about to start work on repairing this poor old house for me. Right! Let's go then Toby, I'll see you this evening Jack." As Toby was closing the door behind her, Jack was surprised to see through the doorway a large official looking car with a chauffeur holding the rear passenger door open.

They were both obviously treating Anne with a great deal of deference, which aroused his curiosity, but it was not his business after all. Yet it now began to explain his sudden orders in some way?

Continuing out to the garden, he found a man he presumed to be Tillys' husband there, holding out his hand he said "hello, I'm Jack Rogers, are you Mr.Tilson?" The man shook hands with him saying "yes, Tilly told me you would be out soon and the name is Arthur, I understand you need some tools."

"Yes please, I'm very pleased to meet you at last, understand you're taking a day off taxiing today? It gives you a chance to get on with you hobby eh?" "That's right" said Arthur, "the trouble is that I'm losing money then, but the cab has to go for these checks to keep my licence, so it's a good excuse."

"Now I understand you're going to try to brighten the old place up a bit, what tools you will need?" he said as he led the way into his sanctuary. "If you don't mind Arthur, just a couple of scrapers, a bucket and an old scrubbing brush for now."

"Of course I don't mind, they're not my tools anyway, they belong to the house, I just try to keep things up together, I can't stand an untidy work area, just a fad of mine." Looking around the walls and seeing each item hanging in its own place, with the shape drawn around it, Jack said "I can see that, it all looks well organised, you can be sure I won't disturb anything."

"You should have seen it when I first came, between the old man, who was too busy with his school, and various part time gardeners, it was a terrible mess, anyway just help yourself in future, all I ask is that things are replaced clean where you get them from, don't worry about any sharpening and so on, I see to that on a regular basis."

He had been collecting the items needed as he spoke, handing them to Jack. Who took them gratefully; he had been expecting to have to rummage through lots of old equipment to find his needs.

He thanked Arthur for his help and headed back into the house, noting on the way how neatly the garden is being kept..

After a good morning's preparation work in the rear hallway, he decided to stop for a cup of tea and a snack, expecting to get it for himself as Tilly would be eating with her husband at home.

Only to find it all laid out for him in the kitchen, 'bless her, he thought, she never forgets' and tucked into the tea and food with zeal.

He then carried on with his work until in the late afternoon he heard a car draw up and the front door opening, letting in Anne and her minder (for this is what he had decided to call him) who was carrying her packages, which he deposited on the hall table.

"Thank you Toby, that's good of you, goodbye now I'll see you next week then?" Toby nodded, and headed for the front door touching his hat, (it just HAD to be a small Trilby! thought Jack).

She then came down the hallway towards Jack and looking around the walls exclaimed "goodness me you have been busy, you must have been working all day!" "On and off" he said, "I met Mr.Tilson for a chat and Tilly kindly left some lunch for me. So I was able get on without interruption you see!" looking pointedly at her.

She laughed and said "I see! You were glad I was out of the way, is that it, well I'm going to have a whiskey, do you fancy joining me?" "Yes please, but you're stopping me working you know!" "I think you deserve a rest after such a long day's work" she replied and led the way into her living room.

He excused himself for a few minutes in order to clean up at the workplace and his own appearance and then joined her for the drink. Secretly glad of the opportunity to talk to her in private at last.

As he sat down, she handed him his whiskey and said "I brought the items you asked for, but we will look at the colours later, after dinner perhaps." Jack thanked her and asked, "Will Nora be in this evening do you know?" Anne raised her eyebrows and replied, "I'm not sure to be honest, I haven't heard from her since she went off on her jaunt.

No doubt she will turn up without ceremony when she needs to change clothes. She may well be here tonight in time for food, but I'll expect her, when I see her."

As if reading his mind, she then asked, "How did you get on with that old file last night, was it any help?" "It was indeed", said Jack, "I was working well into the night studying the papers and making plans for my idea, but I need your consent and help again. Can I explain what I have in mind now, or should we wait until after dinner tonight?"

Anne smiled saying, "now I see why you were concerned if Nora was likely to be in, but not to worry, even if she is, she will be off again quite quickly, so we will talk then."

"Anyway, before that you can come and help me decide what to eat tonight", and standing up she led the way to the kitchen and once there set him to work to help her.

Then as predicted by Anne, they heard the front door bang and Nora came bustling into the kitchen with, "hello you two, sorry I didn't phone, but to be honest I was having too good a time."

Anne laughed at her cheek, "good for you; so the trip obviously went well then. Are you here for dinner or not?" "No thanks' don't bother about me, I'm just here to shower and change, and then off again, we are all going out to a show; see you later" and off she went.

Anne and Jack looked at each other and laughed, "You were right, just as you said, not dull is she?" "Oh! I'm quite used to it by now, she has a new lease of life these days, "

They finished their meal chatting about the decorating he was doing, colours, finishes etc. Then Anne started to clear away the dishes and so on, beckoning for him to stay sitting, as she made coffee. Then as she sat down again, Nora appeared at the door looking resplendent in a bright Red evening gown and Black lace shawl asking "how do I look then, gorgeous or what?" They both laughed with her and together said "Oh yes!" and Anne added "of course you look good, but you know that already, by the way are you being picked up, or taxi?" She arched her brows saying "being picked up! Do you mind?"

"A taxi, it should be here any minute, but you could have put that a little more delicately you know." They all chuckled and just then the front door bell rang. Nora turned to leave saying "that's him now, I shall be home tonight, but don't wait up; goodnight!" and off she went leaving peace and quiet behind her.

Anne poured the coffee for both of them and said, "now then, we can get on with our business, you were going to tell me your ideas for the school property."

Jack began to lay out his ideas in detail, beginning with needing the permission of Mrs. Eden-Smythe being the current lease holder; then explaining his plans for using it as a secure residential car parking area. Using blueprints of the land area within the file, he had produced on paper, the number of vehicles that could be accommodated within the fenced off ground. He would arrange for 24hr. security, using the old school buildings as offices.

He believed it would accomplish several aims. It would ease the problems for residents, by taking surplus vehicles without permits off the square, with short term daily parking for visitors, and lon term security for people going away for longer periods.

On the financial side; he had costed it all with estimated charges for the service based on current figures for residential parking and possible fines for illegal parking. It would pay Anne's outgoings on the school, (council taxes, utilities, building maintenance) and bring her a rental income.

But there would be two main stumbling blocks so far as he could see at present. The first one being; a 'Change of Use' permission from the local planning office and the second; we would need agreement from the Residents Association, as it would not work without their co-operation.

Anne had been listening attentively and now said, "You have certainly been giving this a lot of thought and I would guess much late night work. "On the face of it, your plan seems to be a very good solution to some of my problems and those of the Square's residents if they would agree to it, but if we held a Residents Association meeting to discuss the advantages, surely they could see the merits of such a scheme, providing it was properly operated, and we can stress you're past experience in that field."

"Although I must ask, what would your interest be? It would be a great deal of work for you; I must presume there is a profit to be made for your involvement?"

"Yes there certainly would be, this could be the project I've been looking for. If you are agreeable, we could set up a new company and work on a Partnership basis, which means that you would grant that company a long term sub-lease, we would share the set-up costs and take a monthly salary each, whilst the new company would pay you a percentage rental, based on income."

"Alternatively, if you would prefer, I could set up the same company and pay you a market rental. In that case I would lay out the set-up costs alone, take on all of the outgoings and of course all of the profits."

Realising that it was a lot for her to take in at once and it was getting late, he pushed over a copy of his plans which he had made earlier for her perusal, saying "perhaps you had better sleep on it and we will talk again tomorrow when you have the time. I shall be here all day working on the rear hallway, so will leave it to you."

Anne sat back and thought this over, then said, "Yes; that would be the best way forward, it's a lot to take in. So you are going to be busy here again tomorrow? Well I'm sure you will be pleased to know that I shall also be here all day, and available to help if you need it! So let's leave it at that, I'll say goodnight then."

Jack said his goodnight and departed upstairs to the privacy of his room, to continue with his more detailed planning.

On retiring to her own bedroom, Anne began to think over these exciting new events. Realising that whichever way she chose to go, it needed a lot of trust on her part; after all, she had only known this man for short time.

Yet he had offered two alternatives, one of which meant no financial outlay from her side, and her solicitor Mr. Wetherall would look after her legal interests.

The whole idea looked good and would certainly take a weight from her shoulders, as outgoings and future maintenance costs on the property had been constantly rising, and she was aware of its deterioration since John's demise, but had not paid it much attention, just paying bills as they arrived because she could not be bothered to think about it.

On the other hand, the excitement of being involved in a new enterprise was somewhat appealing, especially in partnership with Jack. After all, it seemed that he had the experience and expertise to run such a business and if he could see it as a worthwhile project to put his own capital into, why should she be doubtful.

She decided to sleep on it, but would contact Mr. Wetherall in the morning to clarify the legal situation, thinking with a smile that his first reaction would be one of caution, as always.

CHAPTER 7.

Waiting for sleep, she let her mind roam over the other work in her day.

Anne had earlier received an urgent phone call from her old boss, asking her to come in to see him.

It was all part of her ongoing reserve duties to the code breaking department of her previous employers, now a very secretive offshoot of the Counter Terrorism Intelligence unit, which she was forbidden to discuss with anyone, no matter how close or trustworthy they might be; In fact when Jack had referred to Toby as her minder, he was spot on.

Toby was one of those highly trained 'chaps' engaged by the secret services to look innocuous, but could be extremely loyal and effective when an occasion was presented. Most people would be most surprised to know that he was firearms trained and carried a small, but effective automatic pistol.

Anne was held in very high regard within that service, as she had a sharp and retentive mind like few others, with a great deal of experience in certain types of code breaking, especially in the more obscure worldwide languages.

Retired at the official age of 55, she had been held on the payroll as a 'specialist consultant' to the M.O.D. due to her unique skills. Hence, she was occasionally called in at short notice to help out on special projects, under a cloak of secrecy, often as a shopping trip to visit her old 'friend' or her 'favourite stores' in the heart of the City of Westminster using a limousine service?

On her arrival at a nondescript building to the rear of Whitehall, Toby lead her via a little used covered passageway, leading to the back of that most imposing and well known building located on Whitehall itself; The Ministry of Defence; then into the very secure inner sanctum of the decoding department.

Then taken to the director's office, and only when that gentleman appeared, did Toby take his leave, saying he would see her later for the return journey.

After greeting her and offering the usual beverages, which she refused, he began explaining the business at hand.

It seemed there had been a lot of telephone and on-line traffic lately between the Far & Middle East, and the U.K. often using even more obscure codes and languages to try to fool the interceptors.

He now asked her to follow him to a special soundproof room, with a security man stationed at the door, where all of the relevant information and equipment had been laid out for her. This was where she came into her own area of expertise and was such a great asset to them. So much so, that she was not normally encouraged to mix with other members of the department unless absolutely necessary and very few people were allowed past the security guard at her door. This was mainly for her own safety, the less people who knew her, or what she did, the better. Hence Toby's close attention on the way in and out.

The director now left her alone, knowing she preferred it that way, as her work required a great deal of concentration, Therefore she now settled down to her pre-loaded equipment to study the latest communications, and worked for several hours non-stop. Solving various conundrums along the way; the only break being an occasional cup of pr-prepared coffee from a flask, and a selection of biscuits.

Until a visit from the director and Toby to tell her it was time to go home.

Her work today had managed to reveal a possible planned terrorist attack, which may well have saved many lives and injuries, so she and her masters were more than satisfied.

Then to her surprise; The Director asked "is your new lodger satisfactory Anne?" "Yes, we get on very well thankyou!" "Oh! That's good" he said.

Anne had by now dropped into a contented sleep, so that her thoughts were merged between reality and dream, which somehow included Jack and his enthusiastic plans.

Meanwhile, Jack had on returning to his room, laid out his original plans and costing sheets, which he began to enter into his computer's, business programmes, in order to produce spreadsheets with built in calculators, as part of a business plan. This would be a necessary tool to convince some people (including himself) of the feasibility of the project. It was also a simple way of factoring in various unforeseen expenses as they arose. He had done this many times in the past, so that he found it to be fairly easy to carry out. Also it always seemed to impress those he was convincing about a particular project in the past.

One of the factors he was unable to consider so far, was the extent of dilapidation inside the buildings, as he had not yet seen inside. He must arrange to do that soon with Anne, as she must hold the keys for access.

He then packed everything away and went to bed, thinking what must be done inside the house tomorrow, as he had promised Anne so to do.

Much later he heard Nora coming home seemingly, trying to do so quietly, which for her was difficult. But he smiled to himself, hoping she had enjoyed her evening.

Making his way down to the kitchen next morning, again dressed for dirty work," Tilly said "I'm doing some porridge for madam, why don't you try some, as you look as if you're going to be hard at it again today, it's good for you!" "O.K. Tilly you talked me into it, I'm sure your right." Anne chimed in with "she is right you know, if you are doing manual work, you should eat accordingly, that's why I'm having some, as I'm going to help you, whether you like it, or not!" With that they both sat down to eat with gusto, discussing what they would be doing.

After working hard all morning and having achieved all the preparation in that part of the house, they were relieved to sit down with tea, and some satisfaction. It was agreed that as Jack would be painting just the undercoats, (which he had found in the workshop); Anne would relax over some letter writing in her study.

So the rest of the day went by, until she came to him to say she would be preparing dinner for half an hour hence. To give him time to clear up and clean himself up, this he did and made his way back down to the kitchen, where Anne was placing dishes on the table for the two of them.

He sat down saying "thank you that smells good." "You should thank Tilly; it's another one of her creations, lamb casserole. She's convinced we don't eat properly when she's not here."

He laughed at this, "I'm not complaining, haven't eaten this well for a long time, including lots of fancy restaurant food." "No Nora tonight then? I haven't seen her today at all." Anne grimaced and said "I think she is regretting last night's jaunt, she probably drank too many 'cocktails' as she refers to her drinks, so spent the day in her room."

They sat together eating with relish, both having had a busy day. 'This is becoming a regular event' thought Jack, but he quite enjoyed the new found comfort and security. It seemed he had been there for many months.

As they sat drinking their coffee, he brought up the subject of his project at the school once more. "Have you been able to give any further thought to our project, as discussed last evening Anne?"

She smiled and said, "as a matter of fact, I gave it a great deal of thought, it seems on the face of it, to be a good use of the property, solving some of my financial problems and being an asset to local residents."

"Do you think it would be possible for me to look over the old school premises sometime, I am presuming you have a set of keys of course?"

"Certainly, I should have mentioned it earlier, you will need to look inside to get a true sense of the work required, I will get the keys out for you in the morning." "Also" he said, "if you are agreeable, perhaps we should contact your solicitor to check on what would be acceptable within the terms of the lease, or any other problems which he can foresee." Anne smiled, saying, "As a matter of fact, I did just that this afternoon. I phoned his office, but he was to be away all day and his secretary promised to give him a message to ring me tomorrow. I think it would be a good idea to meet him together, if that is acceptable to you? Then you can put your plans directly to him. Anyway, he would want to meet you, to make sure you were not the type to take advantage of me. He still thinks of me as a schoolgirl who needs to be looked after."

Jack let out a chuckle, "I don't think there's much chance of that happening do you? But I agree, it's very good idea, we can clear things up much quicker by direct contact." "Good", said Anne "That's settled then. Also I want to put to him both of the suggestions you had on how to set up the financial arrangements, just for a second opinion."

Jack was pleased that she'd been thinking seriously about the plan, he was pleased to know he was dealing with a sensible lady, in fact he thought, 'she would make a good partner to have in a business venture'. Now he said "I will probably need to be out for a while tomorrow, I have a meeting with a prospective client, but any day after that will suit me." Then added; "by the way, I shall be out for lunch, if you could let Tilly know for me?"

"That will be fine, I had almost forgotten that you had another life away from here, you already seem to be a fixture. Now if you don't mind, I must get up to my bed, you have worked me so hard today."

He smiled saying, "you did volunteer you know, that'll teach you! But thanks' anyway, you were a great help; Goodnight then."

He was hoping to get back to his planning, but prior to that he considered the fact that Anne had not mentioned where she had been all the previous day, while respecting she must have good reasons for this, he was still intrigued at the secrecy, and the need for what appeared to be a minder.

He also needed to return a call from Tom Clancy left on his answer phone, asking to meet him tomorrow at his office if possible. There was no reply at the company offices due to the late hour, so he left a message on their answer phone, for the attention of Mr. Clancy, to confirm that he would be there at 10am on the following day.

He then spent some time working at his desk, polishing the figures a little more, until he was tired enough to get some sleep, which he had always found easy to do, but even more so since moving in to this old, but comfortable house.

CHAPTER 8.

Next morning found him refreshed and up early as usual, after showering etc. he headed for the now familiar kitchen, looking forward to breakfast and was not disappointed. Finding Tilly there as usual, busy at the sink. She looked up saying, "morning Mr. Rogers, coffee's ready, could you help yourself?" Jack smiled to himself thinking, 'she's beginning to accept me as part of the household' and said "I certainly will, thank you and I'll just get myself some toast, O.K.?"

Tilly was busy between the sink and laundry room next door, whilst he ate alone, reading the morning paper. Until Anne came in, wishing them both 'good morning' and helping herself to coffee, she sat down opposite Jack, just as the telephone started to ring.

Tilly through from the laundry room, answered the kitchen extension, then held it out to Anne saying, "it's for you madam." Anne took the handset, began to speak into it, and then with a sense of urgency said "yes, I'll be ready, goodbye."

She came back to the table saying, "it seems that neither Mr. Rogers nor I will be in for lunch today Tilly, so as soon as you have finished this morning, you can go down to your own flat. You have the other extension down there, if the phone should ring, but the only call I am expecting will be from Mr. Wetherall and I'll call him back when I get in." "Right you are then madam, but what about Miss Nora?" "Oh! Don't worry Tilly, she will probably going out soon anyway." Now I must go and get changed, the car will be here shortly. I'll see you this evening Jack" and she rushed off to her bedroom with some obvious urgency. Calling back over her shoulder, "I'll pick up that paint that we ordered yesterday, on the way home."

Jack looked after her with some puzzlement, but somehow knew not to ask questions, as it all seemed a bit secretive and if she wanted him to know, she would say so.

Saying goodbye to Tilly, he left the kitchen and headed for the front door picking up a briefcase on the way. He decided to leave the car where it was and take a taxi, as the offices of Canada Parking Inc. were over in the City and he didn't fancy driving across the centre of town.

Walking to the main road, he flagged down a passing Black Cab and jumping in said to the driver, "City Wall please." The driver nodded and as they set off, Jack sat back thinking of what the meeting might be about.

He had made it clear that he was not interested in employment, so presumed they would want to talk about the consultancy suggested at his last meeting, perhaps they had a project for him to look at. But it would have to fit in with the other ideas he was planning at Windsor Square, which at the moment seemed to have possibilities, and would occupy much of his time. Even so, it might be good to have another 'iron in the fire' if that should fall through.

Jack's taxi pulled up at the London Wall address, and having paid the driver off, he looked up at that familiar glass adorned building, which was not looking quite so grand these days, as when he had first entered it all those years ago.

At that time he had been most impressed by this brand new development of modern office blocks, recently rejuvenated from some of the many derelict bomb sites that littered London after the war.

The area was so named after a piece Roman Wall had been discovered there and preserved for posterity; providing a contrast of old and new.

This had intrigued Jack being a newcomer to the great city, as he had been shipped in from the West Country, having learned his trade the hard way from the ground up, to manager, at one of his firm's satellite stations, in Bristol.

He was then to be trained as an Area Manager. It was all a bit daunting to him in those days, never having been to London before, (apart from a recent lunch for he and his wife at the Hilton Hotel, as an interview for the job).

But back to the present; he knew that Canada Parking Inc. had taken over the set of offices vacated by his old firm, as the lease was relinquished by them. He had wondered at the time if this was in order to enjoy some of the goodwill left over within the same trading field, as the address was well known.

The new owners of his old firm UK Parking Ltd, had their own headquarters building in another part of London, and therefore had no need of that property.

Heading for the lifts, he pressed the familiar floor number, knowing exactly where he was going, and on alighting, announced himself at the reception desk, being asked to take a seat. Looking around, he was pleased with the new decor they had added. It had a bright, warm, but professional feel to it, with photographs of several of the company's Canadian and U.S. stations adoring the walls.

Tom appeared from an office door down the hallway greeting him heartily and shaking hands, then leading the way back into a large office, with a gold inscribed sign on the door, reading, 'François P. Calera. C.E.O. where he introduced Jack to the obvious boss man saying, "Sir, this is the guy I've been talking about, Jack Rogers." They shook hands, with 'Sir!' saying in a broad "Hi there! Having heard so much about you since we moved here, I'm really pleased to meet you, and call me Frank, it's easier." Jack was shaking his hand thinking that's a relief, as he was speaking with a distinct French/Canadian accent, but said, "Likewise, I've heard much about you also." He was exactly what Jack would have expected from his past knowledge of the man; a Red tassel haired, hefty looking guy, full of obvious energy.

As he would have needed when his past was considered, having built the company from nothing, in partnership with his brother over the years.

When Jack had first researched this company as a competitor, he read the history of the founder from Québec; who had started with one little site operated by him and his brother, growing year by year to the large corporation of today.

Frank offered hospitality in the form of drinks, which Jack refused with thanks and waited for them to get down to business, which they now did without further delay.

Tom started by saying "as our C.E.O. is over here for a while", indicating Frank, "we thought it a good time to discuss the items you and I talked about at our last meeting, regarding possible consultancy work as you suggested." "Could you tell us if your situation is still the same, or have you made other plans now?"

"My position is the same, in that I don't wish to be employed on a long term basis by another company, but rather as an independent self employed consultant. That way I can follow my own agenda and offer my services as and when required by other parties."

Frank had been sitting back listening attentively. He now spoke up "Do I take it that you have other projects in mind whereby you would be setting up in a similar business, you understand why I am asking?" Jack knew only too well what he was getting at and replied, "Let me assure you that any project undertaken by me would in no way affect the operations of major companies, such as yourself and my previous company, in our field of expertise." "Also may I add that if at any time I am working on a consultancy basis for any organisation, my loyalty would remain with that client then and at any time afterwards?"

Frank let out short laugh, saying "I can see that you are anticipating my concerns before I ask, it seems we understand each other very well. Now I'll ask Tom to put forward the main reason for this meeting, we have a proposition to put to you."

Tom now leaned forward to explain to Jack, "Please forgive my mentioning this, but it forms part of our agreement with you, but I can take it that this conversation is in absolute privacy, whether or not you decide to take on this project for us?" "Of course" replied Jack "it's what I would expect."

Tom looked relieved and said "Right then, the fact is that we have been approached by a major supermarket chain about operating all of their store car parking facilities around the country, including those outside London. We are not as familiar with other major towns and cities as we know you are and would like you to look at a couple of their sites to give an opinion on how best to approach such an undertaking."

Jack smiled at them both, saying "you're being very polite aren't you? As if you need me to tell you how to approach the operation, this is your field of expertise, it's what you do all over Canada and some parts of the U.S. isn't it?" "I think you are asking me more for my knowledge of particular areas of this country and therefore if they could be profitable? This I could do of course."

Frank let out another short laugh at that and said "Tom, your opinion of this guy was right; he's seen through us in one." He continued, "You're right of course, our knowledge is lacking in the geography of the U.K. and the approach needed in a particular population area. We know there can be differences between population mentalities, according to what parking restriction they've been used to in the past. That's where you come in, as we know that you've been involved in the setting up of various out of town projects over the years, is that right?"

Jack thought to himself that they had also been doing their homework on him and said, "that's right, from London to Aberdeen, Glasgow, Sheffield, Leicester, Leeds, Oxford, Cambridge and down to Salisbury, Exeter, even in Cornwall; Plus many areas of London and the Home Counties of course"

"They varied from municipal multi storey car parks and shopping centres to top grade hotels. So you could say it has been an extensive experience."

Tom now spoke saying, "there you are then, now you know why we could use that experience, it could save us a great deal of time and cost before we submit a proposal", then laughingly added, " depending on your cost of course, just in case you get carried away?"

"Don't worry, you will only pay for my time, plus expenses for the period working for you, it would still be much cheaper than engaging new people to travel all over the country, as you well know. Apart from which, there is knowledge of this field of out there, it being a comparatively new profession in the U.K., it's taken me years to gain that firsthand knowledge, from the ground up. As your boss here knows only too well, am I right?" He said, looking over at Frank.

Tom held up his hands and said "O.K.! I know you're right, just thought I'd mention it, I didn't want my boss to think we were offering you 'Cart-Blanch', my job could be on the line then."

Frank then said "quite right too, can't have you throwing my money about. Anyway, I'm happy with what's been said this morning and now I must leave you to it, I've got a lunch meeting over at the Grosvenor Hotel." He stood up and held out his hand to Jack saying, "It's been really nice to meet you, maybe we'll get to together again sometime before I go back." Then turning to Tom, said "you sort out the detail Tom, I'm sure you will work it out, see you later." Then strode out to tell his secretary where he would be.

Tom suggested they move to his office as he had all the relevant documentation there, asking Jack if he would like to break for lunch, but they decided to get on and have sandwiches sent in.

Tom spoke on the intercom to arrange this, after deciding the fillings between them. He led the way down the hall to his office, where he indicated armchairs around a circular table for Jack to sit. Then from a desk draw he took out a file and laying it on the table, sat opposite and said,

"All we have at this stage is a letter from their property development department, inviting us to tender for the operating franchise. They have enclosed details of some of The Major sites with capacity numbers etc. to use in a preliminary survey." He pushed the papers over for perusal.

Jack studied these for a time, whilst Tom dealt with the food which had arrived, ordering drinks at the same time.

Jack had been making notes as he read, then as they settled down again, he began to talk. "You do realise that they will have sent the same thing to your competitors I suppose?"

"We did consider that and asked them, but the guy I spoke to, a Mr. Joseph, the writer of the letter, assured me that at this stage, they had contacted us first, due to our similar operations in the U.S. where they have stores, and know of us through them."

Jack nodded saying, "that sounds reasonable, it gives you a distinct advantage, but you realise, that the only profit for your firm is an operation fee, as major supermarket stores generally don't charge for parking here. But you are obviously aware of that, it must happen all time in your operations abroad, after all, that is your speciality trade mark isn't it?"

Jack picked up a sandwich to give him time to think. He could not see in all honesty what he could achieve for the company that they did not already know. However, they must have gone through all these details before calling him in and if they were willing to pay him, why not just do the best he could.

"Of course" said Tom "we are aware of those facts, but what we want is you're 'out of town' experience. As you pointed out, the cost of time-consuming recruitment of inexperienced staff, supplying transport etc. would far outweigh what you can give us."

He then looked serious and said, "now then, let's get down to business, what are you going to charge us for your services?"

Jack had been giving some thought to this since he first considered the idea of consultancy work. He could only base it on some of the costs that he had been charged when using professional services in the past. He was aware that he had no qualifications to offer, only knowledge gained in a long period of working within a restricted field.

Therefore he now said in as confident a voice as possible; my fees are based on work actually carried out on behalf of a client, at a rate of £50 per hour, or £250 per day, whichever is the lower figure. Plus reasonable travelling expenses. I would not anticipate needing to stay anywhere overnight, unless it would be less expensive than travel costs, I would only incur that expense after agreement with your office.

"I'm sure, (knowing you) that's fair and that the time limits would not be abused, but could I ask you to put those terms in writing, for my attention. I can then write to you with an official acceptance of our agreement, forming the contract between us." After which, you would be free to start at your convenience, but the sooner the better from our point of view; O.K.?"

"That's fine" said Jack, "I'll be in touch in the next few days, and contact you when I've done some preliminary work, to give you an update."

He stood to leave and Tom walked with him to reception, as they shook hands, Jack thanked him for the hospitality, and then stepped into the lift.

As he travelled home in the taxi, he thought over what had happened and began to plan the next steps necessary to earn his money. He would need to arrange visits around the country in the next few days. realising that from having little to occupy him just a few weeks ago, he now had three projects on the go at once, therefore he had better get on with it once he got home. As he now called 47.Windsor Square.

Letting himself into the house and getting a drink of water from the kitchen, he discovered that he was alone there for the first time since arriving. This suited him at the moment, as he wanted to work in his room without interruption for a while, which he did until late afternoon.

Later, he heard the front door being opened and the voices of Anne and her minder, Toby. She was asking him to carry tins of paint etc. into the rear hall. He called down to see if he could help, mainly to let them know he was there, but he was not needed, as Toby called that it was O.K.

Anne was pleased to be home, it had been a long day and she was looking forward to a long soak in the bath and a quiet and relaxing meal. She was pleased to hear that Jack was home, it made her feel safer somehow, as she had seen and heard disquieting things today.

Climbing the stairs, she called up to him from her landing saying, "Jack, I shall be getting dinner in about an hour, is that alright with you?"

He came onto his landing to say, "Yes, that's fine Anne, can I do something to help?" She replied "no thank you, Tilly has left it all ready for us as usual"

With that she went into her bedroom, to bathe and relax, giving her the chance to mull over the day's events.

CHAPTER 9.

After the urgent phone call this morning, she was whisked off to the usual office to be briefed by the director of the familiar decoding department. It was a hive of activity, due to new intelligence received, regarding a possible imminent attack within the U.K. mainland. They were fairly sure it was to be a political target, but were unable to decipher the hieroglyphics hidden deep in an obscure religious dialect of Middle Eastern origin. This was where Anne came into her own, hence the urgent call-up. She settled down to her task immediately as there was an obvious air of urgency about it.

Continuing for several hours, with only a short break for a snack whilst being shown a video film of some of the recent atrocities by the groups they were dealing with; Affecting Anne more than she had realised; During the Second World War years that she was doing this job she could only imagine the effect of their work, but to see what they were actually working against was most disturbing.

After this interlude, she went back to work with remote help from the number crunching department, as computers were known. Then towards the end of the afternoon, she had a breakthrough, by recognising certain phrases, she was able to identify the language and dialect being used. From then on the deciphering section could start making sense of messages and began to nail down target possibilities and the recipients of those messages.

Very soon, anti-terrorist squads became involved and arrests were being made, so that another atrocity could be avoided for a while. The public at large would not be made aware of the true scale of this, to avoid panic.

But also most important, Anne's part would not be known to any but a select few; her knowledge was too precious. Her involvement could never be known to the other side, for her own safety.

Jack was of course oblivious to all this and still so involved in his various calculations that he was somewhat surprised when Anne called up to him that dinner was ready and he should come down straight away, before it was cold.

Walking into the kitchen and its smells reminded him that he had eaten very little all day and was ready for his food. Noting that she was in a comfy looking dressing gown, he said "Evening Anne, had a busy day? I suppose you've been wined and dined over lunch as usual?" She sniggered and said "of course I have what else?" thinking 'if only you knew' but adding, "no doubt you have also been so called business lunching!" "Oh yes! Of course! I was visiting a large, wealthy Canadian company, now occupying my old offices and was treated to a beef sandwich and beer."

"That's good" she said, "Perhaps you will appreciate Tilly's food all the more." "I always do, and frequently tell her so."

Anne was enjoying the banter between the two of them; it was just what she needed after her day. She was still surprised at how comfortable she was with him, after such a short time.

Now she said, "I picked up the decorating items you ordered, so we can get on with it in the morning, if you are free that is." Jack had noticed that she had not mentioned her day out once more, which despite himself, he found intriguing, yet knew there must be good reason.

In fact, he could never know what she had seen, learned, and contributed to that day.

But for now he was enjoying her relaxing company after the work he had completed that day and felt contented.

As they enjoyed the food together, they once more made small talk about decorating, colours and so on, deciding to try to complete a particular area tomorrow. In fact, they were both using it as a diversion, to clear the day's events from their minds.

Jack suddenly stood up saying, "now I insist that you stay there whilst I clear the table for a change and make some coffee. It's time I pulled my weight in that area, I have a feeling you've had a stressful day and it will do you good to be quiet and rest, am I right?"

Anne let out a sigh, replying "yes, thank you very much, you are right and I'm not going to argue this time, but I'm afraid I am unable to discuss my part time job with you. I hope you understand my position, it's not just you, but anyone at all."

Jack was not surprised by this, he had suspected something of that ilk when he saw Toby and the car and now said "not at all, I guessed as much and won't bring it up again, except to say, anytime you need to be alone with your thoughts, I'll understand."

As they sat over the coffee, he changed the subject by saying, "now when am I going to see around the old school, have you had time to look for the keys yet?"

She smiled with a little relief and knew what he was doing to ease her discomfort, "not really, but I don't need to look for them, I'm quite organised you know! Any time you want to go, they are in the top drawer of my desk in the study, please help yourself. I have to ring Mr. Wetherall again tomorrow about it." She had seen messages from Tilly on the clipboard beside the phone from Mr. Wetherall, returning her call, but much had happened since then. Was it really only the day before yesterday? She thought.

"Thank you, I have some letters to post early in the morning, so I might have a quick look then, before breakfast, if that's O.K.? but I promise we will get on with the work straight after."

Anne now stood, saying "that's fine, I shall go up now if you don't mind it's been a long day, but we will get in a good day's work tomorrow, I'll say goodnight now."

Jack said goodnight, cleared the table, for Tilly to deal with in the morning and switching off the lights, made his way up to his rooms.

During that night, a great deal of action was taking place around certain addresses within the London metropolis, having been targeted to an extent by Anne's efforts.

Various suspects were brought in for interrogation and their premises were being searched, which in turn revealed other suspect addresses. Extending searches to other areas around the country. This then resulted in more and more arrests. Then as even more information was forthcoming, other anti-terrorist police around the world became involved and so the whole thing multiplied continuously.

The more this happened, the more it became evident that a major fanatical movement was being dismantled in many countries, who's only aim appeared to be the installation of a particular brand of their own religious beliefs.

Plus other groups were joining in, to follow their own agendas for various claimed rights, at least as they saw it.

This was to be brought about at any expense, including fear, death and destruction through terrorism, of any population who did not fall into their mindset. Indeed, a most unlikely connection had been discovered between Irish dissidents and Middle Eastern arms suppliers.

With any luck, this roundup should delay plans for such an onslaught by some considerable time. But unfortunately, as usual, the m organisers were nowhere to be found at this stage, being the cowards they were, they recruited many young, vulnerable and brainwashed fanatics, to do the dirty work.

Therefore the job of the many intelligence agencies involved, could not be considered complete until those leaders were traced and at least incarcerated.

Many conferences and briefings were being held throughout the night and following days, with this end in mind, including long distance communications between agencies around the world.

One such meeting was being held in the director's office at the 'Anti-terrorist Listening and De-coding Department within that Ministry with which Anne was so familiar. In fact, at one stage she became the main topic of conversation, but not named of course, when only the few people who knew her and her value were present. Although they had now recorded all of her findings and were training new people to follow her lead. They were more concerned than ever for her safety, if her roll in all this ever came to light.

On the one hand she could be placed in a safe house somewhere with 'round the clock protection', which they knew she would baulk at and could be the more dangerous option, as more people would need to know. While on the other, she could stay hidden in mediocrity as she now lived, where she was unlikely to ever be suspected of any involvement, which had worked well so far.

They had discussed this with her in the past, but being a strong minded woman, made it plain that she would not have her home routine disrupted, as she was leading a very contented life now since coming to terms with her husband's death.

The Director now spoke up to ask "I take it that further checks have been made on this new lodger!" Yet being fully aware of his background. The head of internal security was there and said "Yes director, his name is Jack Rogers."

"We have looked into his past and apart from a couple of minor misdemeanours in his younger days, he is clean and hard working in his profession. Also he is now financially sound after a generous compensation package from his last employers."

"Further, during a period of National Service in the Royal Signals Regiment, being as you will be aware, an intelligence arm of the Army. He was posted to Herteford, their H.Q. in Germany, as part of occupying forces, soon after the war, into a secure unit of special dispatch riders, where he was entrusted with highly confidential documents, travelling between Regimental Headquarters units located across Germany We are currently trying to trace his old commanding officer for further, more personal information."

Looking pleased at this information, the Director said "as a matter of fact, my stint of National Service was also in the Signals, in charge of listening posts in the field. They carry out for the Army, a similar service in a theatre of war, as we do for the intelligence services in so called, peace time. As you make your enquiries, perhaps you could look into the possibility of using him, as he seems quite close to our lady and is already installed in her house."

"I will look into it sir" said the security chief, who had been considering such a possibility after talking to his own man Toby, but thought better of mentioning it at this time.

"Right then" said the Director, "I'll leave that with you, perhaps you would be good enough to keep me informed, when you have more to report. But we can close that matter for the time being." "Now then, moving onto the next subject; tracing the original source of these radio and telephone messages." So it continued, until that meeting's subjects were exhausted, and everyone went back to take control of each of their departments, to continue the fight

Meanwhile, from scant information made available to all parts of the media the next day, they made the best of it, with lurid headlines, proclaiming;

'DISASTER AVERTED BY SECURITY SERVICES. TERRORIST PLOT FOILED' 'MANY ARRESTS OF SUSPECTS MADE AND PROPERTIES SEARCHED.'

They knew something quite serious was happening, but were frustrated at the secrecy imposed by security services worldwide, who would not reveal what was really planned for fear of warning various terror groups around the world.

As usual; these news hounds complained that they should be told every detail, without caring that many hundreds of the people involved in the security of their own populations, were at risk of failing to carry out those duties through information leakage.

Also the personal security of many of those people (and Anne was an example) was at risk, when more and more information was released carelessly by them.

The various media were obviously unaware that the momentum of what had started only yesterday was moving forward quickly in many different countries, to block out the capabilities of those groups to carry out more atrocities.

Furthermore, that they were getting closer to finding many of the main organisers and financers of these groups. Including some across the Irish Sea; who it now transpired had also been involved with certain Middle Eastern dictators, in arms running, money laundering, and terrorist training camps.

Jack rose early again next morning, dressing for dirty work once more. Descending the stairs to the ground floor, he went into Anne's study and found the keys he needed, in the desk as instructed. Walking out of the front door, he headed for the post office on a nearby street to post his letters, remembering that this was where his life began to change just a few short weeks ago.

He then headed back to Windsor Square and the school grounds. Letting himself through the gates, he wandered from building to building making notes on a pad as he went, taking into account the general state of deterioration.

Now began stepping out measurements over outside areas. He was there for around an hour before letting himself out again. Then as he was re-locking the gates, a loud, authoritative voice behind him asked, "EXCUSE ME! WHO ARE YOU?"

Jack turned to see an old man of obvious military bearing, bristling with indignation and a moustache to match, plus a strong looking, walking stick in his hand, which he thought could be about to land on him at any moment.

"Well, I am here with permission of the owner, Mrs. Eden Smythe, which is why I'm holding these keys, who might you be?" The gentleman seemed to wilt a little at that, realising that he may have over stepped the mark by not realising the implications of the keys. He now said, in a somewhat quieter tone, "I am **Colonel Batesby-Fortesque, Chairman of the Residents Association** and responsible for security in the square" Jack also relented, realising that this chap thought he was doing his duty and he had heard the name mentioned previously, now said "I am a new tenant at Mrs. Eden-Smythe's house, my name is Rogers", holding out his hand to shake his challenger's.

The colonel willingly shook his hand, saying "my apologies old boy, but you do understand that I must be on my guard, you were a stranger to me, you see?"

Jack was thinking to himself that he would need this character on his side, when it came to getting permission for 'change of use' planning on this property, so decided to make a friend.

He said "of course, I'm very pleased to know that the area has such a conscientious resident's leader, I hope to be seeing you around sometime."

Finally the colonel's curiosity got the better of him and he asked "is the lady owner thinking of re-opening the school then?" "Oh no!" said Jack, "just checking condition and so on" then adding "at this stage." 'That would set the old boy thinking'. "Well, must get back now, my breakfast will be waiting. It's been nice to meet you sir." He added the 'sir' as a clincher to their future friendship. "Same here, old boy, perhaps I'll see you at one of our meetings sometime" and off he strode feeling that he had shown his proper authority to this new comer.

On returning to the house and his breakfast, he recounted his experiences to Anne and Tilly, who both laughed. Then Tilly said "hope you didn't upset the colonel, he makes a bad enemy." Jack replied that he had charmed him, even calling him 'sir'. Now Anne chimed in saying, "Oh well! In that case, you have friend for life" and continued, "I see that your dressed for work again, so shall we get on as soon as possible?" "Perhaps I could just eat something first?" he said jokingly.

They worked hard for the whole morning, apart from a break mid morning, when Tilly brought them tea and biscuits, at the same time reminding Anne of her solicitor's phone messages the day before.

This gave Anne the incentive to do just that and she went into her study to make the call. On her return, she told Jack that she had explained the situation briefly and a meeting had been arranged for the following day with Mr.Wetherall at the school, so that they could thrash out the detail there and then. This, they agreed was the quickest and best way forward, to avoid the delays of drawn out correspondence.

Then back to the job in hand, decorating that rear hallway, which they were, determined to complete before the evening meal.

In fact, it was after seven in the evening before they finished, then as Jack cleaned up, carrying equipment out to the garden shed for storage. Anne set out their food, left by Tilly, in the kitchen. Both sat down with relief to eat in peace, speaking little, being too tired.

But they did discuss the next day's meeting for a while, deciding what needed to be talked about with the solicitor, after which, they retired to their respective rooms. For Anne, a long, lazy bath, while in Jack's case, to carry on with refining his plans for tomorrow, and the up-coming consultancy work.

The following morning, he was relaxing over his breakfast and chatting to Tilly when the morning newspapers were delivered, he sat down to read them, as he had plenty of time, as the meeting was not until 10.30am.

He could not miss those lurid headlines, depicting all the disasters that 'could have been' carried out, had the security and police services not been on the ball. He read on for a while until it began to dawn on him for some un-explained reason, that this may in all probability be part what Anne had been involved in, but that was too preposterous! Surely not quiet unassuming Anne!

Then as he started adding things together, from what she had said the previous night, and from what his solicitor, James had said about her. Add in Toby her minder, and the chauffer driven car, it all began to come together. He was now remembering the odd mention of her life as a young girl in the Ministry of Defence during the war, where she had met her husband. Also her father had been in Naval Intelligence. Just snippets of conversation from their chats together, and his instructions to apply for the accommodation on offer, but it now began to add up.

It was no wonder that she could not discuss anything with him; she must have signed the 'Official Secrets Act' long ago. He now felt even closer to her than before, and a great deal of respect as a person, over and above his feelings for her as a trusted friend.

Just at that moment, she and Nora came bustling in, chattering away, as women do at times. To lighten his own mood he said cheerfully, "good morning ladies, and where have you been Nora? I haven't seen you for days; thought you had been carried off or something?" Nora laughed at this, saying, that's none of your business thank you, but it's nice to know you missed me." Anne chipped in with, "she has been on another jaunt with her friends, to Paris this time mind you!" Nora laughed, "We were invited to a hotel owned by Jocelyn's sister, as it's out of season, and we had a great time." Then "Tilly dear, do you think you could cook me some scrambled egg and bacon, I'm starving, haven't had a proper English breakfast for ages." Tilly replied, "I certainly will, I just wish other people would eat properly in the morning too" said Tilly, looking pointedly at Anne and Jack.

Finishing their food and chatting for a while longer, Anne stood up and said to Jack, "we had better be off for our meeting; it's getting to that time."

As they left the kitchen, she asked Nora, "are you going to be home today madam?" Nora replied "Yes, until this evening, then I'm off to a fashion show in town." I will probably be out tonight though."

Jack followed as Anne walked out to the front hallway where they both put on coats and as Anne collected the keys, he picked up his briefcase with all the documents for the school inside and held the front door open for her.

Mr.Wetherall was waiting for them at the gates of the school. Anne made the introductions and unlocked the gates. Entering the old school yard and buildings, the dilapidation which Jack had previously noted, was all too evident.

They looked around outside for a while, then went into the main building and discussed the urgent requirements. After about an hour of wandering and talking, Anne suggested that they retire to the house for coffee and a detailed discussion.

As they re-locked the gates Jack asked Mr.Wetherall where he had left his car, to which he replied, “that is one of the reasons I have considered your proposal seriously Mr. Rogers, I have been here previously and am aware of the problem, so I took a taxi.”

They then walked back to the house, where Anne showed them into her sitting room saying, please sit down gentlemen; I will just arrange the coffee.

As they sat down, Jack wanted to clear the air between them and he needed the solicitor on his side, so said “I’m pleased to meet you at last, it gives us the chance to get to know each other, as I’m sure you are concerned for Mrs. Eden-Smythe’s welfare in all this. She’s told me of your long term connection with the family and I am after all a complete stranger to you both. That is why I’ve suggested two different scenarios for the way forward with this scheme, so that I am not asking her for any financial commitment unless she so wishes. That is providing we would be able to get the requisite permissions of course.” He opened his briefcase, removing the plans and financial projections he had prepared. But Mr. Wetherall held up his hand saying, “I’m sure your figures are correct, but it is no good showing them to me, I am strictly a legal man, and I’m sure you would not be prepared to invest your own money unless it was viable, this is your expertise after all.”

Anne walked back in to the room and sitting down, said “now then are we talking about the nitty-gritty of this enterprise?” Her solicitor spoke up saying “Mr. Rogers was just explaining his position very clearly and I appreciate that.”

“The way I see the situation is that first of all we must decide how you would like to move ahead Anne.

You are aware of my caution as your advisor, as Mr. Rogers just pointed out, he is a stranger to us, but you know him by now much more than I do."

Just then, Tilly came in with a tray of coffee and biscuits, which she set down on the table between them, saying "may I just ask if the gentleman will be staying for lunch?" Mr. Wetherall answered her, "no thank you Tilly, I have to be back at my office for a meeting." As she left the room, he continued with, "As I was saying, at this stage, we need to decide how much you would like to be involved Anne, as a financial partner, or simply as a landlord? Always providing that we can find a way around the restrictions within the original lease for the property" Anne had been pouring drinks for them all, and now replied, "I have been giving this considerable thought since Jack first put the position to me. If I am expecting the old school to be brought back to some sort of life, which is my responsibility, after allowing it to get into the state it is, and if this were not happening, I would need to be spending a lot of money on the place.

Therefore I should be happy to make a proper investment in a possibly profitable business. So, I would rather make it a proper partnership, also I find the idea quite exciting."

"Well, that sounds quite positive; you have obviously given it a lot of thought. He then turned to Jack to ask, "Have you considered what kind of business set-up is best for the enterprise, a straight partnership, or a limited company?"

He replied, "I decided a company might be better. Firstly it would allow for a proper rent to be paid to Anne by that company, giving her a firm income, secondly that company would become liable for all outgoings, including rates, taxes, utilities etc., which would lift the burden from her shoulders. Then finally, should the business fail, (which we all hope would not happen), the only liability would be as directors of that company, and I propose we each take a fifty percent shareholding by providing half each of whatever initial outlay is required."

Mr. Wetherall sat back in his chair looking quite impressed. He then spoke to Anne saying, "I can see why you have faith in this gentleman, it appears that he knows the business world and has considered your protection in great depth".

If you understand all that and are happy to go ahead, I will draw up the necessary documentation, is that what you wish? Or do you have any further questions?"

Anne mused for a while, drinking her coffee, and then she said, "By all means, carry on with that, it is all quite acceptable to me. I think my main concerns are more to do with, the planning authorities and local residents, who may be concerned how it might affect them."

Here Jack spoke up, I think the best move would be to approach all of the residents together, pointing out the advantages to them and the square in general. Some may wish to park in a more secure compound with day and night staff security, paying for the privilege, which would also release more of the existing space for other members and visitors.Further, there would be no excuse for outsiders to try to dump their cars in resident's spaces during the working day; they would have an alternative, by paying for short term parking."

He went on "once we had the resident's agreement that could be a strong argument with planning authorities. Anything that helps to alleviate parking problems in central London is looked on very favourably, this I know, from my past dealings with them. But all of this depends on how such an ancient lease can be interpreted, which is where we must rely on your expertise Mr.Wetherall."

This gentleman was beginning to feel a little out of his depth, as so much was being said in a short time span, so that wishing to close the meeting now; he said that I will certainly look into; I have a copy stored at my offices.

You obviously have everything else in hand, so I will take my leave, if you don't mind; I have that other meeting at the office soon."

He stood up, holding out his hand to Jack, who shook the proffered hand, saying, "thank you for coming down here, it has helped us a great deal to clarify things and to speed up the process, it was nice to meet you at last."

Anne then gave the lawyer a kiss on the cheek, also thanking him for coming. Tilly then came in to clear away the tray and said, "If you need a taxi Mr. Wetherall, my husband is just off back on duty, I'll ask him to wait shall I?" "Oh yes please Tilly! It would be most helpful."

As Tilly rushed out to catch her husband; He turned again to Jack to say, "I take it you will be informing your solicitor to act for you in this matter?"

"No, I don't think that will be necessary Mr.Wetherall, you will be acting for the new company which is both Anne and I, so there is no need for added expense is there?" "That is entirely as you wish of course, but we lawyers always like to be overly cautious." Then smilingly said "but don't tell me I have another client who complains about our bills?" Jack laughed, knowing this was lovingly said to Anne. As she had said previously, he still thought of her as a school girl. A car horn sounded outside and she opened the door for him to go down to the waiting taxi, waving as he drove off.

She went back into the living room to join Jack, who was busy making notes on the files from his briefcase. She said "Well, we have certainly set the ball rolling now, your ideas are starting to take shape, are you pleased?" Jack was thinking, 'What have I started, there will to be so much to do' but said, "I am, because I feel I have Mr. Wetherall's trust now and that means a lot to me. I didn't want him to think I could be trying to take advantage of your situation with the school, but I genuinely think this is a sensible move for both of us, and I needed a project for the future too." She stood there smiling and felt genuine warmth towards him.

"Believe me when I say that listening to you just now; far from taking advantage I would say you were more than looking after my interests with the structure of the new company and everything you have planned. Indeed, it all sounds almost too good. But I think we will need to put in more than just an initial investment, until we can see some income rolling in. But I'm sure you have prepared for that in your late night calculating eh?" "Now let's go and get some lunch, we've earned it this morning."

Following her towards the kitchen, he was thinking 'this is a very astute lady I'm dealing with; pleased she'll be involved in the new business.' As he sat down to eat, he let out a sharp laugh, saying "poor old chap, I think we left your lawyer a bit dazed, it was a lot to take in so quickly."

Anne giggled a little, "that's just what I was thinking, bless him, he looked trapped in that armchair at the end, but you can be sure he will do what's necessary." "That's all we can ask, I am quite happy to deal with the business side of things, but I wouldn't know where to begin with that historic lease, it will take all his experience to get that 'Change of Use' permission and we're lost without that. So what started as an idea was now on the way to becoming a business and all being well, the future looked rosy for Anne, Jack, and all concerned.

After lunch, they both wanted to clear their minds of business for a while, so Anne collected her list of jobs to be done and they had another look around the house to decide on the next repair project; Choosing indoors for the time being, until the weather warmed and began to dry up. In the meantime they agreed to ask local builders for estimates of work required to the outside building structure.

Eventually it was decided to re-paint the main stairwell area, using much of the unused paint; this work now became a kind of therapy to them both.

CHAPTER 10.

But not all of their respective future was connected to one business venture, they were un-aware that other factors being enacted elsewhere in their name would intervene to disrupt their lives. At times with a certain amount of danger involved, which would draw them even closer together?

At the Ministry of Defence offices, deep within the high security section of de-coding & encryption, a most important conference was in progress in the Director's office. Those present, apart from the man himself, were head of security, (Toby's boss), a chief inspector from the anti-terrorist squad, (protection division) and a major from Army Intelligence, (Royal Signals Regiment).

Everyone present was aware of the main subject for debate.

Recent phone, radio and Internet messages between known terrorist group leaders and local activists had been deciphered, seemingly to instruct a search to be made for a mystery specialist, being used by security forces and responsible for beating their 'unbreakable' coding system.

Although they must have been aware that many of their local members had been put out of action, the fact that they were still broadcasting to many of the contacts, must mean that they were not totally sure just how many.

This meeting had been called as a matter of some urgency, it was feared that there could still be a few fanatical cells left, unknown to them, thus putting their specialist in possible danger, making that person's protection paramount.

After a long discussion, with various suggestions having been made and mostly dismissed; it was agreed that the main stumbling block was in not revealing that identity by use of surveillance people, possibly known to the enemy. It was therefore agreed that the status-quo of this person was the best protection, which had worked well so far.

To this end, Army Intelligence had been brought in when enquiries had been made of Mr. Rogers's ex-Commanding Officer, during his tour as a dispatch rider in Germany and to scrutinise his records. The Major now stood up to explain their findings;

"I can confirm that Corporal Jack Rogers was classified as an S grade dispatch rider, Or SDR, which means that he would be one of a few in such trusted squads, with authority to carry high grade confidential documents, between Regimental Headquarters based all over the South West of that country. May I remind you that it was still considered hostile territory, and we were an occupying force? During his duty in Germany he was based at the Royal Signals H.Q. at Hertford Barracks.

He had no religious or political leanings of any kind, but was capable of bending the rules to suit him when required. From time to time he managed to get into scrapes of one sort or another. But these were mostly overlooked, as to do his job in the atmosphere of that period in Germany, soon after the end of hostilities, he needed to be resourceful, and that was thought to be an asset.

In fact on at least one occasion he was blocked on his journey by heavy German haulage vehicles, with the crews trying to highjack the contents of his message satchel, hoping to find something of value.

Luckily, he was armed at all times (being proficient in various types of handgun and automatic weapons) and able to dissuade them. On this occasion he was backed up by a passing Military Police patrol, who called in the local police. I am telling you this to show that he was capable of thinking on his feet, if the need arose.

Although he is officially still held on the Reserve list, he has not been involved with his regiment, (apart from some of the annual re-unions), since his demobilisation.

I think that covers the relevant information about this gentleman required in this case."

As he sat down, the Director began to speak. "Thank you Major, if no one else has any comments?" he hesitated and looked around the room enquiringly; Then continued, "I would suggest that Mr. Rogers be approached by his own Regiment to get his reaction." He waited a few minutes for any comments, then continued; "It occurs to me to ask, could he still be considered under orders as a reservist, Major?"

Taken somewhat by surprise, the Army man answered hurriedly, "I am not sure if his age would be a factor, but I will certainly look into it, before he is interviewed." (Being un-aware of Jacks' connection to Military Intelligence).

The director smiled and said "if you would be so kind, major, it could make things easier should he prove to be uncooperative." The veiled threat was clear to all.

Bringing the meeting towards its close, he now reminded all of the members present, of, A. the secrecy, and B. the urgency required. Then, asking the two security men to devise some sort of cover for the subject in question, at least until the Army had done its job.

But he then added; "May I add that whatever you decide to do, it must not change the equilibrium in the way that this person is currently living.

Any change could be noticed; I would suggest you keep Toby in place as he has always been, as a sort of un-noticed dogsbody, he has always played the part very well in the past."

He then stood up, saying to the group, "thank you for coming gentlemen, I hope to hear your plans in the very near future." With that he moved back to his desk, dismissing the conference.

The chief security officer for the department and his colleague from counter terrorism, moved into the former's office to decide a strategy, aware that this was a very delicate situation, with the lady's safety at stake.

After mulling over several ideas for her protection, all of which seemed to carry risks of exposure, it was decided a better solution would be to use Toby in a more involved capacity, as temporary protection, hidden within the community. They were aware that a lot of renovation was about to be carried out at the subject's home; and he was therefore to be 'promoted' to become a labourer as part of a builder's team, employed to carry out work on the exterior of No.47 Windsor Square.

They knew from Toby's regular reports that the lady in question had been asking for tenders for its renovation from local builders and decided that one of their own, vetted contractors would win that work, as they would cover the major cost from within that department's budget. It would be a discrete way of covering her until Mr. Rogers had been approached and hopefully put in place.

This plan was immediately put to the director and approved for instant action, with a note to the effect that he would inform the lady in question personally.

Consequently, on the following morning, Anne received a phone call from him, (which she knew would always be scrambled), informing her that the department's local building firm, had decided to offer a very reasonable tender to carry out her house renovation, backed by him, as a 'thank you' for help received. But of course it must only be between the two of them.

Then as an aside, he added, "by the way, don't be surprised if you see Toby working there. Put it down to work experience!" Then, before she could get into an argument, he rang off, but could swear she heard a chuckle! Sitting back in her desk chair, she began to absorb this. Something was going on, of that she was sure, but knew better than to argue with them, once they had put a plan in action.

Then she thought to herself, 'why should I complain, I'm getting my house done up cheaply, and I don't need to talk to all those different builders'. It then occurred to her that she would need to explain it to Jack, as he would have been involved in the decision, but she would talk to him later. Secretly, she was mostly pleased at the cost saving as always.

Within the next few days the whole plan would swing into action, with builder's vehicles delivering scaffolding and materials and men permanently on site (including Toby), assembling the scaffold and erecting storage and rest cabins. All of which created a more secure environment, the more people around, the better, hiding what was in effect a protective security situation.

So for the time being, her protection seemed to be under the control of the internal security services, without it being obvious.

Furthermore; Anne was more than happy, seeing all this action to improve her house; but finding it hard not to acknowledge poor Toby's presence, as one of the workers. She felt rather sorry for him, knowing he was used to a much more genteel lifestyle. Yet, she was also aware that he was most capable of looking after himself and her, in any situation.

On the same morning that Anne received her phone call, Jack had a letter from Canada Parking Inc., acknowledging his letter and confirming the arrangements discussed with Tom at their meeting. It confirmed that this formed the basis of a contract between them and asked him to start his work at the earliest opportunity as they were looking forward to receiving his report in the near future.

He smiled to himself, thinking 'that's a polite way of saying, GET ON WITH IT NOW'. But he had previously decided to make a journey up to the Midlands to cover several of the client's larger Supermarkets in the first instance, as he could visit those units in a couple of days, planning to set off the next day.

As Anne and Tilly had gone off shopping for new curtains or something, he was alone in the house. This gave him an opportunity to gather the things he would need for the job to be done and pack a few clothes for overnight stays. He could also plan his journey and itinerary, for the next few days. To this end he phoned a couple of hotels that he had used in the past, to book overnight accommodation.

As he completed this, he received a very strange phone call; it was an old friend from his service days, **Bill Knightly**, with whom he had loosely kept in touch from time to time over the intervening years, but mostly at Regimental re-unions. He was a regular career soldier and had now risen to the rank of Lieutenant Colonel.

He started by saying; "Sorry Jack, can't chit chat, but I'm afraid this is an official contact, I'm phoning, rather than writing to you, as it is a matter of some urgency." Jack was shocked at his tone, it sounded most officious, so he replied, "O.K. then Bill; better let me have it, whatever it is."

Bill cleared his throat before saying, "could you meet me as a matter of some urgency, somewhere well away from my office";

Jack knew that meant Regimental H.Q. near Ripon, in Yorkshire. “I could come down to London if you wish.” Feeling confused, but intrigued, he thought for a couple of minutes and then said, “as a matter of fact, I am due to travel up to the Midlands tomorrow, so could meet you halfway if that would help?” Bill appeared to let out a sigh, “That would be most useful, where shall we meet?” Jack said “I have a hotel booked just outside Birmingham, would that do?”

Bill agreed that would be ideal and after Jack had given him the name and directions, he said “see you tomorrow morning then, about, 10.30-11.00 O.K. with you? Can I add that this is to be in the strictest secrecy?” As Jack concurred, the phone was disconnected rather abruptly, but he presumed this was to stop any questions.

As he made his morning tea, all sorts of ideas were tumbling through his head. Why should anyone from his old mob be interested in him? He was aware that Bill was involved in the Army Intelligence side of The Royal Signals, being an electronics wiz, but that’s all he knew.

But he would find out tomorrow, so there was nothing more he could do until then, apart from speculate of course, as he had to admit that the secrecy aspect was most intriguing.

Therefore, to keep himself occupied he decided to spend the rest of the day maintaining his car ready for the journey tomorrow, as he always preferred to do himself, knowing the Monza as well as he did, after many years and almost 200,000. Miles of ownership, he had no desire to change it, or allow others to mess with it.

As he was working outside on the car, Anne and Tilly came home in Arthur’s taxi, and he could hear Anne insisting she pay him for the journey, although he claimed to be on his way home for lunch anyway. He then heard her say, “Tilly, you go in with Arthur to get him some food, I can get a sandwich for Jack and I.” Thanking her, Tilly and Arthur carried the items that had been bought into the house.

She then came over to Jack saying, "You are a 'Jack of all trades' aren't you?" He laughed and explained about his journey the following day and that he would be away for a few days, leaving out the meeting with his Army contact, as ordered.

Anne nodded and realising she was a little disappointed at his not being here when the building work started, which again she was not allowed to discuss with him. But instead, she told him lunch would soon be ready, so to get cleaned up and went off up the steps into the house. He smiled at this, thinking, 'she gets more like a mother (or wife), day by day'. But if he was honest, he quite enjoyed being fussed over now.

As they ate their sandwiches together, Jack expanded on his trip and why he had to go now, under a contract agreement, asking for urgency. He added "I'm sorry to delay the decorating we had agreed on, but I am hoping to complete this job quite quickly, and we can get on with it once I get back."

Anne said "don't be silly, that is unimportant, our agreement was that you would carry out that work when possible, your own career must come first." Then she added, "Whilst on that subject, I've had a very good quote from a building firm that I know, for outside work on the house. Apparently they have another job in this area, which helps with costs, so I have agreed with them to go ahead."

Jack was surprised at this news, as they had not discussed it for some time, but it was her decision after all said and done. He replied, "It sounds like a good deal, to get someone to start quickly is most un-usual. I should be back in time to help you, all being well."

"Not to worry Jack, this building firm is trusted by several people I know, who have had work done by them in the past, so that I'm sure all will go well."

He now stood up to say that he had paperwork to do upstairs and would see her at dinner time.

After he had gone, Anne mused on what had been said, hoping that she had not broken the promise to her department chief, (though she did not know the real reason for that), but thought it to be the best way to make Jack aware that things were about to happen.

Then she and Tilly had a busy afternoon sorting out their purchases and preparing a meal for that evening, which was to include Nora for a change, as she had phoned to say she would be home.

Meanwhile, upstairs; Jack went through the information he had regarding tomorrow's trip.

The more he looked into the possible business, and based on knowledge gained over many years in that profession, he became more convinced that there was little profit to be made. He knew this because he had produced feasibility studies in the past for his company, proving just that fact. Yet he had tried to warn his clients of this, without wanting to break confidentiality with his past employers. But to no avail, they seemed to feel that they had more expertise from their similar overseas operations and the same should apply in the U.K.

Yet he would do the best he could by producing an up-to-date précis of the facts, and then leave the decision to them.

He carried on working on the other main project figures and plans, of the old school business for some time, until he heard Nora's strident voice calling up to him that dinner was ready.

On entering the kitchen, he was met by an exited babble of conversation, mixed with the smell of a traditional roast dinner, which was just what he was ready for and it all made for a homely atmosphere.

He started with, "good evening ladies, this is all very pleasant and welcoming to a poor old bachelor. It's Nice to see you again Nora after such a long time."

The lady in question rounded on him with a smile, "I do hope you're not being sarcastic Jack, you're probably just jealous because you haven't been enjoying yourself as I have, and what's with the 'poor old bachelor bit, you are enjoying the life, be honest?"

Anne laughed at their bickering and said, "Now then Nora, he has been working very hard you know! Even made me work too; have you seen the rear hallway, since we re-decorated it?" "As a matter of fact I did notice it, most impressive, perhaps he has earned his dinner." She was secretly amused at the happy note in Anne's voice, they were obviously getting on together, as she had hoped; She could now break some news to them both.

As they settled down to the meal together; She began, "this may or may not come as shock to you Anne, but if you feel that you can manage, I would like to take up Jocelyn's offer to move in with her." She now stopped to see Anne's re-action, who seemed quite nonplussed and just smiled, saying "I am not at all surprised; it is obvious you are happy over there and why not? You have a new life now and so it should be. You have been a great help to me over the years and I am most grateful, but that was my life, now this is yours, just be happy darling." Nora jumped up, rushed around the table, to give Anne big hug and a kiss on the cheek. "Oh Anne!" She exclaimed "I'm so glad you're not upset, I haven't been able to tell you before, for fear of hurting your feelings."

"But I'm hardly ever here these days and Jack is here now, to keep you company, although I know that may be only temporary. I hope we shall always be friends." She was babbling a little by now, so stopped talking abruptly, dabbing her eyes.

Anne smiled and cuddled her back, "Of course I shall miss you, but I am fine these days and quite capable of running my own life you know. Much as I am pleased to have Jack here now, he is a paying tenant after all and I must not rely on someone else to be a part of my life." "Just believe that I am very happy for you to live your life in your own way, and I wish you luck in the future."

Then in order to give Nora time to recover, she turned to Jack and asked of him; don't you agree? You have gone very quiet for a change!" He laughed at this and replied, "Well, I'm not really involved, so thought I had better keep out of it. But let me say Nora, I'm also pleased for you, it's obviously what you want to do and good luck to you. After all; your old enough to make up your own mind now, aren't you?" he said with a grin. This was also met with a friendly kiss on the cheek from Nora and a 'thank you' from her.

Anne now stood up to say, "Jack, could you open a bottle of wine for us," pointing to a wine rack in the large corner unit. "We should celebrate a little, don't you think?" and began clearing the table and starting the coffee lay out. Then as an afterthought said, "No, let's have a liquor with our coffee instead, it's in that cupboard beside the wine Jack."

Smiling to himself, he replaced the wine bottle and selected a Cointroue, realising that Anne was giving Nora time to collect herself.

After Anne had filled the cups and Jack, the glasses. Nora picked up her glass, saying simply, "thank you both; this makes it a lovely evening after all."

The other two picked up theirs, with Anne Saying, "here's to your future darling", with Jack adding, "Hear! Hear!"

He then asked Nora when she planned to leave, explaining that he would be away for a few days, starting tomorrow. She replied that it would take her about a week to pack and make the move, so it shouldn't be a problem.

Anne butted in here, by saying, "If you don't mind, I am quite capable of looking after myself you know! So don't organise your movements around me." They both laughed and Nora said; "That's true, I should know better, sorry my love, just didn't want to let you down too suddenly that's all, and I feel better now."

A little while later, Jack excused himself and stood up with, "I shall be leaving very early in the morning, so I must say thank you and goodnight ladies, if you will excuse me." They both returned his 'goodnight', and he left, leaving them to talk privately together for the rest of the evening.

This they did, deep into the night, recounting their life together, remembering the good and the not so good times with, and then without John, over the years.

Then Nora asked, "Tell me, Anne, what are your feelings toward this new lodger of yours? Is he just that, or more?" Anne looked surprised at that and said "Oh! Nora, don't be silly! He is much younger than I, he wouldn't think that way about an old lady like me, I have a lot of trust in him and I enjoy his company, but at the moment he has plenty of other things going on in his life".

"As a matter of fact I will probably be his business partner soon." Her friend replied, "It's just that you both seem to get on so well together, right from the start, that's all. I suppose I was being selfish in hoping you would have someone else in the house, when I decided to move on."

"I have told you before, Nora, I am quite alright and happy with my life as it is. With much more to look forward to now, so stop worrying about me."

Of course, Nora was totally unaware of the other part of her life and all the excitement it brought. Which was just as well perhaps, as then she would have had something more to worry over.

CHAPTER.11 .

Jack set off early the next morning intending to beat the rush hour traffic heading in and out of London, which indeed he did, all the way to Birmingham. So much so that he arrived at his hotel in time for a leisurely breakfast. After which, he retired to the lounge area to read the morning newspapers and await Bill's arrival.

Spot on 10.30 a.m. Lieutenant Colonel William Knight of the Royal Signals Regiment; strode into the hotel lounge, and although he was wearing a suit, there was no doubting his profession. He spotted ex-Corporal, Jack Rogers and headed across the room to him, holding out his hand, as if greeting a long lost friend. As Jack stood to shake the hand, Bill said, quite loudly, "how nice to see you again, after so long, what a co-incidence." Jack felt that he should follow the lead, although he had no idea why, and said "yes indeed, what a lovely surprise!" Then indicating an armchair asked "won't you join me for a while?" Bill thanked him and sat down.

He then leaned in towards Jack and said much more quietly, "good, thanks for falling in with that little charade, now we can talk sensibly. Luckily you have chosen a table out of the way." He then produced a folded document holder from his inside pocket saying, "sorry about all the subterfuge, but I have to ask you to read this before we start." Adding in a slightly louder voice, "would you give me your opinion on this idea of mine?" As Jack sat back to read, Bill called a waiter over and ordered coffee for them. After it had arrived, Jack put down the papers with as straight a face as possible, but inside his head was utter confusion.

The main page was a photocopy of 'The Official Secrets Act' in his name, with his signature, from many years ago, taking him completely by surprise.

The second item was on his old regiment's headed paper, officially reminding him of his duty under the 'Army Reservist Requirement', which he also vaguely remembered signing on his release, many years ago.

He must have been showing some concern as he looked up, because Bill sniggered a little and said "I thought that might shock you, but I'm afraid I must have your signature, before I can explain." But Jack was still unsure what was going on and said so, "and what if I don't want to sign?" Bill looked a somewhat embarrassed saying "Again, I'm afraid you have no choice under military law, but I can assure you that once I fill you in on the details, you will want to help. It concerns your landlady."

At last! Thought Jack, I see a chink of light. If Anne was in some trouble, he would be to help. So he signed page and initialled the letter from his old mob, as he called it, wondering at the same time, what he had let himself in for.

Bill picked up the documents, before he could change his mind and replaced them in his inner pocket, somewhat relieved that it had gone that easily, which was why he had mentioned the lady in question. He had surmised correctly that Jack had a lot of respect for her.

He now began to outline the details of what had been going on in the other life of Mrs. Eden-Smythe, of which Jack was only vaguely aware. For that matter, even Bill was not too sure of the details of what she did within the M.O.D, only that she was a very important person to them and in need of high priority protection. To this end he had been given his orders, using his past relationship with Corporal Rogers, to coerce him into co-operating in this matter. Using whatever methods were available.

"Did you know that your landlady was involved in a top secret occupation at the Ministry of Defence? Apparently she works within a very hush-hush department where she is highly respected."

Now Jack did look shocked, although he had suspected something, it was never anything like this and he said so to his co-conspirator.

"Well! I can assure you that this information comes from the very top, and I'm not privy to the detail, only to say that you are the only person who is in a position to carry out this duty.

Jack was nonplussed and said "how on earth can that be, I am simply a lodger at her house and a comparatively new one at that. What can I do to help?" (He was not sure if Bill was aware of his other occupation with Military Intelligence.)

Bill explained the situation regarding her anonymity, the possible risk to her safety and how important it was that the status-quoi was maintained, that her lifestyle did not change from its current routine, so as not to draw attention to her.

Therefore, his residence at the house gave a unique opportunity to provide close surveillance, without it being obvious. They simply wanted him to be aware of any strangers turning up around the house, or anything that could be construed as unusual, keeping in mind the knowledge he had been given.

"Could you give me a few minutes to absorb this information Bill? It's a shock to find out that Anne is such an important person. I suspected that she was bright, but not to the extent you are telling me and she puts on a convincing act of the simple gentlewoman."

"That's O.K. I need to visit the Gent's anyway, I'll be back shortly." He was pleased to have a break, giving him time to contact his superiors with a progress report. Which at this stage was reasonably positive, but he still had a way to go, to convince his friend of the seriousness of the situation.

As for Jack, he was totally bemused by what he had heard; yet it confirmed some of his thoughts on what he had thought of Anne and her other life.

He was now seeing her in a different light altogether, but then realised that this is exactly what he must not do. The aim was to keep things just as they were and not to do anything to draw attention to her.

What the security service was asking, seemed quite a simple task, as it didn't interfere with what he was already doing, apart from being more observant.

Bill now returned, reseating himself and asking "what do you think then, do you feel able to do as we ask, or are you perhaps unhappy at the thought of being responsible for her safety?"

Jack replied, "That's just my quandary, apart from being a bit more aware, I don't see what I can do to help, I'm not a trained bodyguard. But I can assure you that I am fond of Anne and would try not to allow anything to hurt her, if I were capable of doing so, but there is my dilemma; just what am I capable of?" Am I to presume that the people wishing her harm would be most capable in that field? Who exactly are these people anyway and why Anne?"

"All I know at this stage is that she has a unique skill, which has caused certain factions huge setbacks to their plans for terrorist acts in this country. They are making efforts to find out who is able to decipher their very special coding system, based on their various obscure languages. Information gathered by our listening experts, here and abroad, points to them believing that they have a mole in their own ranks at the moment, but they are also looking for an expert within our own security services."

Bill took a sip of coffee and continued; "Up to now she has been kept hidden within her very normal looking lifestyle, of which you are aware. In fact you, and now me, are two of a very select group of people allowed to know her identity. So much so, that until you just told me, I was un-aware of her first name. She has been very carefully protected over several years and only used when it was imperative.

Jack had been listening attentively and now said, "Just tell me if you can Bill, is it to do with all these arrests we've been hearing about lately on the news, and how are the Royal Signals involved?"

Bill simply nodded his head and added, "As for our involvement, we have been using our communications outlets abroad in certain countries where we have military personnel on the ground."

"Secondly I am now authorised to say, you have been under scrutiny by the Anti-Terrorist crowd ever since you moved in, hence they contacted us for your past record. Then when this latest intelligence came in we were asked if you could be trusted."

Jack let out a chuckle at this saying, "if they looked into my past record in the mob (Royal Signals Regiment) that would have put them off completely. Nice to know that I've been scrutinised though, all I wanted was a comfortable home for a while."

"They were more interested in the fact that you were able to think on your feet and that you had a high security rating as an SDR." 'Army slang for a Special Dispatch Rider'. "You should be flattered! You could have been quietly turned down for the tenancy. Now let's get back to the matter in hand. Are you up for this assignment? I need your answer today, as my superiors are hanging on for my call, so that they can set things in motion. It's a matter of some urgency."

Jack replied, "Of course I'm up for it, just tell me what I need to do? Do I need to cancel my current project or what?" Bill was relieved, he had achieved his main purpose for being here this morning and asked? "Can you tell me what it is you are up here for, or is confidential?"

Jack then explained his consultancy work and although he had a duty of confidentiality to his client, it in no way interfered with their subject.

Simply car parking advice, he then added, "but if this is all so urgent, what about Anne's present safety, should I cut my business short to get back to London?"

Bill was pleased at the way he had now grasped the urgency and to put his mind at rest, explained that the Ministry department she worked for had let him know that they had plans in hand to cover that period and she was well protected at present.

On being told this, Jack suddenly remembered that a firm of builders were due to turn up in the next few days and wondered if this could present a safety risk. He pointed this out to Bill, who smiled and said. "Did it all happen rather suddenly do you know? I think you'll find that's the cover I mentioned."

Then it dawned on Jack, he had thought it to be a bit strange that the building company were known to her employers and were conveniently working in the area at that time. He laughed and said "they are a devious crowd! We just don't know half of what's going on under our noses, do we?"

Bill now asked, "can you tell me are you on a fixed time table on this trip, what I mean is have you fixed up any appointments today?" Jack had not, as he was more on a fact-finding trip and wanted to arrive at the various sites as an anonymous customer, therefore didn't have any set plans in mind. He told Bill and asked him why he needed to know? Bill said he needed to telephone his superiors to bring them up to date on what had been decided and would probably receive further instructions. "So why don't we have some lunch. I wonder if you could get us a discrete table in the dining room and I'll join you the shortly."

Jack agreed and set off to arrange it, finding a corner table again where they would not be overheard, this amused him, he was already thinking like a sleuth again, though this was not so new to him.

A little later, as he was perusing a menu, Bill returned and sat opposite. They ordered the food, and after the waiter had left, Bill told him that his bosses were very pleased that he had agreed to do as asked, and would be informing the other agencies involved. As to his precise duties, Jack was to simply be aware of the possible danger to Mrs. Eden-Smythe, without changing their normal routine, but to look out for strangers around the area, not including the current builders on site, as they had all been previously vetted.

Before he left the hotel, he would be given an emergency telephone number to call at any time, should he have a problem.

The food now arrived and they talked as they ate, discussing further detail of the job in hand.

Finally Bill smiled at him and said, "I'm sure you will be pleased to hear that during this time, you will be 'On Strength' salary-wise, based on a grading of 'Military Intelligence Special Covert Agent' the exact details of this will be sent later. It won't make you wealthy, but it's worth having."

Jack was most surprised at that, payment had not occurred to him and said "so I am going to be paid by the army, (he almost said TWICE, but stopped) without even asking for it! Now that is surprising!"

Bill chuckled, "well, after all, we can't ask you to put your life on the line without paying you can we? Anyway, as you're on the strength, you can't sue us."

Jack exclaimed "Hang on a minute! No one mentioned my life being at stake previously; it's a bit sneaky to slip it in now isn't it?" Bill laughed at this saying "well you don't think we'd pay you for nothing do you? Just think, you're better off now than you expected to be, I'm even going to pay for your lunch." He then called the waiter over to deal with the restaurant bill.

Jack snorted! “Some deal! But I don’t know that I’m better off, when I came here this morning, I was quite contented with life and safe!” Yet thinking to himself, that he didn’t really mind, it was quite good to feel useful, especially being able to help Anne, after she had been so good to him. But it was good to have a moan at the army, just for the fun of it.

They stood together and shook hands, with Bill saying “thanks for listening, this all must have come as quite a shock to you, not knowing what was going on under your nose. All I can say now in all seriousness is please be aware of what I’ve told you, in the strictest confidence.

You can’t even mention it to your landlady; she mustn’t be spooked out of her everyday routine.” If I should need to get back to you, in the next few days, will you still be in this hotel?”

He replied “yes, I still have to complete this job for my clients and I’ve already lost a most of the day thanks to you! But I am surprised that you say Anne knows nothing about all this extra security, she’s not silly you know. Perhaps she’s worked out why the builders arrived so conveniently, don’t you think?”

“That could well be the case, but unlike you, she will be used to being aware of things around her and won’t change her routine without good reason. Well I must get off, it’s a long drive back to H.Q.” With that, he turned on his heel and strode out of the hotel as he had entered earlier in the day.

After he left, Jack looked at his watch, surprised to see that it was only 2.30pm. It seemed as if he had been talking to Bill for much longer. He therefore decided to get back to the job he came to do, knowing that one of the sites he wished to visit was within a short drive from the hotel.

He therefore finally booked into his room, had a quick swill and then picking up his briefcase, headed out to the car park.

Finding the required supermarket easily, he carried out his survey inside and out making Dictaphone notes all the time, spending in all some two hours there.

Deciding that there was no reason to contact the manager, as it was all pretty standard stuff so far as he was concerned, he had seen it all so many times before.

On the way back to the hotel, he toured the area looking for competition which may affect his findings, but there was nothing of any consequence, and he headed back to the comfort of his room.

After showering and changing into more casual wear, he decided to phone Anne before going down to eat, just to check that all was well and that Nora was staying with her. Despite himself, he now felt somehow responsible for her welfare.

Anne answered after the third ring and was obviously pleased to hear from him, saying "how nice of you to telephone, I thought you would be far too busy to think of us down here, with your power lunches and so on!" "Not really Anne, just boring business meetings about of all things, Supermarket car parking would you believe! Not exactly something to shout about." Then trying to introduce his main concern, he asked, "is Nora with you then, or is she gadding off again?"

Laughing at that, she replied, "as a matter of fact she has been very busy all day, packing things into boxes and deciding what she should take or not. She is just setting the table for our meal and said she will not be going out tonight, she's too tired." He was relieved to hear this and told her he hoped to be back in the next couple of days. To this she said, "When you do, you'll be surprised to see what is going on here.

The builders have already arrived today with much of their equipment and intend to start fixing it all up tomorrow; they are even leaving a night watchman on duty to protect it all."

Jack smiled to himself, now being aware of what was really taking place, but said "now that's what I call efficiency, you must have some very good friends; I'll say goodnight then Anne, give my love to Nora." She said goodnight also and rang off.

The following morning saw Jack out and about early, wanting to get his task over with quickly, so that he could return to London as soon as possible, now that he had other duties to consider.

He continued with the survey of several sites around the Midlands area, up to a 60 mile radius of his hotel, for the next two days. In some cases meeting with store managers to discuss local customer requirement; but they invariably confirmed his original conclusions.

He therefore decided not to waste another night at the hotel and telephoned the house to tell Anne he would be home that night. But as she was not there, left a message with Tilly.

Booking out in the early evening, he set off for the journey back down the Motorway towards what he now called home, looking forward to the new found comfort.

The journey being un-eventful, he arrived at 47 Windsor Square well into the evening and was most surprised by what had transpired so quickly.

The house appeared to be totally surrounded by scaffolding, all well lit by hanging electric spotlights, there were also four small Portacabin type buildings double stacked on the roadside. He eventually found a space to park elsewhere in the square and walked back to the house, carrying his cases.

On arriving at the front door and attempting to unlock it, he was approached by a solid looking chap in workman's clothes, who asked him who he was and what business he had there. Just as Jack was about to ask him the same thing, the door was opened by Anne, saying "it's alright Jenkins, this is Mr. Rogers, my lodger, he's been away for a few days, so you wouldn't know him."

"Oh! I'm sorry mam! But I need to be sure, I'll say goodnight then" said Jenkins in a subdued voice. "Thank you for that; Are you alright for beverages and food, or would you like something sent out?" said Anne. "No thank you mam, I've got all I need in the office." With that, he touched his cap and slipped away.

As she held the door open for him, Jack stepped into the entrance hall, put his cases down and turned to Anne with an enquiring expression on his face. "Well now that's a nice homecoming I must say! What on earth has been going on while I was away, and who is the bodyguard?"

She laughed at his demeanour and said, "take your coat off and come on into the kitchen, I'll tell you all about it." As he entered, Nora was busy at the stove, she turned and said "Hello there wanderer, nice to see you back. Come on sit down, the food's ready." She and Anne started to lay the table and they all sat down to eat. As they tucked in, Jack looked at Anne and asked "So what's happening out there, it's all a bit sudden isn't it?" Although he was well aware of it being part of the security operation for her protection, that Bill had told him about.

Anne told him that it had all happened on the day of his departure. The builder had phoned her that morning to say, the materials and equipment were on their way, but it should not interfere with her routine, as it was all exterior work, apart from the parking area being taken up.

She was most surprised at the speed of it all, but pleased at the same time, also that they were employing a night watchman to look after the materials and equipment. The builder had told her that there had been a great deal of pilfering on their sites and it was necessary these days.

Jack absorbed this and was thinking that her employers seemed to have covered everything, but then he thought, 'they do this all the time and are professionals'. But he said to Anne, "Well I think you have some good friends to have arranged it so well and so quickly but it looks expensive to me."

"But that's the beauty of it Jack, the quote they have given me is so much cheaper than all the others, I couldn't refuse it. I think my old bosses might have had something to do with it mind you, as this firm does a great deal of work for them, but I'm not going to complain."

'I'll bet it's a good quote', he thought, 'even free if I'm not mistaken'. "So long as you are happy Anne, but then, you would be if it's a bargain eh!"

Now Nora chipped in with a chuckle, "he's already got you sussed out Anne! We all know how you love a bargain, and hate paying out. Right I'm going to make some hot chocolate to take to bed, anyone else?"

They both said they would, so she made herself busy clearing the table etc. while they sat and chatted about Jack's trip and the report he needed to prepare over the next couple of days. He explained that this would need to be completed, before he could carry on with the rest of the internal decoration that they had agreed on. "Of course you must," Anne replied, "that is your business, which comes first; our agreement was a few hours whenever you can fit it in."

Placing their hot drinks on the table, Nora said "I'll say goodnight to you both, I have much to do tomorrow. See you in the morning?"

They thanked her and said 'goodnight', as she picked up her drink and went off to her bedroom.

Jack asked Anne if that meant that Nora was leaving tomorrow and she nodded saying "I think she may have been waiting for you to return, although I told her not to. But she is looking forward to starting a new life and I would rather she did, than hanging on to help me."

"Yes, I agree, if that's what she's decided, it seems she is happy with her new life, so why not?" You're bound to miss her after so long, but seem to be happy for her to go now, is that right Anne?"

"I have thought for some time now that she would need to move on soon and I'm pleased for her so to do. I shall miss her, but I'm back to normal now and quite capable of caring for myself." They carried on chatting for a while longer, until it was time to retire.

As Anne went on up to her room, he made sure all the locks around the house were in place, with more care than previously. Then carrying the cases up to his room, he settled down with some relief. It had been a very long day.

Three days earlier, it had also been a long day for others involved in the security operation to protect Mrs. Eden-Smythe.

Anti-terrorist and M.O.D. officers had been involved in the building operation at No.47 Windsor Square, by instructing Fred Appleton, Managing Director of F. W. Appleton & Sons, (General Builders and Decorators), on the urgency of this job, and that they would be adding to his workforce with a few of their own men. This would include overnight security, and that was all he was told.

This did not faze Mr. Appleton at all, he was quite used to receiving similar instructions as part of the contract he had with the M.O.D. and all of the staff he employed had been cleared by them. As was his site manager, Jim Macready; who by now knew the routine for using these men as normal, but being aware that they had other, more urgent duties at times.

He was most happy to have the overnight security problem removed from his responsibility; it was always difficult get a reliable night-watchman. He had been instructed that this chap's name was simply 'Jenkins', though he doubted this being his given name in 'real life' anymore than the other 'new employees' joining his workforce. Fred Appleton had also been instructed to phone the lady of the house that morning to advise her of the immediate action they would be taking. Then to proceed A.S.A.P. with delivery and setting-up of the job in hand; as per his written work instructions, with an emphasis on never leaving the site un-attended, at anytime.

This entire activity taking place whilst Jack was away in the Midlands for only three days in total. Including, his own recruitment of course; which was a major part of the whole operation?

This had all been reported to the Director of Anne's department, who was pleased that all had gone so well and had been discretely carried out.

Again at around that same time, Lieutenant Colonel William Knightly of the Royal Signals Regiment was being de-briefed about his meeting with ex-Corporal Jack Rogers

His Commanding Officer of that section of Army Intelligence was most searching in the questioning, seeming to be very interested in the man's character and how far he could be trusted to carry out what had been asked of him. Bill assured him that Rogers seemed capable and obviously thought a lot of the target lady, but it must be remembered that he was no trained bodyguard.

Then the C.O. surprised Bill by saying, "in your opinion, would he benefit from a short refresher training course in firearms, and to be licensed to carry a small handgun, Just in case?"

Bill had to think carefully before answering and said, "At this stage, I would not consider it necessary to approach him and it seems a bit drastic to suggest it yet. Perhaps we should wait a while to see if the threat becomes more imminent? I don't think he would be keen to carry a firearm again, unless absolutely necessary. Smiling to himself, he could just imagine Jack's reaction to such a suggestion.

"Right then", said the senior officer, "we will leave it at that for now, but keep an eye on things and me informed at all times." "Yes sir," said Bill, as he stood up to leave and make his way back to his own office. On entering the outer office, his admin corporal and clerk stood smartly to attention, and he told them to relax, asking for any important messages. "On your desk sir, but one person in particular has phoned several times, and is very persistent; he won't leave his name." Said the corporal, "He just keeps saying it's most urgent that he should speak to you, but I didn't think I should interrupt when you were with the commanding officer."

"Quite right corporal, the C.O. wouldn't like that!"He walked on into his office, picking up the messages, several of which were from his contact at the anti-terrorist squad, asking him to call A.S.A.P. as a matter of some urgency.

Picking up the phone, he dialled the special number he had been given previously and was immediately put through to his contact. No names were used there, only a code word, 'Hertford'

"Thanks for calling back, I take it you are using the scramble button?" Bill confirmed that he was and asked what the urgency was. His contact was most anxious to know the outcome of his meeting with 'the lodger' and if he was willing to carry out the assignment as discussed.

Bill smiled at the obtuse language being used; they seemed to have their own, in their quest for secrecy. He explained what had taken place at the meeting and assured the contact that all was resolved at present.

It transpired that more phone and radio conversations between the suspects had been intercepted, (which it was now possible to translate), showing that they were perplexed at the amount of information known to the U.K. security services. The fact that they were still using the same coding system proved that they were unaware of the breakthrough.

It appeared that they were now convinced of a traitor in their midst and were looking to find the mole at present. Which suited the protection unit, as the pressure was off their target for the time being, but they must still be vigilant.

To finish the conversation, Bill assured him that 'The Lodger' had been given the emergency phone number and code. So that there was no more to be done at this stage and with that aside, he rang off.

He then sat back to consider the implications of what his C.O. had said, with regard to possibly arming Corporal Rogers. Bill had never considered things to be that serious, just a matter of surveillance by him, not as some sort of bodyguard.

Yet it showed the level of anxiety felt by some of the top brass.

But he had plenty of other work to deal with, which had been neglected over the last few days due the sudden orders to contact Rogers after all this time adrift.

He called out to the Corporal to come in, so that they could begin to clear up the work. Including information gathering from Signals listening posts in other

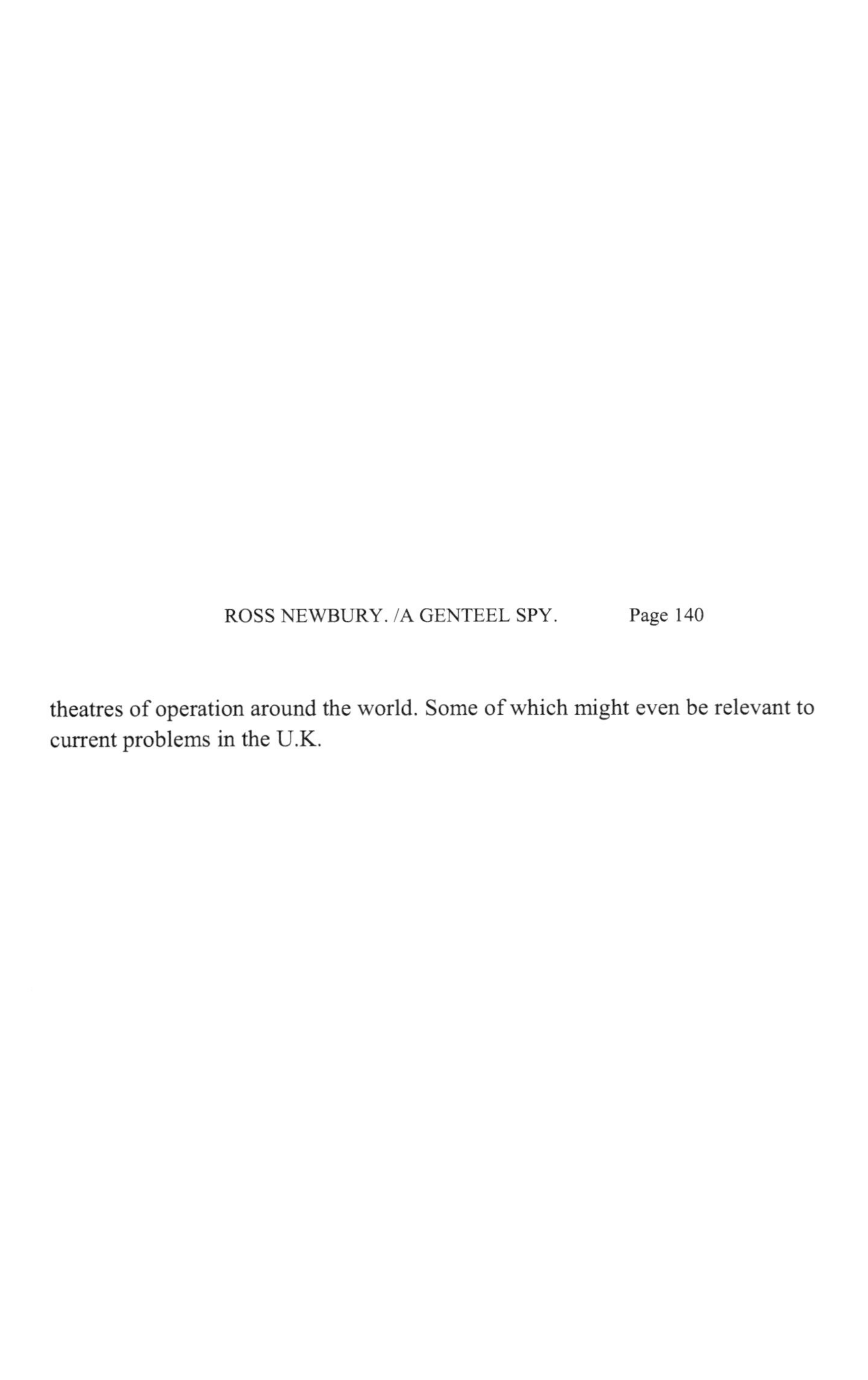

theatres of operation around the world. Some of which might even be relevant to current problems in the U.K.

CHAPTER 12.

Anne awoke early to noises emitting from workmen busy on the outside of the house, which was somehow a comforting sound, knowing that the work was being carried out at last.

After preparing herself for the day, which she knew would be busy one as she had received a message the previous day from the Director, asking her to come in to the office for a special job!

She was aware of what that might entail. Usually a brain-storming session on some new encryption language that had been discovered by the listening posts, which tended to take several hours of intense concentration.

Descending to the kitchen to prepare breakfast, she was surprised to find Nora already there, cooking herself a hearty meal. Now! Nora was not known for early rising of late, as she was more likely to be just coming home at that hour, in her new life. But then, Anne remembered her retiring early, as she was moving out today, and greeted her with, "Good morning darling, preparing for a busy day then?" "That's right" she replied "Just thought I would get fortified, after a lovely long sleep," adding, "can I get you some?" Anne declined, pouring them coffee as they both sat at the table.

As they were chatting about Nora's moving out and the arrangements she had made for transportation, Tilly came bustling in, apologising for not being there before them. Anne smiled at her and said "you were not to know we would be early were you? So stop worrying, do! You know that Nora is moving out today?" "Yes she told me and I shall be sorry to see her leave madam." Then turning to Nora said, "I'll help to bring the boxes down and Arthur is ready with his taxi to take you over to your friend's house, whenever you're ready."

Jack now entered with "Good morning all you ladies, it seems I'm the lazy one today, why is everyone up so bright and breezy?" Anne chuckled, saying "we all have lots to do today thank you, not like someone who will be sitting at his computer all day!" She then said. "By the way Tilly, I shall be out all day and Mr. Rogers will be working in his room, so you organise things to be done as you wish."

Tilly answered "yes madam, I know what needs doing" and turning to Jack, asked "would like me to make you some lunch Mr. Rogers?" "No thank you, I'll probably get myself a sandwich if I need it, I would rather keep working today." She nodded bustling out to start her work around the house.

As the three of them chatted, mostly about Nora and her plans, Jack was musing over Anne's remark that she would be out all day, wondering if she was covered, although he was quite sure that was pre-arranged.

Just then the door bell rang and Anne stood up saying "that will be for me", hurrying out to the front hall. On opening the door, she was pleasantly surprised to see Toby waiting as always and immaculately dressed as usual, with the car and driver double parked out in the roadway. As Toby wished her a 'Good morning', she said "it's nice to see you here Toby! I thought you would be much too busy on your Building Work?" giving him a quizzical look as she was getting into her coat. He realised that she was 'pulling his leg', but was far too serious and polite to say so; replying "no, not today madam, I have a day off for this duty."

She called out goodbye to the others and went through the door, just as Jack appeared, to check who had called for her, trying to carry out his new duties, but realised he should have known it would be covered and called out "bye" in reply. He waited for her to get into the car, and then closed the front door.

Returning to the kitchen, he chatted to Nora for a while longer, who tried in her own way to ask him if Anne would be O.K.. He assured her that he would be looking out for her friend after she was gone, which seemed to satisfy her. "Now, I had better get to work, let me know when you're ready to leave, I'll give you a hand."

After which he made his way upstairs to get on with that report on his findings over the last few days. He had decided that there was little point in visiting any more of the Supermarket sites, as they were all of a similar ilk and he didn't think it fair to keep wasting time (and his client's money) on a foregone conclusion. Even so, he worked all day producing the best feasibility study possible, from the information gathered, now and in the past, but without much enthusiasm.

Apart from an interval when he heard Nora in the process of leaving and went down to help with her boxes etc. But Tilly and her husband had things well in hand, so after the taxi was fully loaded, he gave her a kiss on the cheek, saying "Aurevuior Nora, I'm sure you'll be visiting Anne regularly won't you, so I'll see you then? But best of luck anyway" and was surprised to see a little emotional tear in her eye. Yet had he thought more about it, he would have realised it was big step in her life, she had been connected with Windsor Square for many years now.

He returned to his room and the production of his masterpiece on behalf of Canada Parking Inc.

Sometime later, Tilly called up to him to say that she was off now, but had left a sandwich for him in the kitchen. Calling down his thanks, he smiled to himself thinking, 'thoughtful as ever Tilly.'

Apart from a further quick break to make a cup of tea and eat the food, up in his room, he continued to work until late in the afternoon.

Finally, completing the report, showing proposals for a comparatively small profitable outcome, should they decide to pursue that particular contract?

He produced three copies of a professional looking document; parcelling two of them for posting and retaining one for himself, he finished up for the evening.

Looking at his watch, he realised he had not heard Anne come in, although it was quite late and went downstairs to look for her.

At that time, Anne was actually in the car on her way home after a very hard day, almost dozing in the back seat.

On arrival at the Ministry this morning via the usual back door methods, she was immediately shown into the director's office by Toby, who then left with a polite aside of "I'll be here to collect you whenever you are ready mam." She thanked him and walked to the chair held for her by her boss, who had obviously been waiting for her. He then sat across from her over the conference table, so recently used to plan for her protection. Of which she was totally un-aware of course.

He started by saying "Thank you for coming Anne, I'm afraid we have another stinker for you to solve. It seems our opponents have become somewhat paranoid about our infiltration into their communications, they seem convinced that they have more than one traitor in their midst. So much so, that they are going to extraordinary lengths to weed them out. Hoping we think to isolate the imaginary traitors, by going deeper and deeper into their ancient languages, known to a few faith teachers only, for use in their coding system. We are frankly at a loss, as we thought we now had all of these installed in our computer memory banks, but they are floundering at the moment. You studied many of these in your university days, but I doubt you went that deep into the culture?"

Anne replied "I think I covered most known dialects around the world in my university thesis, but it's impossible to know them all of course. Yet I did find that as in many languages, dialects often merge as far apart as Latin and Gaelic or Egyptian and Chinese, due to the worldwide trading carried on through shipping, and overland caravans." she suddenly stopped, saying " I'm sorry Director, I was on my Hobby-Horse again, I do get carried away on the subject."

"Please don't apologise dear lady, it's fascinating to a code cruncher like me and that's why we value your expertise so much.

Your knowledge is born of enthusiasm for this subject which makes you a unique asset to us. Each time you reveal a new language or dialect being used in the hieroglyphics of coding, we are now able to record it into our memory banks, for future use." "For instance, this time it appears that they are probing various Nationalities with differing phrases in the hope, we presume of trapping their targets."

"But they are also persisting in plans for wholesale destruction of the fabric of certain Governments around the world. Occasionally they even try to contact cells which have already been taken out, unknown to them, thanks in part to your previous work."

I have arranged for the information we have gathered, to be placed in the 'Private Room' for you under guard, are you happy to work there or here, in my office?"

The 'Private Room' was a specially designed space, securely protected from prying eyes, ears and electronics, even from within that secretive section of the Ministry building. With several recording and playback machines, plus display screens connected to the main computer system and a secure internal communication system.

Anne replied that she was quite happy to work in that room, as she could concentrate without interruption there. Then she added, "By the way Director, may I thank you for the kind gesture of having my house repairs seen to, it's a great weight from my shoulders."

"It's the least we could do to thank you for all your efforts on our behalf, dear lady. Is Toby enjoying his new employment, do you think?" Anne chuckled, saying, "poor boy, it's most unfair you know, he is so good at his main duties and hates being grubby."

The Director smiled and said, "Commander Tierney, his boss, tells me it will be good for him to harden his body a little more and it's not for long." He then stood up and came around the table to escort Anne to the secure office, necessary due to the tight security surrounding her.

Having delivered her past the door guard and made sure she had all that she needed, also introducing Clare; her assistant for the day, (a young lady that Anne had not met before), to be available at Anne's beck and call, via the intercom between them, (but she would not be told Anne's true name). It would be Clare's job to feed the relevant information to the screens for her attention.

Anne now knuckled down to her task. With other de-coders having pre-sorted the more straight forward information, from the complicated language deviations; she could get right down to her specialisation. Which was much too involved for anyone outside that expertise, it was all down to her and she soon became engrossed in the intriguing detail of separating language peculiararities, and occasional similarities. In fact she was so engrossed that she was surprised when the intercom buzzed; it was Clare asking if she would like lunch brought in. She asked for just a sandwich and glass of milk, as she didn't want to break her concentration too much.

On delivering the food later, Clare asked if she could stay and have hers there also, as unbeknown to Anne, she had been instructed so to do; whilst the guard on the office door was discretely being replaced.

Anne was quite pleased to have the company for a short while, and as they chatted, realised that this young lady was most interested in the subject also, and most willing to learn. As Clare must have the highest security to be there, she saw no harm in this.

After some 20 minutes, Anne hinted that she wished to get on with her work, by beginning to clear her part of the table. Clare took the hint and collected the crockery etc. and as she left said, "I'll bring you a cup of tea about three OK?" Anne nodded her thanks, already absorbed in her studies.

So it went on until late into the afternoon, when she called Clare, to ask her to bring the Director in, when he could spare the time.

Soon afterwards, they both arrived with an air of expectancy, with the Director asking, "before we start, did you wish for Clare to be present or not?" "Yes", said Anne, "I think she could be helpful now and later."

They both sat down either side of Anne eager to see what she had discovered, during the day.

She had drawn up a rather complicated chart, showing obscure connections between phrases from differing languages and various similarities between dialects used therein and how a rough code could be developed from those key phrases.

But the most important item she had discovered, was the use of obscure certain Religious Text Books that she could not name at present, but knew she had read at some time in the past; they may even be in her own library at home.

After that it became deeper and deeper, until they were both lost in the detail, and said so.

When Anne said to Clare, "surely your number crunchers could write a programme, or whatever you call it, and feed it into your computers, to sort out the detail for you?

Once it starts to marry up my findings, it could produce a whole range of codes that the opposition are using." She then sat back with a sigh, saying "I really do feel that I have extracted all the information you should need, for now and well into the future, once that computer programme is up and running," continued, "I will give it more thought at home, using the books I have there."

"As I cannot meet these people, I will rely on you and the Director to supervise that work Clare, and now I am going home to relax."

They both looked at her charts in amazement, quite unable to understand it all, but realising she was right, and the computers could now do the 'donkey work' required.

The Director now spoke, "well Dear Lady! You've done it again, although I don't pretend to understand half of these languages you've used, I'm sure you are right." Turning to Clare he said "will you be able to convey what you have been asked by this lady." She nodded enthusiastically, "I think I get the gist of what she has discovered and I'd like the opportunity to work further with the computer programmers, if I may sir?"

The director was somewhat relieved, as he was not so sure that he had grasped the concept, but said, "Certainly my dear, you show me what you are capable of and make this an absolute priority job, I will ensure that your supervisor is instructed." He then added, "You will keep me informed on your progress at least daily, and I must stress again the need for discretion, as to the source of this information. You will not! I repeat not! Mention this lady to anyone but me. Do you understand?"

Clare was shocked at this, but could see perhaps the reason why, replying, "Yes sir, I fully understand what you say and will follow your instructions."

She was pleased at being made privy to something very big here and was determined to do her best not to abuse that trust. She continued, "Where should this information be held sir, in the office safe?"

The director thought for a while and said, "No, it will be placed in the hands of the chief security officer and held in the department's vault. I will see to that now." Picking up the phone he arranged for the documents to be collected from him, there and then, so that he could instruct that department to release them only to Clare, or himself. He then asked for Toby to collect Anne (although her name was not used of course), to see her home.

Five minute later, reliable Toby arrived to take Anne home. She said goodnight to Care and the Director, who thanked her profusely, and off she went, through the usual back entrance, looking forward to home and bath; Feeling that a good and successful day's work had been completed.

On the journey home, sitting quietly in the back seat of the car, Anne considered what had happened today, and hoping that this would be her last visit to the ministry for some time, as the work tended to mentally drain her these days.

Also she preferred the comfort of her own home much more, although Nora would not be there now. Which reminded her that her friend would have moved out while she was not there, feeling a little ashamed that she had not given it a thought all day, with all that had been going on. It was after all, a major change in both their lives, after many years together. Then she closed her eyes and relaxed.

As Jack came down downstairs from his room, he called out to see if anyone was at home, but it remained very quiet, even the builders had finished their work, as it was now dark outside.

Anne was obviously not yet home, so he became a little concerned at her whereabouts, although he knew she was in good hands.

Then it dawned on him that, here he was as a so called protector, yet he had no way of contacting her, as he wasn't even sure where she was and had been so engrossed in his own work, that he hadn't given her a second thought until now.

He could only guess that she had also been busy late into the evening, and well protected.

He could do nothing about it at the moment, so decided to help by getting a meal ready and headed for the kitchen once more. He could smell something cooking as he entered, and sure enough, Tilly had been as efficient as ever. A Cottage pie was simmering gently in the oven, with vegetables prepared in a steamer, ready for just placing over the heat, which he now did. Then began to lay out crockery, cutlery etc. so that he could have it all prepared for when Anne came home, as he imagined she would be tired after such a long day.

As he completed this, he heard voices at the front door and on walking through to the hall, saw Toby ushering her through the door, looking up to see Jack and accepting that Anne could be left in his charge. He therefore said, "I'll say goodnight then madam." She replied "goodnight Toby and thank you very much, will I see you in the morning, at your other job?" He smiled at her joke and said "you probably will madam." He then touched his hat and closed the door.

Jack helped her remove her coat, saying "you've had a very long day, come and put your feet up, the meal will be on the table in a few minutes" leading the way into the kitchen.

As she sat down with a sigh, Anne exclaimed, "Oh how lovely! You have it all ready, I wasn't expecting this, but I am certainly not going to argue tonight, it's just what I needed."

Busy at the stove, Jack said "You must thank Tilly, as usual, she left it all prepared. But you had me worried when you were so late, I've just realised that I have no way of contacting you when you are out, as I don't know where you are."

Anne smiled to herself at this, "well it's very nice of you to be concerned, but you can be sure that when I'm with Toby, he has it all organised, and I'm afraid I am unable to say any more, if you don't mind?"

"Not at all" said Jack, "I do understand, but you ought to consider getting a mobile phone you know, it could be quite useful, for other times. Especially when we go into business!"

"Yes, I have considered it, but never bothered to get around to arranging for one. Perhaps I'll have a word with my telephone contacts sometime. Now then, let us eat, shall we, I'm starving."

They sat for a while, chatting over their meal, mainly about Nora's leaving, and the work Jack had been doing all day. Until he got up and said, I'll just clear this lot away and make some coffee."

Anne stood also saying, "Not for me thank you, I'm going up to take a long bath and get into bed to read for a while, if you don't mind. Thank you for doing all this, it was most appreciated, I will see you in the morning will I?"

"Yes. I shall be in all day, apart from going to catch the early post, before breakfast. Goodnight now!"

After clearing away, he once more double checked that all doors and windows were secure, noticing as he did so, the duty night watchman strolling around by the Portacabins outside.

He was not to know that that man on duty had been given instructions to be extra vigilant that night, just in case the car had been followed, without being noticed. It was a million to one chance, but they were being even more vigilant now, if that were possible.

After what he had learned today, the Director had become almost paranoid about this Lady's safety, she was so important to the current project.

But he need not have worried, as Toby; sensing the extraordinary importance of his job and the day's events, had already spoken to his chief of security and arranged to spend the night there also.

He really did take his job very seriously, and had a great deal of respect for his charge. Mrs. Eden-Smythe.

The next morning saw Jack up early once more and quietly leaving the house, he strode off towards the Post Office to deposit his report, for priority post; then circled back via the Old School to take another look at his future business venture, making a mental note to ask Anne about the solicitor's progress.

He then returned to the house for his breakfast, noting that there was already a great deal of activity from the builders, who seemed to be getting on well with the required work.

As he let himself in through the front door, he was surprised to see Toby by the works manager's office and in working overalls at that! But guessing why he was there, made no attempt to acknowledge him.

On entering the kitchen he was greeted by the usual delicious smells of coffee etc. and the chatter of Anne and Tilly as they worked to prepare it. Tilly was telling Anne about Nora's departure the previous day and laughing about some of the things she had said earlier in her life with them.

Not wanting to intrude, Jack started to pour himself a drink, when Anne said "good morning Jack, you're quiet this morning," he replied "I didn't want to intrude on your reminisces, but good morning to you both. Did you sleep soundly Anne, after your hard day?" She nodded saying, "I did; thank you, and feel refreshed this morning."

Tilly asked him as usual if he would like some breakfast cooked, "No thanks, but I see you have some fresh Croissants, could I have one of those, with some toast?" Anne said to this, "I've told you to help yourself to whatever you wish in the kitchen, you mustn't feel that you need to ask." Jack now helped himself and then something occurred to him and he said, "These are really fresh, have you been out to get them Tilly?" She giggled at this saying, "When do you think I've had time to go out this morning, the milkman delivers those three times a week. He collects them on his way round, from the local bakery."

What Jack had in mind was, how did the poor chap get through security, but of course they would know him as regular. But thinking to himself, it just shows how his mind is working now, a few days ago it wouldn't have occurred to him.

Tilly excused herself, saying she was going to be cleaning upstairs today.

Anne had been opening the mail and said "you would like to read this I'm sure, handing him a letter from the solicitor. Jack began to read and was encouraged by the content.

It seemed that their lawyer had been busy, as he had drawn up papers for the new company and asked that they come to his office to sign them under witness, when they could also decide on a name.

Also to discuss matters relating to the school lease, having been researched in some depth by the historic department, with some positive results.

Handing the letter back to her, he said "that looks good, we should make an appointment to see him as soon as possible; don't you think?" Anne agreed and said "I'll phone this morning, but do you have any times, when you may not be available in the next few days?"

"No, I'll work around it, this is much more important, so the sooner, the better. Things are looking quite encouraging from that letter, so with luck, we can get moving soon."

"Now I had better get on with some work in the house, there may not be much time in the near future. I'll carry on painting the stairwell where we left off, are you OK with that Anne?"

"So long as you can manage to fit it in, but don't neglect your other work will you. If need be, we can always get a firm in to do the work?" "Not at the moment, I have nothing pressing to deal with now, and I did promise you as part of our agreement, which I intend to stick to."

Changing into work clothes in his room, he made his way out to the garden shed, to collect the tools and equipment he needed, then set to, for a solid day's work on the staircase.

Meanwhile, after clearing the breakfast items away, Anne went to her study, to telephone the solicitor's office to arrange an appointment, which was set for the following day at 10.30am. So she walked through to inform Jack, who was pleased it would be so soon, as he was eager to get going at last. Anne then went off to see Tilly upstairs, saying as she went, "I'll be back later to help."

After working with Tilly for some time, she suggested that they have a break over a drink in the kitchen, and went down to make some tea, telling Jack to join them in a few minutes. For the rest of that day apart from a couple more quick breaks, they worked hard together until finishing well into the evening, but managed to complete the job they had set out to do.

Before settling down to another quiet evening meal together which was becoming something of a ritual, but a time they both enjoyed. It gave them the chance to go over the day's events and plan ahead to tomorrow's meeting.

Jack thought they should decide on a name for the new company and after much soul-searching and innovative ideas, they came up with the grand title of **'Windsor Auto Storage'!** (The first name they had considered).

After further time chatting, they both stood, each intending to clear away, but Anne insisted, pointing out his efforts last night.

On the following morning, after the usual breakfast scene, but without Tilly, (as she was taking young Peter to the dentist); Anne and Jack left the house together (which was noted by Toby up on the scaffolding), to walk a few streets to the offices of Ainsworth, Smith & Wetherall. Arriving well in time for their appointment, made their way up to the reception floor, were acknowledged by the severe looking lady behind the desk with a short "good morning Mrs. Eden-Smythe", and sat down to wait. Jack had noted that Anne did not need to give her name, being obviously known and expected. Most impressive, he thought, this lady is full of surprises!

On seeing them leave the house, Toby had called in to his chief to report the matter, as per his instructions. He was informed that providing Rogers was with her, he need not be concerned, just be aware of them being shadowed by others.

Anne and Jack were not made to wait for long, as within a few minutes Mr. Wetherall appeared from his office saying, "Good morning to you both, thank you for coming so promptly," giving Anne a peck on the cheek and shaking hands with Jack, and ushering them into his office. He indicated two old, but comfortable looking elbow chairs across the desk from him. As they all settled, he said "now then I think we should start by telling you what we have discovered within the terms of the school lease. It is a somewhat complicated old document, written in historic legalese, being constructed for the purpose of protecting the new residents of

Windsor Square at that time. Obviously what you are now proposing was never envisaged"; He paused, to let out a small chuckle, (un-characteristically); "after all they were still using horses in those days, cars were unheard of as everyday transport." "In fact some of the newer properties have been built on what was the stabling and coach, housing area. There was even a resident Blacksmith installed there."

Jack spoke up here, saying, "that hadn't occurred to me, but it must have been that way, wasn't that one of the main reasons for these estates being so popular? Due mainly to the inconvenience of travel at the time; I have operated parking garages in several parts of London which were originally stables.

Here Anne butted in, with "The history is all very interesting, but how will it affect our plans? That's what we need to know Robert." Mr. Wetherall smiled at her, "Don't be so impatient Anne, you know I like to indulge in the past, whenever I get the chance!"

Looking at Jack he said, "This is her impatient side coming out as you will find out, as a business partner. She will complain that I am costing her money next." (Jack now realised how close they had been over the years).

"But you're right, we must get on," said the lawyer. He now passed over a two page conclusion prepared by the research department, which laid out what they thought could be carried out under the lease and how best to go about it. "As you will see, providing it is interpreted in the right way, the use could be changed, so long as it is for the betterment, and by the agreement of current residents.

Though to do this; various legal interpretations have to be put forward, and I have prepared such a document for you to place before your resident's meeting and the planning authority."

"So!" Said Anne, (still a little miffed at his leg pulling) "You have been busy after all Robert; this seems to be just what we need to get started, thank you."

She turned to Jack to ask "what's your opinion, do you think this will be sufficient for your plans?" "Yes, it looks OK, much more than I was hoping for, to be honest. So our next move would be a meeting of the Residents Association, don't you think?"

"I agree," said the lawyer. "There is no point in approaching the planning department without agreement by residents."

Now we must get your Limited Company set up, I have the papers drawn up for you to sign. All you need to do now is decide on a name, have you had any thoughts?"

Jack replied "Yes we have discussed it and we would like to use the name; **'Windsor Auto Storage'**, is that OK?" "That's fine, providing it is not already in the 'Register of Companies' domain." But we will complete the documentation using it, and see what happens." With that, he pushed more papers across the desk and asked them both to sign where marked.

After which he took them back and witnessed their signatures, saying, "Now to complete matters, all I need is a cheque from each of you for 50% of the initial investment, then I can then get your share certificates drawn up." I just hope you are both aware of your responsibilities as directors of the company. I suggest that you read this leaflet, explaining your commitments" passing over yet more paper.

As they each handed over their personal cheques for the agreed amounts, Robert said, "I take it you would like my invoice made out to the company name, after all is complete?" He was looking at Anne, with a quizzical smile on his face.

She rose to the bait by saying, "Oh! I might have known you wouldn't forget that, you old Scrooge." They all laughed as they stood up to leave.

Showing them through the door, the solicitor said, "I will register the new company today and let you know in the next few days when you can commence operations. Goodbye to you both." Giving Anne another affectionate peck on the cheek and shaking Jack by the hand. They thanked him and left the offices, walking down to street level.

Stepping out onto the pavement, Jack said "I think we should go somewhere to celebrate, do you fancy having lunch somewhere nice Anne?" "Oh! What a lovely idea, I fancy somewhere expensive, do you?" He laughed and called for a taxi, saying to the driver, "**Hilton Hotel, Park Lane** please"

As she climbed in to the taxi, Anne said "you know how to impress a lady don't you, I haven't eaten there before, do you know it then?" "Oh yes" said Jack, "I know it very well, the underground car parking there was one of my operations."

The taxi pulled up to the front entrance to the Hilton Hotel, and its door was opened by a uniformed doorman, allowing Anne to step out as Jack was paying the driver. Then as he walked around the car the doorman grabbed his hand saying, "Hello Jack, how nice to see you again, it's been a while."

He smiled saying "Hello Oscar, it has been some time. I just thought I would take this lovely lady to lunch in your Roof Restaurant." Oscar looked at Anne and doffed his hat, saying "Bon Appétit madam." He then moved to open the swing door for her.

As they ascended in the lift, Anne commented about his reception by Oscar the doorman saying, "You seem to be well known here don't you?"

Jack chuckled, "I should be, I was here many times a week, often in the early hours of the morning, for the last 12 years. My company runs, sorry; used to run the parking here and it was under my control, first as an Area Manager, then as the Company's General Manager.

After a pleasant lunch in the Roof Restaurant, and finishing with coffee out on the balcony admiring its impressive panoramic views across Hyde Park, they chatted about the new venture and its potential; providing all went well. They then toasted Windsor Auto Storage Ltd. in wine and coffee, both in a happy frame of mind.

Anne then excused herself to 'powder her nose', while Jack dealt with the bill and the waiters. As he was waiting at the entrance foyer for his companion, his mobile phone rang and on answering it, was surprised to hear the voice of Toby on the line.

He said "excuse me for calling you Mr. Rogers but I have been asked to check that all was well with you and Mrs. Eden-Smythe?" "Yes, we are fine thank you, just finished lunch at the Hilton, we will be home soon, OK?"

He replied apologetically "I'm very sorry to trouble you, but as you had not been seen for some time, we were concerned." "No problem, Jack replied, we'll see you shortly, tell your bosses we're fine."

That was a shock he thought, it brought him back to reality with a bump. But before he could think further, Anne came out and they headed for the lifts once more.

On the way down to the ground floor, Anne spoke up with "that was most enjoyable, thank you for thinking of it Jack. He replied looking very serious, "you do realise that we have probably just blown half our first year's profit Anne." "I don't care", she replied, "It was well worth it, if we could do just that once a year, it would still be worth it!"

Jack laughed and said "You've had too much wine and your past caring, wait until tomorrow when you start adding up the cost!"

As they came out of the hotel front door, Oscar called a taxi for them, and as he let them into the car said, "nice to see you again Jack and you madam, hope to see you again." "Oh! You will!" Said Anne, it was marvellous and we shall be back!" she had, perhaps had a little too much wine, but still didn't care."

Jack tried to hand Oscar a tip, but he said, "Not from you sir, please" and closed the cab door touching his hat. Anne said expansively, "What a very nice man he is." Yes! She was happy indeed.

Back at the house, Toby was reporting to his superiors on his conversation with Mr. Rogers, assuring them that all was in order. His chief was most relieved, as they had been out of view for too long and no one seemed to know where they had gone to, after visiting the solicitor.

But what the hell were they doing at the Hilton Hotel? It was not at all in their normal sphere of life? Yet, it appeared that she was being well looked after by their protector, Corporal Rogers.

The Director was perhaps showing even more concern than usual, (if that was possible) as there had been considerable developments since the revelations on Anne's last visit.

The following day had seen a great deal of activity, when computer programmers had got to work; with Clare's help, they followed the direction of Anne's notes and charts. Producing a suite of search programmes, to utilise all the information held in their huge computer data bank, pointing to all the obscure international languages and religious phrases, that Anne had uncovered.

An immediate response was startling, as they were beginning to decipher many more new coded messages.

The immediate fear was that as the opposition might begin to be aware of this, they would then intensify their efforts to discover the source of what they would consider to be a serious leak in their ranks at the moment. But if not, they may look elsewhere for a source, outside their organisations.

They may even start to think it was from within the British Intelligence Services? Therefore, the Director's concern for secrecy, and the protection of his expert decipherer.

On their return to the house, Jack let Anne in through the front door and saying fairly loudly, "I'm just going to check on how the builders are getting along, won't be long."

Casually walking around the outside of the building and stopping to look at the completed work, chatting to workmen on the way, until he met up with Jason, apparently to quietly discuss his work. But in effect to assure him that all was well and they had just decided to have some lunch out.

He apologised for not being able to let him know where they would be. Toby replied that it would not be expected normally, but his boss had told him to find them as there was some sort of panic on at H.Q..

Then Jack drifted on around the house, had a chat with the site manager in his office, and moved on to let himself in via the rear garden door.

Calling out to Anne as he stopped to admire the work they had done on the stairwell the previous day.

She was on her way down those stairs, having been up to refresh herself and change clothes.

"I think we did a good job there and I like our colour scheme, do you?" "Yes, it's not a bad job for a couple of amateurs" he replied. "What should we tackle next then?"

"Nothing more today Thank you! I'm going to sit quietly in my study and write some letters, I need to recover from all this excitement" exclaimed Anne. "Anyway I'm sure you have plenty to do, now that your plans are taking shape?" "By the way, are they getting on with the work outside to your satisfaction, after the inspection?" She said this in a laconic way that showed she was still happy from her 'lunch'.

"They seem to be getting on well and doing a good job too, but then they would be, as your boss suggested them, didn't he?" Cocking a quizzical eye at her, "Right then I'll see you again tonight."

At that moment, Anne's phone rang and she went off to her study to answer it. Nora was on the line and they spent the next hour, exchanging news, with much giggling and chortling going on.

Jack went up to his room to check for phone messages, just one, from Tom Clancy of Canada Parking Inc. to confirm that they had received the report and could he arrange to meet in their offices in the next few days, to discuss it, there were questions about its content.

This he did immediately, and as Tom was out of the office, he arranged with the secretary to be there the following morning at 9.30.

He then settled down to planning for what needed to be done next, in connection with the new company. Most urgent was to arrange a meeting of the Residents Association through Anne, as soon as possible.

It was some time later that he realised the workmen had stopped their operations outside and darkness had fallen, when he heard Anne calling him, to say dinner was ready.

As he walked into the kitchen, Anne said "I have only prepared a sandwich, as we had a big lunch, is that alright for you?" "Yes, thanks'."

Chatting as they ate, Anne told him about Nora's phone call, and how happy she seemed to be in her new life. Saying "it was nice to talk to her it feels as though she has been away for ages, rather than just a few days. We must have been on the line for almost an hour, exchanging news."

"That's good" said Jack, "I'm pleased she's OK, I suppose you told her about our celebration today?" "Of course I did, she was most surprised at our extravagance." He laughed and then said, "By the way, I shall be out tomorrow; I'm meeting my clients again. Hopefully that will be the end of it and I can settle down to work in the house and be getting on with our new venture. Do you think you could get the resident's meeting set up, sometime soon?"

"Yes; I'll contact the Colonel in the morning; He will enjoy being able to arrange an 'Extraordinary Meeting' it will make him feel important again. But I shall have to give him some inkling of the subject, to let him know the importance of having everyone there, is that alright?"

Jack hadn't thought of that, it was important to get a unanimous vote for the Planning Authority. He said "Of course you must, I would stress the 'New use for the Old School' angle mainly, in case they get the wrong idea before we can explain fully. He'll need to place it on the meeting agenda."

He then stood up and started to collect the dishes and without arguing, Anne helped. She then said "I think I'll ring the Colonel now, it's not too late. Shall we have coffee in the sitting room for a change?" "Nice idea," said Jack, "I'll make it now and bring it in."

Anne went off to her study to make the call. When the phone was answered and she announced herself, the Colonel was obviously surprised and said; "My dear lady, very nice to hear from you, how can I help?"

As Anne explained the need for an Extraordinary Meeting and the reason for it, he was obviously hoping for more information, but she explained that it would be better to put the detail to all residents at the same time, as it would affect them all. He enthusiastically agreed, and promised to arrange it within the next few days. Anne thanked him and replaced the phone. She then joined Jack in the living room, where he had laid out the coffee.

They discussed what should be said to the residents and how best to explain what they wanted to achieve. Then deciding to retire, Jack told Anne to go ahead, as he would clear things away and lock-up the house. Once again he assured himself that the night watchman was around as he secured everything, before going up to his room.

Outside, Toby had been replaced by another such protection officer, to act as night security, so as to allow him some relief. He had been on voluntary, almost none-stop duty for several days and nights now, with little time for sleep.

Elsewhere, positive action had been taking place in several countries, as the new M.O.D. computer programming results were transmitted between international agencies.

Producing a deeper understanding of the more obscure communications between certain groups, whose sole aim seemed to be, to strike terror into the populations of any, organised civilisations not in tune with them and their outdated beliefs?

On his arrival at the offices of Canada Parking Inc. at exactly 9.30am. Jack was obviously expected, as Tom was already in reception chatting to the girl on duty behind the desk, asking her to arrange for refreshments in about an hour. He saw Jack entering and met him with his hand out, saying, "great to see you again, my chief is in his office, expecting us." Jack shook his hand and followed him into his previous boss's office once more. The big chief stood up from behind his desk, also with his hand out. "Hi! There! Jack, thanks for coming in so quick, we sure appreciate it."

Walking over to the desk he again shook the proffered hand, saying, "Good morning Frank; I just thought you would like to make your decision as soon as possible now." Frank moved around the desk to sit at the conference table, which was much more informal for a discussion. As they all sat down, each produced their copy of the all important report and settled down for serious work.

Frank opened up with "Tell me if I'm wrong, but do I get the impression from your wording in this," pointing at his copy, "that you aren't thrilled with the idea of this deal?"

Jack replied, picking his words carefully; "As I have mentioned previously, I've studied these kinds of sites in the past and could never see a great deal of profit coming out of them, but you are far more familiar with these operations than I am." He paused to see if they wished to interrupt, but as they were listening intently, he continued; "The only obvious income is an operating fee which the supermarkets are reluctant to consider to any great extent, as they are offering free parking to draw their customers." "Your superstores in Canada and the US are much more willing to subsidise this."

"The only other possible income is from a fines system being imposed on non-customers or non-payers. But as you are aware, the costs of imposing and collecting them can often be higher than the take."

"My apologies for the negative nature of the report, but I must express my opinion as a consultant, for you."

Having listened intently, Frank now spoke up, "Yes, your report certainly expressed that opinion and we were sure surprised! But I'm glad you were frank. We don't want to rush into a contract before we are sure of the economics. Tell me why you think it is a different operation over here?"

"Two reasons, mainly that the British supermarket shoppers have become used to free parking, since in the early days, most such stores were built out of town through lack of space and planning permissions."

"Therefore potential customers had to have an incentive to drive out to them; another reason for so many of them building petrol stations on site, providing subsidised fuel."

"Secondly, with land costs, taxes, both local and National, so much higher over here; Retailers are more reluctant to pay a decent operating fee for the service you would wish to offer."

Tom now spoke up, "How would you suggest we go about applying for this contract, if so decided, to ensure it's worthwhile to us then?"

Jack replied "in the first place I would say, don't, it's more trouble than it's worth. But if you did decide to apply, you would put forward a generous operating fee request for each site; to be sure it was worth your efforts." "You know better than I, what the operating costs would be and how to approach a fee. If they refuse your figures, back away.

Then concentrate on more lucrative operations, where a parking fee is paid by the customer. Railway Stations, Hospitals, Shopping Malls, Council owned sites, etc."

Frank said, "I take it you looked into this with your old firm and were un-impressed?"

"Quite right" said Jack, "we spent a great deal of time and effort looking into it and never bothered again. It's only of use to much smaller firms than yours."

Just then the coffee arrived and they relaxed for a while, chatting generally for a while about operating differences between the varying countries they were involved with.

Eventually getting back to the matter in hand, they discussed more detail until Frank spoke up to finalise the meeting by saying, "Well Jack, we'll discuss it further within our organisation, but I think you've saved us a from making a bad move and I think we may well take your advice."

Standing up, to shake hands with Jack, he said "let Tom have your invoice and he'll take care of it right away, you've earned it."

Tom showed him to the lift and again shaking hands said, thanks' buddy, you've been a great help. If we need you again can we call on you?" "Of course; I shall be quite busy for the next few months, but I'm sure I could be available." As the lift arrived, he stepped in waving to Tom as the doors closed and he descended to the ground floor.

Stepping out from the lift doors and heading through the foyer towards the main doorway, he noticed a small, slight man sitting on one of the couches reading a magazine. This was only because he had noticed the same chap sitting down there and picking up that same book, as if he had just entered at the same time as Jack, when he had gone up in the lift earlier.

It was the fact that as he sat down, he revealed high heeled cowboy style boots, with pointed toes, under a Brown sports jacket and Jeans, smiled to himself, thinking, 'not the attire for a business meeting in that part of the City'. But just presumed he was probably a visiting American.(*which in fact had been the contrived image)*

Now he wondered why the man would still be there after such a long delay, but then dismissed it from his mind, seeing a Taxi outside the doors, dropping off a client. He rushed out to catch it, giving the matter no further thought.

On his way home in the Taxi, he mulled over what had been said at the meeting, reminding himself to make up an invoice for his services, to be sent off the next day. Then he must get on with his other plans.

However, when alighting from the Taxi outside number 47. Windsor Square and paying off the driver; he noticed a small Green Citroen car pulling up across the road. Surprised that no one got out and when he saw the driver just sitting there, felt sure he had seen the man before, but as he was dealing with the Taxi driver, paid no further heed to it.

After Jack had entered the house, the driver of that small Green car called out to one of the builders working on the house, asking the way to a particular street. Toby walked over to help him and leaning into the driver said, "Everything OK Charles?" "Yes all OK" said Charles, "he was a long time in the meeting, but there was no one else interested in him all the way." "Right then" said Toby, "you can leave him with me now, go on home, I'll report in for you." He now stood back and made a gesture as if pointing out the way to another street, and the car drove off.

He then entered the site office in order to report to his superiors on Charles's comments, and to confirm that Corporal Rogers was safely back in the house.

He was instructed to hand over to another operative for overnight duty at the end of his shift, when he could finish for the night.

There had been some concern that Corporal Rogers's contact with Lieutenant Colonel Knightly in the Birmingham Hotel may have been observed through sheer bad luck, by certain dissident factions in that area who may be aware of a connection with Army Intelligence.

Targets under routine surveillance had been spotted near the hotel used, soon after the meeting, but it was somewhat inconclusive. However, to be on the safe side it was felt that an eye should be kept on him for a while, for his own safety. Hence the extra surveillance, if not perhaps to the highest standard!

Charles's bosses were not yet aware of what he had considered the best of taste in dress in a business environment. He was very much a rooky in the surveillance field and on probation at present. But he was very keen and conscientious in his own way, just needing to be taught the finer points of his job. One of the reasons he had been chosen, was for his slight stature, so that he could melt into the crowd. But he was only too aware of his size and tried to improve on it in his own way, with negative results.

On entering the house, Jack was pleased to hear Anne on the phone in her study, as he had been hoping she would be at home for the evening, so that they could talk for a while about the new project. He really wanted to get going now that his other work was completed. He called out that he would be in his room for a while and would see her later, which she acknowledged with a wave.

He worked for a while preparing the invoice for Canada Parking Inc. ready for posting the next morning. Then set about drawing up a list for discussion with Anne later, on what to do next.

The front doorbell rang and as he went onto the landing to check who it might be, but was relieved when he heard Anne say, "Oh hello Toby, I'm glad you had my message. Could you please see that these books are delivered immediately?"

Handing him a small parcel, "they are most important." Toby took the parcel from her saying, "Yes madam, I have instructions to take it myself at once." He was gone as quickly and quietly as he came.

Anne had also been busy that day, having spent the day reading through parts of her library, which contained many obscure tombs on ancient languages and religions.

She had finally found the two items that she had referred to on her recent visit to the Ministry. They were both more modern variations on ancient religious texts, used for present day teaching.

But these 500 year old teachings were what the fanatics believed to be the correct way to live and wanted all governments to revert to; but conveniently laying the blame at mainly Western civilisations for the 'Moral Decline' of their subjects, whilst ignoring the fact that they were quite happy to use modern travel, technology, and armaments, to get their way.

Anne had enclosed a letter to the Director pointing out how these books were the coding reference points they had been looking for and how to decipher them; for use in the new computer programmes. They should then find that many of the previous obstructions would be 'ironed out'.

Later, Jack heard Anne calling up the stairs to say that dinner was ready and closing his work down, descended to the comfort of the kitchen, and as usual, to the smell of hot, homemade food.

Anne opened the conversation by saying, "I have spoken to the Colonel again and he is arranging for the meeting to be held on Friday of this week at 7.30 pm in the old school hall, if that's alright with you?"

"That's fine by me; does he think that all residents will be there?" "Yes, he told me he had made it plain that it concerned everyone in the Square and that it needed the consent of all members, he felt sure that there was serious interest and all would be there."

Jack smiled and said "Good; in that case all that needs to be done now, is to make sure they are well fed and watered, so that all will be in a receptive mood."

Anne laughed and said, "You shouldn't worry on that score, the Colonel is a very good organiser and likes the responsibility of it. He used to be a Mess officer in the army."

"In that case, it only remains for us to make sure our presentation is good and that we explain the benefits to the Square and its population, in the hope that they agree with our plans." Jack had no qualms on that score as he had made many such presentations in the past.

They spent the rest of the evening chatting about what to say and how best to approach the members of the Residents Association. After which, they watched some television to relax, until it was time to retire.

When Jack made his usual security checks, prior to going to bed.

Friday morning arrived and Colonel Batesby-Fortesque was on the doorstep of No 47 early, to collect keys for the school. As Anne handed them over, she had the temerity to ask if she could help in any way. "No thank you madam, all is in order as always" answered the Colonel, in his best brusque and efficient manner, almost affronted by such the suggestion; Adding, "it seems we shall be having a full turn out, there is much curiosity about what you are about to propose?"

Realising that he was fishing for more details, Anne replied "That is good to hear! I'm sure you have arranged things as efficiently as ever Colonel, we'll see you there about seven this evening then?"

The evening of this crucial meeting arrived; Anne and Jack made a point of arriving early to be sure all was as they wanted. They need not have worried; although the old assembly room had seen better days, the best had been made of it by thorough cleaning and wall drapes.

Tables and chairs were laid out informally, plus a top table from which to command the room for the presentation and a long table at the rear, laden with finger food, cutlery and crockery. They could hear activity in the adjacent kitchen where hot drinks would be dispensed later. The Colonel emerged looking busy as ever, (never happier than when he was organising) looking around with contentment, he said, "is all to your satisfaction Mrs. Eden-Smythe?" Anne had learned long ago how to keep him happy and replied with enthusiasm, "it is indeed, most efficiently done! Thank you Colonel." Jack thought he should join in also and walked over to shake his hand, saying "yes indeed, many thanks' sir, obviously well organised."

The Colonel preened, thinking 'perhaps this young man was genuine after all', he had not been too sure about the stranger up to now, because he had not been informed about the new resident, as he felt he should have been.

Thinking he should know all about everyone in the square, being an important member of the community; (at least in his own mind.)

Anne went into the kitchen to say hello to the ladies working there. She had come to know them over the years at other such occasions.

Jack started to set up his charts and so on for the presentation; realising that being a stranger to them, it would be necessary to sell himself before they would trust him enough to accept the proposals. This was no difficulty to him, as he had been doing just that for years, learned from his days spent selling, in various forms.

Association members began to arrive, greeting each other as long lost friends, although they were near neighbours, Anne in the middle of them mingling in her best hosting manner and introducing Jack as she did so. They treated her with great respect, being one of the longest serving residents, and owner of the present venue; therefore accepting Jack as genuine. He now realised how lucky he was to have her on his side.

Spot on 7.30pm. The Colonel stepped up to the top table to call the meeting to order, asking all to be seated and saying that, as this was an extra-ordinary meeting, they would forgo the usual subjects for discussion at this time, and then handing over to "Mrs. Eden-Smythe and Mr. Rogers" in his best master of ceremonies voice.

Anne stood up first as previously arranged; in order to introduce the main agenda, explaining that as the old school was now in a poor state of repair and in need of extensive work, she had been looking into other ways of utilising the property, in order to bring it back into use and refurbishment.

"To this end, I am lucky to have had a proposal from Mr. Rogers, (indicating him sitting next to her) who you will know by now is my tenant, to resolve the problem to all our benefit. I will now ask him to outline his plans, and hope that you will agree with me that they show initiative for the square."

As she resumed her seat, Jack stood, saying "first, may I thank you all for coming this evening; I hope you will all feel it was worthwhile. I shall first explain my recent background to you, so that you will see where my proposal originates."

He spent some time explaining his past employment and how he had come to reside at No.47, as a temporary base while looking for a new business venture, and how he had discovered the old school on his strolls around the square. Not realising until then that his landlady was the owner.

Then began to lay out his proposals to the group in detail, using a large wall chart he had prepared showing a map of the square and the school grounds. At the end of his lecture, he made a point of mentioning the company structure, in which he and Mrs. Eden-Smythe were to invest an equal amount. This was to avoid the inevitable doubt about him taking advantage of his landlady.

He now asked for questions from the members; which began when a somewhat officious looking gentleman stood to say, "I am Lord Swinburne from number 92; may I ask the cost to the residents for the use of the secure parking service you are proposing?" Jack replied that it would not exceed the present cost of charges made by the local authority to park on the street. But there would be some added cost to cover overnight security, should that service be used. Adding that residents and their guests would at all times have preference in its use and cost.

Another member now stood to say "my name is Jim Parker of No.53. I don't wish to tell you how to run your business, but how would you propose to subsidise the residents, and can we be sure that prices won't change over time?"

Jack replied, "We will be able to cover those costs by charging short term daytime parking from outside the square at a higher rate, comparable with other such facilities in the area. As for the prices for residents of the square, these will be on annual, guaranteed contracts."

The next person to stand up announced himself as "Sir Clive Simpson of No.88. (Retired Minister of Culture) "Surely if we take up your service, we would lose our resident bays on the road, outside of our property?"

Jack had anticipated all of these questions and replied, "The idea of this facility is mainly for the many surplus cars appearing here, as there are only two official bays per property at most. If you should prefer the security of 24 hour parking in the new facility, I'm sure it would be possible to sublet your space."

After answering more searching questions, and they eventually came to an end, Jack asked the Colonel if he would break up the meeting for refreshments, allowing time for members to discuss the plan amongst themselves, before a vote was taken later. The Resident's leader did as asked and was received with good humoured applause from the audience.

As they all broke into groups to discuss what they had heard for the very first time, and to decide how it would affect them personally, Anne and Jack sat at separate tables (which had been previously arranged) representing the old and newcomers to the square. So that residents could feel able to approach them individually with personal questions, according to their own concerns.

After some 20 minutes, the Colonel stood at the top table asking if they would regain their seats. He waited until they had done so and order had been restored; re-introducing Mrs. Eden- Smythe to chair the meeting further.

Anne stood up, thanking him and saying, "if there are no further questions ladies and gentlemen?" here she paused, and receiving no queries, added "I would suggest we now vote on the proposals put before you by a show of hands."

To her surprise, there seemed to be an almost 100% show of hands, and quickly declared the motion as passed, looking at the Colonel and seeing him studiously noting it down. Then adding, "Those of you who are not too sure, are welcome to clear any doubts you may have, with me or Mr. Rogers, at the end."

"For my part, I would be most pleased to see the Old School property back in use again and looking tidy once more, as an asset to the square, as I am sure my husband would if he were here. It has been derelict too long."

"You will be kept informed at the progress as we move forward, once we have planning permission of course", she grimaced here to show that all was not yet finalised.

At this time Miss Gloria Coltrane, (a retired actress and resident) stood up at the back of the hall to say loudly "may I thank you and the Colonel, on behalf of present members, for the splendid organisation of this meeting and the refreshments provided."

There was applause all round the room. As Anne nodded, holding out a hand towards the Colonel and applauding with them.

The meeting then began to break up, although no one seemed to be rushing off, staying to nibble at the leftover food, and to chat together, with generally positive comments on plans for the new use of St.Stephens School, and the effect on parking congestion in the square.

As the hall emptied, Anne and Jack searched out the Colonel, finding him in the kitchen with two of his assistants clearing away.

They offered to help, but were again refused, therefore thanking all concerned for their efforts, they left the Colonel to lock up.

Knowing all would be secured and the keys returned as always; when everything was ship shape.

As they sauntered back to the house on that pleasant, Spring evening, discussing the night's events, they were contented at the outcome, which had been better than they could have hoped for, when this scheme had first been muted, just a few weeks ago. They were aware that this was only the first hurdle and that there was still much to do.

But for now they were happy just to get home and open a bottle of wine to celebrate this success; chatting quite late into the night.

As they entered the house, it was recorded by a duty night officer sitting in the works office.

The following morning saw them arranging over breakfast to contact Mr.Wetherall (the solicitor), to inform him of the previous evening's decision, so that he could take the next step toward obtaining planning permission. Anne informed him that apparently Robert had an old golfing friend in that department, so it should not be too difficult?

Jack could do no more at the moment on that project, so decided to try to complete more of the internal work around the house to keep him busy. After changing, he collected his equipment from the garden shed, saying good morning to Arthur who was happily working in the garden. He came over to chat, which was unusual when he was at his hobby. "I heard about the meeting last night, all went well then?" "Yes" Jack answered, "Didn't see you there though." "No, I had a late job at the airport, but I hope your plan goes ahead, I should be interested to know when it's up and running, I may be thinking of expanding to another one or two taxis." "Good for you, I'll let you know as soon as things get that far ahead Arthur." He nodded and sauntered off, back to his garden.

Jack smiled to himself, he had not thought of Arthur as the ambitious kind, but could be one of his first customers for the future!

He kept himself busy for the rest of the morning, until Anne came along with a mug of coffee. She said, "Mr.Wetherall has returned my call just now, I explained last night's result, he assured me that he would be contacting his friendly planner, immediately for a 'change of use order' but would need a copy of the official Resident's Agreement."

"That's good to hear" said Jack, "now if you have nothing else to do, you can put on an overall and get painting." Anne smiled at his tone, saying "yes master, but can I drink my coffee too?" then hurried off to get an overall and her drink!

So the comfortable day went; the only interruptions being, Tilly calling them into the kitchen for lunch and later in the day, the Colonel returning his keys for the school. Plus a neatly typed copy of the meeting's minutes, which Anne brought back to Jack, handing it to him, and arching her eyebrows said "there you are then! I'll bet you didn't think of that, did you?"

He had to admit he had forgotten about a written confirmation of the positive vote result, knowing the solicitor would need it for his presentation to the planning authority. Replying with a smile on his face, "OK, so I'm not perfect after all!"

"I do know that" said Anne, "I shall write to Mr. Wetherall later and enclose a photocopy." And picking up her paint brush said, "but for now I had better get on with my work Sir!" She was enjoying this complete change from her normal life and the relaxed banter that went with it.

Later that evening whilst in his room working out more details for the future of the new company; Jack's phone rang unexpectedly. Picking up the handset, he was surprised to hear the clipped voice of Major Kingston-Green of London Parking Ltd. (his past adversary and the new owner of his old firm); saying, "Is that you Jack?, hope you don't mind my calling you during evening?"

Jack smiled to himself at this comment, The Major never had cared if he was upsetting someone or not, it was not in his makeup. Also, he only ever used a first name if he wanted a favour.

He politely replied, "of course not major, like you I am working anyway, what may I do for you?" The Major cleared his throat, "I understand you are a free agent these days and would like to meet for a chat sometime, you may be able to assist with a problem we have. Would you be free for an hour or so sometime soon?"

Jack was aware that he needed to be careful with this gentleman; he was notorious for trying to get something for nothing, although a multi millionaire. So replied; "That's correct, I am now self-employed working on a consultancy basis, when would you like to meet? I'll fit in with your timetable if it's urgent." Thinking 'that tells him I am not for free' and asking how desperate the crafty old devil was.

His reply was typical, "of course old chap, I'm sure we can work something out, if you find yourself able to assist. Could you possibly make it tomorrow morning, unfortunately I have to be in another part of the country on the following days?" Jack was thinking 'what a good job it is that I know him and his tricks', the reply meant that he did not want to commit to payment, unless pressed and that it was an urgent matter. So to turn the screw a little further he said, "I could make it then, but it would need to be local to my next appointment in the West End. Shall we say the Hilton at 10.30? Let's say Mezzanine lounge?"

As Jack was well aware; the Major preferred to hold meetings at his palatial offices, where he could feel superior sitting behind that huge desk. However, because he was the one in need of help, he accepted brightly saying, "of course dear chap, if that is the only way you can manage it. I look forward to seeing you there then," abruptly replacing his phone. Again Jack smiled at this, knowing how The Major hated to lose position in a conversation, and enjoying the pleasure of winning, though he was aware of how petty that was.

Descending to the kitchen on the following morning, the extension phone rang and as he was the only one there, answered it. A clipped and well rounded male voice asked if Mrs. Eden-Smythe was available to speak. As Jack started to say that he would find her, Anne walked in and he beckoned to her, handing the phone set over. As he walked away, he heard her say "Oh! Good morning Director", hearing no more until she said "yes, I will be ready, goodbye."

As she sat down at the table she spoke to Tilly (who had now entered from the utility room), "I shall be out for the day, but in for dinner tonight, just leave something in the oven as usual will you." Then turning to Jack said, "What about you, then, in or out?" He replied "Out at a meeting for at least part of the day, I'll probably have something to eat then. But back in for the evening meal."

Anne nodded and said, "I have written to the solicitor and will post it when I go out. Now, I must go and change, my car will be here shortly"; leaving Jack once more to wonder about her other life.

As he was leaving the house later, he met Toby on his way up to the door. They exchanged greetings and as he moved off to find a waiting taxi, instructing the driver of his destination, Toby nodded to his driver by the car gesturing for him to call in to H.Q. to let them know that Corporal Rogers was leaving the house.

Anne was delivered to 'her friend's shop' once more, which was the cover for the un-obtrusive rear entrance to the Ministry of Defence coding dept. and then to the Director's office, where she was obviously expected.

The Director came around his desk smiling, "Good morning madam may I thank you for coming so quickly, would you mind if we moved directly to the special room?" She agreed and followed him to that room next door, noting that he seemed to be in an unusually tense mood this morning.

He led her past the guard into the familiar space, motioning her to the conference table and comfortable leather padded elbow chair.

As Anne sat down, she said to him "I am intrigued by the new urgency, as I was under the impression that things were under more control since our last session."

"We would like you to look at something and advise us further if possible." He went back to his desk and pressed the intercom, speaking into it he said, "Would you please send Clare in now."

Within a minute she entered the office and greeted Anne like an old friend, who smiled at her, saying, "I understand you have been very busy since we last met?" Here the Director spoke up to say "she certainly has, having a team of dedicated computer programmers under her control."

We introduced your books into the system, but would now like to show you the results and ask for comments on a few phrases and language dialects that seem to be blocking some of the results we are getting.

We are in direct contact with the annalistic department. Are you ready to continue now?" Anne nodded, and he again pressed the intercom switch, asking that the process be started.

Almost instantly, the screens at the back of the room came to life, showing question and answer formats, also a selection of incoming communications control screens.

With the help of Clare and the Director, describing what was going on, Anne studied how the system used her particular expertise, making notes on the pad provided.

As she began to grasp what they were doing, she pointed out certain errors in the pronunciation and hieroglyphics of the languages held within the data base, being monitored by the computers. Especially certain words and phrases in the very old religious language of the books she had sent in, confusing the programmers? She was able to adjust the faults via a keyboard connection directly to them, to solve the problems they had been experiencing.

Eventually the Director considered that they had achieved all that could be expected for the day, asking Clare to close the session. Turning to Anne he said, "We have achieved a great deal again today, thanks to you dear lady, now you must go home and relax."

Relieved, Anne stood up saying, "thank you director, I should like that. Are you likely to need me again in the near future?" He considered for a while, thinking to himself, 'the less often we bring her in, the less she will be exposed to scrutiny' he replied, "No I don't expect so madam, I will only call you if we can't manage, from now on. You seem to have set us up very well and I am hoping we have learned enough to carry on with what we have from now on."

At that moment, Toby arrived quietly as usual, to escort Anne to the car, for which she was grateful. She always felt safe and comfortable with him by her side.

She thanked Clare for all her help, said goodbye to the Director, and followed Toby out to the car, then relaxing in the back seat, closed her eyes until they reached home.

As Toby opened the car door for her, she looked up at the building work around her house and noticed that some of the scaffolding had gone. As they walked up the steps to the front door, she mentioned this to Toby and asked if it meant that they had finished. He told her there was still a little to do, just a few more days to complete the work.

Then as he saw her into the house, and added, "By the way madam, the site manager will need to come into the house tomorrow with specialists, in order to complete the security installation."

This surprised Anne, as she had not ordered any security and told him so. Toby replied, "I believe it was arranged by the director" with a faint smile on his face. Then closing the door, said "goodnight madam, I shall be down in the works office should you need me."

Walking down to the car, and dismissing its driver, he went to settle into the office in order to keep the house under surveillance; at least until he could be sure that Corporal Rogers (as he was known by security) was home.

He was somewhat relieved to have been told by his chief that his charge, Mrs. Eden-Smythe would not be travelling to the Ministry so often in future. He had been concerned that it had only needed one slip in the security around his charge, or a touch of bad luck, to reveal her connection to the Ministry of Defence, putting her at great risk. So far they had managed to keep her a secret, but the longer it went on, the more chance of a mistake.

Apart from taking his job seriously, he had grown fond of his charge, admiring her skill and courage, and it was a great shame that the world at large would probably never know of her true achievements in defence of the UK.

Jack arrived in the Mezzanine lounge of The Hilton Hotel promptly at 10.30am and found to his surprise, Major-Black already there. He was surprised, because it was known by those who knew The Major, that he liked to make the late and great entrance, showing his superiority (in his own mind), by keeping people waiting.

As Jack walked towards his table, The Major stood to shake his hand, saying "how nice to see you again old chap, you're looking well." Again surprised, as this was not the usual approach by this gentleman,

Jack wondered why and replied noncommittally, "yes, it's been sometime since we last met", sitting down at the table, as a waiter arrived with a coffee tray and began to pour for them both.

The Major sat opposite and began the conversation by asking about Jack's current position and how he worked within his new role as a car parking consultant.

For instance, did he still have a responsibility to his old employers with his departure contract? Or as Jack would have put it, phishing for free information! He now explained as he had to his last clients, making it clear that he would not be prepared to reveal the intricacies of his last job. But in general he could use all of the knowledge gained.

Seeing that he was not going to get any more information for free, The Major decided to get down to business. "We are having problems with that Car Wash installation at the Vauxhall site. As you are well aware, it is a good profit spinner and we need to incorporate it into the new development there.

I have been told that you had some ideas about that when you left. I wondered if you would be able to work with us on this problem."

Jack now realised where this was going and smiled to himself, no wonder the crafty old devil was trying to ferret out his ideas for free, but decided to go along with the game.

"To be honest Major, I haven't given the matter any thought for some time; I've been very busy over the last few weeks on other projects. However, I could try to find time to look into it if you like; that would be on a consultancy basis of course." He reached out to pick up his coffee cup, watching The Major's re-action.

The Major attempted to smile, saying "of course old chap, I appreciate what you say and that you are keeping busy, but we don't need to get too formal at this stage, do we?" picking up his cup to drink also.

Jack made no reply, waiting for him to continue; seeing that he was not going to get any joy from that comment, The Major continued, "We have come to you for advice, as we are aware of your expertise in the field of drive through car wash machines in this country. I understand that you were the first to understand their value here, as in America?"

It was obvious to Jack that the phishing expedition was still going on by The Major, hoping to get what he needed for free, which was his normal approach to any negotiation. It was not that he couldn't afford it, more a matter of pride, to get something for nothing. But Jack knew him of old; he therefore replied in general terms, playing the game for its own sake.

"Yes, I had always considered that it was a waste of profit potential, to have several thousand cars sitting for many hours at any one time in our car parks; so I looked for ways to improve our income from them, at the same time providing further services to our customers. But you are aware of this, as a car washing service is provided at your sites.

Although it is normally carried out by hand by your attendants as a sideline to supplement their wages, which I feel is the wrong way around, as they were not concentrating on the job they were there to do."

"Having made enquiries into throughput numbers of vehicles in other countries, and the profitability against capital outlay, I looked into available manufacturers.

Most were happy to help, as they were eager to get established in the U.K. The Vauxhall site was ideal due its location, neglected appearance, and land cost."

The Major had listened intently, now saying, "Thank you for your frankness, I agree with your concept and the profitability angle, so our decision to retain it. But my main interest is in how to incorporate the existing site within the new development there, how would you consider resolving that?"

Again Jack smiled to himself, thinking 'now the sparing begins' and replied, "I could certainly carry out a survey for you and produce a detailed report for consideration between yourselves and your architects; in my capacity as an independent consultant of course."

The Major sat back with a scowl on his face, the niceties over, he realised that he was going to be asked to pay for the information that he needed after all, which hurt his pride somewhat. Finally asking, "and how much is it likely to cost us for your 'services' then Mr. Rogers?"

Jack had been ready for this and calmly passed over a copy of his standard contract and charges. As he read the document, The Major pulled several faces, as if surprised at the size of charges.

But Jack was not perturbed by this; he had seen this gentleman in action on several occasions around a negotiating table. Therefore he said nothing, allowing the old devil time to absorb the contents.

The last time he had been involved in such a meeting, was when his late employer had been selling the U.K. holdings of 'New York Auto Storage Inc.'. Jack had been invited by his boss to assist in the negotiations.

The Major had not forgotten his input, which had not been favourable to London Parking Ltd. as he had hoped.

Eventually, with a sort of 'harrumph'! The Major said reluctantly, "Well this seems rather expensive for the little help I need, but I shall have to discuss it with my board of directors, to get their reaction."

"Fine!" said Jack, standing up and holding out his hand, "I'll wait to hear from you, if you should wish to proceed." After shaking hands, he turned on his heel and walked away. He was not prepared to get involved in a bartering session; he knew full well that The Major was simply playing for time. The Major had no need to consult with his directors; they would do whatever he decided, as always.

As he left the Hilton Hotel out onto Park Lane, a taxi pulled up, but he refused it, deciding to walk through Hyde Park opposite, stopping for lunch on the way at the Serpentine Restaurant, which was one of his favourite eating places, due to its position, with views over the Lake and Park.

His next appointment was not until later in the afternoon, when he was due to meet a land agent he knew, whose office was located in the Edgware Road, at the North end of the Park. So to walk there would be a pleasant use of the time available, he thought and good exercise too.

Much later in the day; apart from his walk in the park and enjoyable snack lunch, he felt somewhat deflated after a wasted afternoon, with no sensible information coming from his meeting with the agent.

Flagging down a Black Cab he headed home,

Toby noted his arrival from the site office and reported it to his H.Q. They informed him that Rogers had done a lot of walking and had two meetings, with no un-welcome followers during the day. He now felt confident enough to hand over to a night duty colleague and head for home for some badly needed rest.

Aware that he would have other duties in a few days, as he knew the builders had been told to start removing themselves from the property at last, having completed the work ordered by his charge Mrs. Eden-Smythe, plus lot more not ordered by her?

Number 47 Windsor Square would soon be a very secure property indeed. With direct monitoring connections to the anti-terrorist squad's offices and local police control rooms.

Anne and Jack were unaware of all this going on in the background, however, they were aware of a lot more internal work being carried out in the house than had first been planned for, but Jack had put this down to the renewal of electrical wiring, being such an old installation and probably recommended by Mr. Appleton. In fact parts of the house had been more like a building site for some days now. But it was all necessary work for such an old property, and would soon be over.

Jack had seen Toby heading away from the site office soon after he had arrived home, wondering why he had been working so late again, although he could hazard a guess.

CHAPTER 14.

The property now under surveillance was a derelict warehouse, located behind rows of empty shop units on the outskirts of a down-at-heel London suburb, awaiting re-generation. Giving the surveillance team some problems trying to look inconspicuous, they were sitting on old boxes in the back of the dirtiest, scruffiest old van they could find from the vehicle pool, painted Red and very rusty and it was proving most uncomfortable. Even more so as time elapsed, as they were unable to leave the van for fear of being spotted as strangers to the area, (but the bottles and chemical toilet were almost full!)

Anti-terrorist officers were acting on information handed down to them from the M.O.D. listening and decoding department, that a meeting was about to take place between suspected leaders and members of a local cell. Also an important finance and arms supplier recently arrived from a Middle Eastern Country, via Switzerland; notified to them by the Border Protection Agency.

There was a great deal of excitement over the airwaves amongst members of this terrorist cell, over the imminent arrival of this very senior leader. Further, that this bomb plot was to be their destiny, with a most devastating result against the U.K.

That they should wish to destroy the country that had taken them, and their parents and family in, was beyond understanding. But then, these men were not thinking in a normal, civilised way.

It was known from overheard conversions, (deciphered by the latest computer programmes installed after Anne's last meeting with the Director at the M.O.D.) that they were planning to build at least one large mobile bomb, and the possible use of suicide bombers, to target an upcoming important event.As yet the target was unknown, but considered imminent, from the information gathered.

What was known was that the particular people being watched, were dangerous fanatics who were quite happy to die for their cause, having been brainwashed by their so called 'teachers and protectors'?

Therefore, everyone involved in the surveillance and eventual containment of this action, was armed and protected as much as possible; but with speed and surprise in mind, due to the use being made of explosive materials, which could be instantly ignited in the case of a raid.

There were cameras located on each side of the van using small air grills which had been placed there for its previous trade of transporting vegetables many years before (and the smell still lingered). Using cutting edge technology of the period, images were being fed back directly to the M.O.D. and Scotland Yard listening rooms, where comparisons could be made to information held on computer records when a target person was spotted. Senior officers in charge of the operation could then issue instructions directly to teams on the ground.

Suddenly the quiet tension in the van was broken by Chief Inspector Theo. Thompson who had been sitting impatiently cracking his knuckles for some time; in a vain attempt to appear calm. He now burst out with "how much bloody longer are they going to be with that sodding Surveillance Equipment? The bloody targets will be here and gone before they've finished!" The rest of the team barely looked up, they were well used to his outbursts and use of expletives, it was just his way of relieving tension and it had not been all that long since the technical team had gone in.

Earlier in the day an innocuous looking British Telecom repair van had pulled up outside another empty warehouse on the other side of the block, which shared a connecting wall with the unit under surveillance. Two men in scruffy looking BT. overalls casually alighted, opened the rear doors and began to unload free standing signs which declared, "Warning, Repairs being carried out above and below ground." These they erected around a manhole in the pavement.

They then removed a ladder from the rack on the van roof and propped it up to a telephone pole alongside.

Next they unloaded a selection of heavy looking tool bags and boxes, which were carried in to the now unlocked warehouse unit. It all looked to any casual onlooker a perfectly day to day, B.T. telephone repair operation. Once inside, they had set to work on the real reason for the visit.

An attempt was to be made to install listening devices and if possible a small camera, (without detection), from that adjoining property, currently unused. But this was not proving easy, as the incumbents of the target premises under surveillance, were constantly checking the surrounding area, prior to their meeting. They were obviously very nervous with such an important contact due soon.

Finally a message came through to say that audio contact had been made and that they could clearly hear conversations going on, albeit in a language they could not understand; but it was now being beamed back to headquarters, where it could be translated by experts and the computer banks.

A short time later the translated conversation was being fed back into earphones of listeners in that old Red van.

It was clear that the men inside that target warehouse were most excited about their visitor. The hapless, so called terrorists were speaking of him with great respect and awe, almost as a Godlike figure, but at the same time with a sort of fear of what he could do to them in the event of failure on their part. They had obviously been conditioned into doing as they were told, even to giving up their lives, with no thought for their families, or victims.

They were simply conjecturing on the possible target for their assignment, so that the listeners were now aware that they had not yet been told. This made it even more important that they should remain incognito until it was revealed.

Now a large, Dark Brown Mercedes Limousine with tinted windows, displaying a CD (Diplomatic) number plate, arrived at the warehouse entrance, looking very much out of place. It was followed by an inconspicuous White Ford Transit van of medium size, with two men in the front seats of indeterminate race.

As they drew up, the waiting men from the warehouse came tumbling out, showing a great deal of excitement and deference to the first vehicle, almost bowing to the passengers, even before the doors opened and two very large and menacing looking gentlemen stepped out. Whilst one was keeping a wary eye on the surrounding area, the other opened a rear door to allow what was obviously the 'main man' to alight.

He was a somewhat slight figure of possible Arab/Iranian appearance, dressed in an immaculate Navy Blue Western style suite, (probably Saville Row made) with a short Light Blue coat of some silk material, thrown across his shoulders. Even from their surveillance position many yards away, the watchers could sense an air of authority exuding from this gentleman; he was obviously used to being obeyed without question. Almost ignoring the simpering menials in front of him, he gestured for them to lead the way, and following them into the warehouse,

a bodyguard in front, and behind him. At the same time, a man from the van also followed, the driver staying with the vehicle and its load.

The surveillance team were now able to concentrate on conversations taking place inside the targeted premises. Even before it was translated back to them from H.Q. listening experts, it was plain that the newcomer was issuing instructions to his underlings, with no preliminary niceties.

When the translated version did get back to them, the amount of information was astounding. The principle man who had recently arrived was the supreme leader of all the groups involved in terrorism in Europe and the U.K. He was also supplier of finance and armaments (which it seemed the White van contained) and it became evident that this was not the only operation he was planning in Great Britain in the near future. But it transpired that the poor souls in that room were to be given the 'Honour' to lay down their lives in a very important attack.

There were to be two consecutive attacks on the seat of authority in Britain to hit at the heart of what was thought by them to be a corrupt institution within the core of British Parliament itself.

Within days the Ceremony for the 'Opening of Parliament' by the Queen was due to take place as everyone was aware, but it had not been a consideration by the security services, as it had previously been thought secure and everyone attending had been vetted to the maximum extent.

However it now appeared that somehow this group had infiltrated some minor positions around the royal and religious attendants within the entourage and there would be two suicide bombers ready to sacrifice themselves for the 'greater good' (as they saw it).

Although they listened and scrutinised every word, the experts back at H.Q. were un-able to discover just how this infiltration was to be carried out and as there were literally hundreds of possibilities among such a large congregation, it was decided that the seriousness of the possible outcome, made it necessary to stop it here and now.

This meant a hard decision had to be made by The Director, but it was so serious as to need the permission of at least the Ministers of Defence, Home Office and possibly the Prime Minister.Also the fact that the Mercedes vehicle was carrying CD plates made it doubly important to be doing the right thing, although as yet they had been unable to verify which Embassy the vehicle belonged to, but they could also be bogus plates to avoid a challenge.

He made his way back to his office in order to use the Red secure telephone line in a locked steel drawer of his desk.

That Red phone was answered immediately by the Minister's personal private secretary, having cleared the Director's security and confirming that the line was scrambled, put him straight through to the Minister.

A familiar voice said "good morning Director is this about your current surveillance operation?" 'Good' thought the recipient, no time wasting small talk as usual'

He replied "good morning to you Minister, yes it is that operation. I have to make an urgent decision and would appreciate your input." He then outlined the situation, which was obviously a shock at the other end of the line, ending that it was now or never, as all of the culprits were at present in one place for a short time only, and it would be expedient to put a permanent stop to their plans, rather than risk losing sight of them later, with such an important target at risk.

The Minister was shocked at the enormity of what he had heard and realised that there was no time to waste by contacting other members of the government or security departments, that could be done later. He therefore made an immediate decision and answered with "I must agree with your analysis Director, I feel sure that you have considered all of the implications against the urgency of the matter and can only advise that you go ahead with your plans to eliminate the danger, (polite speak to stop it at all costs), I will inform the P.M. of what you are doing. Perhaps you will keep me informed as to the outcome when you are able."

The Director replied with "thank you minister, I will see to that."

Replacing the phone in the desk drawer and locking it, he next contacted his chief of security, who had been waiting for his call. "Would you please put the alternative operation into effect immediately" was all he needed to say, knowing that all parties were well aware of the urgency.

He returned to the communications room to supervise proceedings as they progressed. Where the on sight surveillance team had reported that the White van had now been unloaded into the warehouse and that all members of the group were busy planning how to build and prime the various bombs to be involved, for use in a few days.

That team was informed of the decision to implement the alterative operation and that they were to proceed with the pre-organised routine at once, which basically involved clearing out the area as soon as that alternative operation was underway.

Shortly afterwards, a second BT. Van pulled up behind the first one, disgorging two more 'BT. engineers' who appeared somewhat larger in stature and somehow menacing.

Again, they moved to the rear doors of the van, removing two bags and a large box which they carried between them into the empty property to join their colleagues. Who were by now busy dismantling their video camera and listening devices, apart from one tiny unit resembling a very ordinary electrical box which had been left in place in order to keep tabs on the miscreants right up to the bitter end.

There was little conversation between the two groups, as the original technical engineers were well aware that the newcomers were in fact SAS. Explosives experts and did not encourage personal contact. Apart from establishing that an old gas pipe cut off at one end and feeding through a hole in the dividing wall which had been used for locating the camera, could be activated. This they were assured could be done, with a bit of tweaking at the mains intake.

The original men now left, carrying their tools and equipment, wishing the soldiers good luck, they casually walked out to their van and while one loaded up, the other scaled up the ladder leaning against the telegraph pole and installed another video camera encased in an innocuous looking junction box.

After which, they removed the ladder and warning signs from the road, also loading them onto the van. Climbing into the front cab, they stopped to light up cigarettes and then quietly drove away.

Back inside, the soldiers got to work, placing various highly flammable materials around, which would leave no trace.

Next, as one man attended to the mains gas intake ready to activate, the other man set up another old piece of pipe beside the sawn off gas pipe feeding through the intervening wall.

Making sure that it was pointing directly at the group of men clustered around the pile of explosive materials on the floor of the adjoining warehouse, he placed a small, but highly volatile projectile, shaped like a small rocket, with a timed fuse in the old pipe and after checking with his colleague that all was ready, he set the timer for 5 minutes. At the same time the other man turned on the gas supply. They then calmly collected their bags etc. walked out to their van and also quietly drove away.

By this time the tatty old Red van containing that original surveillance team had quietly pulled around to the road in front of the row of empty shops, well away from danger, as they thought. Although they were still able to hear what was being said by the target group, by use of the sole listening device left in place.

Chief Inspector Theo. Thompson and Sgt Helen Bligh alighted from the van to get some fresh air and watch for any passing member of the public, who would be diverted for their own safety. But that was unlikely, as no one frequented that area now, being so derelict and un-inviting.

Back at the MOD control room the Director had been informed that all was now in place and the final result was imminent, therefore all involved were now aware of the current situation and were waiting for the big bang.

Even so, when it did happen, it still took everyone by surprise!

Listeners first heard a whooshing sound and a small explosion like a firework rocket going off. Then a split second later the audio went dead just as the most almighty **'EXPLOSION'** Happened!.

From their position on the far side of the empty shop units, (in what they had considered to be a safe distance), the first thing Theo and Helen knew, was when several of the glass shop fronts imploded around them with shards of glass flying around; but they were lucky, as the unit in front of them had been boarded up. Simultaneously they saw parts of the target warehouse roof rise into the air, above the height of the shop units with a huge cloud of dust and fire, and then disappear from sight as it settled again. For all of three seconds, they froze, before springing into action. Dashing to the van, they climbed in through the back doors with Theo shouting at the driver to move, adding that he should drive around the block quickly, to view the result and have the cameras running.

As they did so, the scene before them was of utter devastation. The building itself was razed almost to the ground and burning furiously, as was the building next to it, (where the 'BT. Engineers' had been working). The Mercedes car and White van still standing outside were both badly damaged and covered in debris. There was no sign of life, which could not be expected after such an explosion. Virtually every piece of glass within eyesight was smashed and there was dust and debris everywhere.

Chief Inspector Theo. Thompson now spoke very quietly, saying "O.K. chaps, let's get the hell out of here, you can turn off the cameras now and report in that we are on our way home."

The whole van interior had suddenly gone very quiet after seeing the devastation; Until Sgt. Helen Bligh expressed all their thoughts by saying; "My God! However much explosive did they have in there to cause that much damage?" Theo. Replied "just be thankful it went off there, rather than where they had planned. Let's just get home now." Now the van fell silent once more.

A similar atmosphere was present in the control room back at the Ministry; there too was a shocked silence at what they had just seen on the screens.

They had been listening to chatter in that warehouse amongst the planners, with the 'Main Man' ranting impatiently at the poor souls being shown how to blow themselves up efficiently. Just as drivers of the White van were being shown how to set the large mobile bomb in their vehicle, for use on the second planned target.

They would also be giving up their lives 'for the cause' of course. It needed two drivers in case one was disabled as the target was approached. But then life was as nothing to their leaders, (when it was not their life).

This second target was to be the mounted military escort waiting outside for the Queen's return journey, after opening the House of Parliament. The mobile bomb was to be driven straight into the middle of the Cavalry, or at least as far as they could get before being stopped, then exploded; creating as much carnage as possible, with no regard for live and injury to the soldiers, their horses, or spectators.

They could still be heard chattering, as the listeners heard the first **Whoosh!** and **BANG!!!** Just before all communication was cut; then the screens filled with pictures from the camera placed at the top of the telegraph pole outside, until it too stopped operating.

Next pictures to appear were from the old Red van as it drove past the aftermath a few minutes later, showing results of the explosion, which took their breath away for a few minutes.

No one knew what to say. It should have been a great moment of exultation as they knew a possible catastrophe had been averted, but somehow they felt almost deflated at such devastation and loss of life.

Perhaps that was the difference between the two factions, had the planned terrorist attack succeeded, followers of that belief would certainly have celebrated over the mayhem and multitude of death and injury caused.

The Director simply thanked all concerned and told them to be available in the conference room after lunch at 2pm. for a de-briefing session, then retired to his office to make necessary phone calls. His first contact was with the Minister for National Defence, (his boss).

He dialled on the Red phone, and was connected immediately with the Minister, who had been awaiting his call. Before he could speak, the Minister said "I am with the Prime Minister and other Cabinet colleagues involved, the phone is on speaker for all to hear, perhaps you could give us a brief résumé of the situation at this moment, the full report can follow later, after you have de-briefed your team." 'That's good' thought the Director, nice and succinct again. He replied, "Thank you Minister this is the story so far":-

He then gave an account of all that had happened that morning, right up to a description of the pictures he and his team had just witnessed in the control room.

After a short delay, the Minister said "Thank you that was most succinct, perhaps you could arrange with my Private Secretary to come up to my office sometime tomorrow, when you have collated all of the necessary information? She will adjust my diary to accommodate your visit." Then he added, probably prompted by the PM. "Can you confirm if there were any losses to our services"? "Happily none sir," said the Director.

Again the minister asked "Can you confirm if there were any survivors amongst the miscreants at this stage?" "None sir," said the Director, "Thank you," again. A pause, then the phone was replaced.

His next secure call was to the chief of security and as the connection was made, he said "I take it that you have seen the video pictures etc?" "I have Director, most successful, but shocking." "Yes indeed, and are all of your contacts back safely?" He was of course referring to the SAS men and surveillance teams. "All back safely and compiling reports on their activities sir."

The Director was relieved, "Very good, could you arrange to be in my conference room at 2 pm. for a de-briefing session between heads of department?" "Certainly sir" came the reply, as they both replaced their telephone handsets.

Having done all that he could at the moment, he decided to go for some lunch in the senior civil service restaurant within the Ministry building, (advising the duty secretary of his whereabouts), in order to relax before what would be an intensive fact-finding meeting at two o'clock. He had been at his desk since early that morning; it had already been a long day.

His only regret was that he could not reveal to anyone, the important part played by Mrs. Eden-Smythe CBE. Without her input, they would not have been able to break the language codes in time; and yet, for her own safety, it could not be revealed to anyone.

Meanwhile the SAS explosives experts had returned their BT. Van to an underground MOD vehicle pool, collecting their own anonymous Black 4x4 Range Rover, also with tinted windows, (to protect their identities), taking their specialised tools and equipment with them.

They quietly returned to a military depot somewhere in the North London suburbs, where they would be secretly de-briefed by the commanding officer.

It had been a dirty, but necessary job, efficiently accomplished.

Similarly the other 'BT engineers' returned their vehicle and its contents, (minus the devices left behind), but including the uniforms, for use at some other time. Then headed back to the anti-terrorist H Q. to report what they had seen and done. Their job also successfully completed.

Theo Thompson and his squad were more than pleased to return that dreadful old Red van, glad to see the back of it and the primitive toilet arrangements. Then dashed off to the nearest facilities for relief and a wash up; before also reporting upstairs to H.Q. where they handed in their guns, protection garments, and technical surveillance equipment.

The 2pm. de-briefing in the Director's conference room was a sombre affair. What had started out as a routine surveillance operation, based on information gathered by the listening and de-coding department over the airwaves? Where the best they could have hoped for, were identities of senior members of the last known, London terror cell and hopefully, a location for the next planned target.

Yet the enormity of what was being planned by their terrorist targets had taken them all by surprise! They were all aware that having to take such a mammoth instant decision to put a stop to the planned operation could well have gone wrong, with other members of the public being put at risk.

But an even greater risk was that the terrorist operation should have been allowed to go ahead, considering what was at stake, for the very existence of the leadership of Great Britain both Royal and Government!

Due mainly to the location of the terrorist meeting place, and the expertise of all protection services involved, the operation had been a complete success in evading a catastrophe.

It was appreciated by all concerned that the Anti-Terrorist squad had arranged what they called an 'alternative strategy!' just in case of unexpected developments, in exactly the manner that occurred. They had suggested at the time the operation was being planned, that whenever inexperienced fanatics and explosives were together, anything could happen, which might involve innocent parties.

The Director concluded that they should all be pleased by a successful outcome to the operation; by averting a major catastrophe to the British way of life;

the removal of a most vicious group of Radical killers, their leader, and a main supplier of arms and finance.

He finished by saying, "you can all relax a little now, but not for too long, you know our enemy never stops plotting against us." He then added with a slight smile, "that is of course, after your written reports are completed and handed in!"

"Thank you all for a job well done." He then stood up from the table, left the room, and headed for his office. He had his own report preparations to make for the meeting next morning with Ministers.

That concluded the meeting and they stood to leave, there was a quiet murmuring amongst members, remarking, 'that was praise indeed from the Director, most unusual?'

Un-aware of all this, the previous day had seen Anne and Jack enjoy a nice evening together; discussing what they had been doing through the day, at least, as much as Anne could reveal. She had apparently been shopping again looking for more furnishings to go with the new decor, which had been completed by the builders after installing the new electrical wiring, lighting and of course, alarm systems.

She was happy, because the site manager had informed her that all work was now complete and they would be moving out over the next few days. Also that the original price quoted would stand, as extras were to be covered by the Ministry. This appealed to her even more!

Jack listened intently to her chatter, pleased to see her happy, although she was obviously tired. He knew she had had a hard day and took the shopping story with a pinch of salt, being aware that she couldn't reveal her true actions.

She then asked how his meeting had gone and he light heartedly related most of the conversation, intimating what an old rogue The Major was, which took some time, until he thought she was looking even more tired. He suggested that she might wish to go to bed and relax, but she was reluctant and said, "Not just yet, shall we take our coffee into the living room and watch a little television?"

This they did, and after watching a selection of casual programmes, the evening news came on with a Breaking News caption across the screen.

MYSTERIOUS EXPLOSION! SUSPECTED TERRORIST ACTIVITY

AT A WAREHOUSE ON THE OUTSKIRTS OF LONDON!

The news announcer was re-iterating the caption and adding; "During mid morning today, a large explosion took place at a disused warehouse located in a rundown area awaiting re-development." A full size picture of the site, showing the devastation, sprang up behind the BBC announcer;

It showed a large area of destruction, and it was obvious there was very little of the original structures left, with much burnt out timber scattered over a wide area. It also showed two badly damaged vehicles parked outside. A large expensive looking saloon, and a non-descript White van.

"The explosion was followed by an all consuming fire in the subject premises and nearby buildings. At first, a gas leak was suspected as the cause. "

"However, on further investigation by the fire department after it was brought under control, at least eight badly burned and dismembered bodies have been discovered, inside the premises. From their condition and other factors, it seems there was little doubt that the destruction had been caused by the detonation of high explosive, military type materials. This had in turn ruptured the gas main, causing a fireball, which has apparently destroyed any possible forensic traces."

"Initial conclusions by Home Office experts have presumed that it was some kind of terrorist bomb making factory, and a mistake was made during bomb manufacture. So far, no other injuries have been reported, as the area luckily was deserted, being due for future development."

"Further investigation will take place and we will bring you any information, if and when it becomes available." "Now for other news":-

Jack glanced over at Anne, who had a shocked look on her face, but he said nothing, as he simply didn't know what to say. Officially he was unaware of her involvement with security forces.

Meanwhile, all kind of thoughts were racing through Anne's head, wondering if this had anything to do with her contributions in the tracing of those kinds of people. Could she possibly be any part of such a loss of life?

Or was it simply as reported, an accident caused by the illicit making of bombs, in order to create an even larger loss of life among innocent civilians?

To break the silence (and perhaps her thoughts), Jack commented on what they had just seen saying "well if that was as reported, it serves them right don't you think?" "I suppose so", said Anne.

"It still seems to be a terrible loss of life. I am only thankful that no innocent pedestrians or local residents appear to have been affected."

"Agreed," Said Jack, "but we have to consider who may have been affected if they had been able to use their bombs." He then added, "Anyway, perhaps it's time to call it a day; there will be a lot of noise and action tomorrow, with the builders clearing out."

Anne was only too pleased to go to bed and standing up, said "Yes, you're quite right, goodnight Jack, can I ask you to lock up again please?" "Of course" he replied, "see you at breakfast."

As he moved about the house checking on the security of doors and windows, (noting that the new system had yet to be switched on), he considered what might be going on in Anne's mind at the news they had just witnessed, but could only guess, knowing so little about her involvement with that side of life.

On reaching his bedroom, he decided to take his mind off such things and started to make a few notes about what needed to be dealt with in the next few days, 'most importantly the Old School project, it was time that was on the move', he thought.

CHAPTER 15.

The builders began early next morning to carry on removing scaffolding from around the house, and generally making the noise associated with workmen moving equipment and loading it onto vehicles.

So the household were up and about early as usual and were in fact in the middle of breakfast, with Tilly busy at the kitchen sink and stove, chattering about events of the previous day and how it had affected her husband Arthur, in his taxi work, due to traffic snarl-ups.

Anne and Jack smiled at her chatter, which was unusual for Tilly; but they were pleased for her, if that was the extent of her families' concerns. She then excused herself, rushing off to the laundry room.

This gave Jack the chance to bring the conversation to what was on his mind and to change Anne's train of thought. He started by asking her, "Have you heard from Mr.Wetherall yet about the 'School Project'? We should start to get it moving now, don't you think?"

"Yes indeed, I will telephone later to remind him." She chuckled; "I don't think Robert is aware of the word Urgent! I know it's no use to phone before 10 am, but I will try later.

I'm afraid I have been thinking of other things of late, and it slipped my mind somewhat. Perhaps now that the builders have finished at last, we can concentrate on our NEW COMPANY, eh!"

Jack was pleased to see her enthusiasm; perhaps it would keep her thoughts away from the macabre.

He now added, "I was wondering if we should approach them for the work which will be needed to convert the school; presuming we get our planning permission of course!"

Anne mused for a while thinking that F.W.Appleton & Son were usually busy carrying out contracts for the Ministry of Works, but answered, "we can always ask them before they leave. I have to see Mr. Appleton senior anyway, in the next couple of days he will need to be paid"

Just as Anne was clearing the table, the front doorbell rang. Jack called out to say he would answer it and walked into the front hall to do so. It was Jim Macready, the site manager, together with the security engineer, whom they had come to know as he worked around the house. Jim asked if he could speak to Mrs. Eden-Smythe, so Jack showed him in, calling out to Anne as he did so. But as he started to move upstairs to his room, Jim suggested that this might concern him.

As Anne came in, Jim said "good morning madam, we've come to set the alarm system and I thought Mr. Rogers should be here, if that's alright with you?" "Certainly, I would probably forget how to use it anyway!" she replied. Jack grinned inside thinking, 'there she goes again, using the dotty old lady act'. It was more likely to be the other way around; her mind being the sharper by far.

The engineer now moved to show them a hidden box installed behind a panel located in the wall beside the stairs, and began to explain how the panel was opened to reveal the alarm control box, code numbers were entered to set or disarm the system. "You will have to decide on your own numbers, no one else must know them, and this is how to set those numbers."

The process seemed quite easy to Jack, he had used several different systems in his last position, as he knew Anne had done too. As they both affirmed that they had understood, he said "there is an addition to this system too, you will not be able to just open the front and back doors as you just did Mr. Rogers.

You will need to verify the person at the door via the illuminated mirror screen above the door and release the electronic door bolt with this button", he indicated an innocent looking second light switch by the door. "There is duplicate system inside the back door also." Next, he produced from his tool bag several sets of slightly unusual looking keys.

"Your old keys will no longer operate from today. These are designed to cancel the electronic bolts when used by the registered user only, due to a built in electronic recognition. Is that all clear to you both?"

"My goodness!" exclaimed Anne, "we shall be more like a secure bank vault or something! But, what about Tilly when she comes up from the basement? Will she have to go through this rigmarole?"

The engineer smiled and said, "Mrs. Tilson has been issued her with her own key for both doors and she and her husband still have access to the garden direct from their flat", and added, "I suggest you try it now using the code already installed, ABC1234." They both did without incident, and then were shown again how to change the code.

After which, the engineer warned them about not leaving windows unlocked, which would set off the alarm when set. He then handed Anne an instruction manual containing contact information in an emergency, and thanking them, left.

The site manager now explained what was being done as the workmen left the site, before excusing himself. As Anne thanked him for the quality of work carried out and moved to let him through the front door, he added "Mr. Appleton asked me say that he would be along to see you later today, if that's alright madam?" "Yes that will be fine," replied Anne, about to close the door behind him.

But then on seeing the postman on his way up the steps, waited to take the mail, thanking him.

Closing the door she said to Jack, "This letter could be what we were waiting for, and headed for her study, indicating he should follow. Sure enough, there was a heavy looking package from the solicitor containing a copy of the Planning Permission they had hoped for, with the usual covering letter from Mr. Wetherall explaining the obvious in detail, and that he would hold the original document in the new company file; Namely: 'Windsor Auto Storage Ltd.' in the firm's vault.

They smiled at each other, knowing they could now get on with their new venture in earnest. Jack Said, "to be honest, I'm relieved, I wasn't totally sure we would get the permission so easily. But now I can get cracking with the re-furbishment at last."

For some time they discussed the next steps in the development of their enterprise, agreeing who should do what and when. Until they heard the front door bell again, and as Anne stood up to answer it, Jack said "the door alarm is not on at present, but we must re-set it before this evening."

Anne answered the door and said "Oh! Hello Mr. Appleton, how nice to see you again, do come in. Closing the door behind him, she led the way to her study. "I was just about to have some coffee, would you care for some?" "Thank you madam, I would." She asked him to sit down and Jack offered to get the drink, but was stopped by Tilly on the way in with a tray, anticipating things as usual, and after pouring for three, she left them to it. Anne turned to her visitor saying, "Now then Mr. Appleton, I owe you some money, don't I?" "Not at the moment madam" he replied "I have been told not to invoice you until the Ministry has settled their end. I just wanted to be sure you were satisfied with the work done, or if you require anything else at this stage?"

Anne exclaimed, "No thankyou Mr. Appleton! You have already done far more than I expected and I am very satisfied with the work done, your men have been most careful and thorough. Please let me know as soon as possible, how much I owe you."

The builder nodded, saying "thank you for those kind comments madam, we like to do our best."

Here, Jack chipped in with "could we put something else to you Mr. Appleton, Anne and I are setting up a new business venture, using the old school premises in the square and we shall need quite a lot of work done to renovate the buildings and grounds. Would you be able to fit that work into your schedule in the near future?"

Mr. Appleton thought for a while as he drank his coffee, then said "Depending my other commitments and on the type of work needed, perhaps we could fit it in. As I remember the school, it is all single story building, am I correct?" "Yes," replied Jack, "it would be some roof work and general renovation, including electrics. Plus extending, re-surfacing, and securing the outside areas."

"The low elevations will make it easier, with very little scaffolding required. But first let me check what work we have planned for, back at the office, and then I'll contact you to come down and do a survey of work required with you, if we can fit it in. Is that alright?"

"That will be fine" said Anne, "we will wait to hear from you then? Now do let me know when you need some money won't you?" "Thankyou madam, I will, but there is no hurry at the moment. Now if you will excuse me, I'll get on." He stood up to leave and Jack went with him to open the door, thanking him once more as he left.

They settled down to discuss what could be done in the meantime and Jack suggested he should go down to the school and produce a list of requirements for whichever builder was eventually used.

This he now did, making copious notes and sketches on paper and reminders on the Dictaphone, taking up the rest of his day.

On his return to the house, he was pleased to see that most of the scaffolding and all but one of the Portacabins had been removed. He chatted to Jim Macready who told him that they would be leaving a man on duty in the remaining shed overnight, then they hoped to complete the clean-up the following day.

On entering the house and finding Anne in the kitchen, sat at the table to discuss what he had been doing, and what the site manager had told him.

He started to explain what he had noted about the improvements and repairs needed at the school, which she listened to intently for while, showing interest, as she laid out the meal and started to eat. But she was beginning to show signs of tiredness, Jack realised that he was being a bit selfish talking about his plans, which he tended to do with a new project, and she had been through a great deal in the last few days; he could see that it was beginning to tell on her.

As they finished the food, he stood up to say, "Why don't you go into the living room and relax. I'll clear up and bring you some coffee and liquors; we can either watch TV or listen to some music, whichever suits you?"

"Oh that would be nice! Thankyou, it's just what I need at the moment; we will forget business and all the other things for tonight.

So they were able to forget the trials and tribulations of the last 48 hours, with the new security installed and set, feeling very cosy and safe at that moment.

Yet, outside in the builder's storage shed, vigilance was still continued by Jenkins the 'Night Watchman'.

CHAPTER 16.

Making his way up to the Minister's office the next morning, having made an appointment earlier with his Private Secretary, the Director considered the change of venue that had been arranged since his last contact. He was to travel with his boss to No.10. Downing Street where the meeting would be held, which proved the importance placed on his report.

He was wondering into what depth he should go with his review of what had happened the day before. It had been a most dramatic incident, and he was convinced that the action taken had been warranted in the circumstances, but would they agree?

On entering those hallowed halls of the Prime Minister's offices, they were greeted by the Private Secretary and ushered straight into the Cabinet Conference room, where to his surprise several well known and important faces were seated, awaiting his arrival, at least proving that they were aware of the gravity of his news.

His audience consisted of several Ministers from such departments as Home Office, Foreign Office, Armed Forces, etc., plus Heads of Internal Security, Anti terrorism and Joint chiefs of defence staff. All presided over by, the Prime Minister himself! What an audience? 'He thought'. He was not normally of a nervous disposition by any means, but this was a bit daunting, even for him.

The P.M. stood up to greet him, saying "good morning Director, we are all waiting for your report, I won't introduce you all round, it would take too long, but I think you know most people here by reputation and they have all been briefed on our participation. So I would be obliged if you could now give us the facts about yesterday's operation, in your own words."

The Director sat down as indicated, opposite the P.M. so that he would not miss anything, and began to speak, occasionally looking at his notes for detail.

He described the original surveillance operation, acting on information gathering by his own department; and the installation of audio and video links into the warehouse meeting place.

How, after the arrival of a very senior member of this terrorist group, (recently arrived in this country); and a van load of munitions, and the following conversations were translated; they had been astounded by what was being planned.

The targeted event was to be the upcoming, **'Opening of Parliament'**; It was to be an attack on the Queen, her family, and her Entourage, Also the Seat of Government, and Religion, during the ceremony inside, and the World wide historic Image of Britain's Armed Forces; The Guards Cavalry; outside; A crushing blow to the United Kingdom!

A drastic decision had to be quickly made, to avoid an escalation of events by these fanatics. He explained how he had obtained permission from his Minister; (indicating his boss) urging that there were only minutes to make that decision, before the meeting broke up and the miscreants disappeared. It was agreed that an alternative contingency plan, (previously arranged) should be used.

This was immediately set in motion; the resultant explosion and its consequences shocked all concerned in the operation, but proved the amount of munitions being used and what damage could have ensued, had the operation been allowed to go ahead; even more so when the target was considered and the repercussions of that being successful.

He decided that he had said enough for the time being and ended with, "I'm sure you will all have seen the television coverage of the devastation caused, but thankfully no innocent members of the public were involved.

I think I should stop now, to answer any questions you may have;" picking up a glass of water, as his mouth had suddenly become very dry.

There was a distinct pause, as the people around the table absorbed all that information. The Prime Minister was the first to speak, saying "Thankyou Director, that was a most succinct report, we understand that you are unable to go into too much operational detail of the actual means used, but could you enlighten us on what, and why was a secondary plan required on a surveillance operation?"

"This was advised by the Anti Terrorist Squad Sir; they have past experience of some of the groups involved, and advised that volatile materials, plus excitable, volatile fanatics, can result in serious accidents. Which in turn can be dangerous to the public at large; it is also sometimes necessary for a planned terrorist operation to be 'nipped in the bud,' as in this case."

"Thank you, I understand what you are saying, may I take it that certain members of our military would have been used, as explosives were involved?" (The P.M. was referring to the S.A.S. of course). "You would indeed be correct in that assumption Sir." He replied.

It was now the turn of the Foreign Secretary to speak, "When watching the TV coverage of this incident, I noticed the one of the vehicles involved carried a CD plate, have we ascertained if it was a genuine plate, and if so, which Embassy?"

The Director was surprised that this detail would have been noticed in the devastation shown by those pictures, but was ready for the question. "We decided that it would be advisable not to pursue that line of enquiry, for diplomatic reasons. Especially as the CD and number plates mysteriously disappeared overnight."

From the Head of Internal Security the question was, "Can I take it that our explosives experts erased all forensic from the scene and it will remain 'an accident' in the eyes of the media?"

"That is correct sir, which is why we have not returned to the area since the explosion, so that there could be no connection."

The Prime minister now brought the meeting to a close by saying, "I thank you gentlemen, I believe the Director has given us all that is possible at the moment, I will thank him and his team on your behalf for a job well done in averting such a serious incident. May I suggest those of you who have departmental details to iron out, remain here to do so? The rest may return to other duties, and I feel sure there is no need to remind you all of a need for absolute discretion in this matter." He now looked around the room to press the point home, then added, "I shall inform Her Majesty during my next regular meeting at the palace."

Standing up, he beckoned through a window to a hovering waiter to start serving refreshments. He then looked directly at the Minister for Defence, saying "shall we now retire to my own office? I should like the Director to be there also." He walked out of the room, and beyond the door, the Director and his boss waited for him to lead the way.

After sitting down in a comfortable armchair and indicating that they should follow suit, obviously intending this meeting to be less formal, and the office door securely closed, he got to the point by opening up with, "I understand that you have had considerable success of late in locating terrorist cells, and added to this latest success, leads one to believe you have had a considerable breakthrough in your code breaking department, is that so?" The Minister was a little taken aback, as he had not expected this approach by the P.M. He replied by saying "I must refer to the Director on that matter, as this department is under his control, and I am aware of his concern for secrecy." He now turned to that subject to offer him the chance to speak.

The Director was unsure just how much he wished to say on the subject, but as it was the Prime Minister asking, he had to say something of substance.

Therefore he started to spell out how the computerisation of code breaking, made it possible to store huge amounts of data, including almost every known worldwide language and dialect.

The ability to sort millions of numbers and combinations of letters in a very short period of time; enabled them to decipher coded messages quickly and accurately now, rather than the old pencil and paper method.

The P.M. had been sitting patiently, listening to what he was already aware of, but being no fool, fully aware that he was being 'Blinded with Science', he asked, "Yes that's clever work I know and we would be nowhere without computers these days, but there has to be a human element in order to supply them with that information for storage, does there not?"

The Director nodded, accepting the P.M.s' assumption, but thinking, 'Oh Dear! He's heard a rumour about our sources and is asking for details'. So replied, "Yes, we have our experts in many areas of number and word manipulation, but they are precious to us and at risk should identities be revealed to our enemies. We go to great lengths to protect those identities."

"Yes, I agree with your reasoning and would not wish to intrude into your security, but to be perfectly honest I am being nosey. I am aware that things have happened rather suddenly of late and have a feeling that there is one person in particular who may be responsible."

"In fact I have wondered if it could be a friend and colleague of mine from the old days at Bletchley Park. In fact, a particular lady with an extraordinary grasp of obscure languages?"

"I have also received information that a previously unknown ex-Royal Signals Corporal has been re-activated after many years out of the service, for no other reason than he has become a resident of that lady's house? You may just nod if I am correct;" Ending with a quizzical smile.

This rather threw the Director as he was unsure how much to reveal. But then if the Prime Minister couldn't be trusted, who could?

He looked over at his Minister who nodded imperceptibly, so replied "We do have such a person, but she is no longer a full time member of the M.O.D. Assisting occasionally as required, she has made several important breakthroughs of late. In fact, I can say that without her help, this latest atrocity may not have been averted."

The P.M. said "thankyou for your frankness, I do understand your reluctance to place this person in danger; it is simply that I know and respect this lady, and wish to mention her part in this action, to the Queen when I report to Her Majesty tomorrow, as the planned attack would have involved her."

Rising to his feet, he said "Once more I must congratulate you and your teams on the recent successful operation, please keep up the good work;" Thus closing the meeting. Both rose to their feet and headed for the door, saying 'good morning Sir'.

On the way back to the MOD building in their official car, the Minister turned to the Director saying "well that was a surprise! It was the last thing I would have expected from him; especially that he would know our lady personally. I was unaware that he was ever at Bletchley Park, did you know that?" "As a matter of fact I did Sir, it came up in conversation with her at one time, and she told me he was particularly good decoding German languages."

The Minister continued, "You realise what this means don't you? She is likely to be in for a further honour in the future." Smiling at this, the Director replied, "I'm very pleased to hear that, she deserves to be acknowledged. It is a shame that for her own security, she cannot be recognised for her exceptional work."Then as the car stopped, added, "If that's all Sir; I must get on now, there is much clearing up to do after this operation, in order to preserve its integrity from the Media; and others?"

"But of course Director, you must have a great deal to do, just keep me informed should there be any repercussions, thank you for all the help you have given us this morning." With this, his colleague let himself out of the car, to return to his own office elsewhere in the building, as did the Minister.

Seeing the 'In Tray' on his desk was overflowing, the Director started to go through the pile, and found that they were mostly memos and reports concerning the operation of the day before. 'Was it really only yesterday he thought', so much had happened since he had authorised the surveillance operation on that morning?

After initialling each one and moving it into the out tray, he added a memo of his own to the top of the pile, asking that they be transferred into the Secure Vault. He did not want the information contained to be hanging around the department.

Settling back in his chair to relax for a while, he went through all that had occurred over the last two days, and satisfying himself that all was complete as possible, he thought that it could be 'put to bed' and that was the end of it.

He now called into the de-coding and computer and listening rooms, speaking to the heads of department. There was nothing exceptional to report; it seemed that communications between the terror cells had gone very quiet after recent events.

But of course, there were less of them to talk now.

He spoke to Clare as she sat at her computer screen feeding in more programming information; to congratulate her on her work between Anne and the rest of the experts, and what had been achieved.

He then continued to his lunch, with a light heart. All seemed to be going smoothly at the moment, but he knew only too well that it would not be too long, before another emergency presented itself.

CHAPTER 17.

Several days after the building team had left and things were getting back to normal at No.47. Windsor Square, Anne had a telephone call from Mr. Appleton senior, to say that he would be down on the following morning with a colleague to discuss work required on the old school, and could he meet them there at 10.00 o'clock. This was agreed by her, knowing that Jack had been awaiting his call and would make himself available.

He was away most of the day at a meeting with 'The Major' at the Vauxhall Bridge Site which had been arranged the day before via a phone call.

Whilst she and Tilly were busying themselves hanging new curtains and continuing a general clean-up of the house, following the builder's retreat. She was quite happy to be doing this work as a total break from past events, and pleased that the interior of her house was looking more like its old self, but much improved. Her only regret was that John was unable to see it, as it now was.

On arrival at the Carwash site in Vauxhall Bridge Road, Jack was greeted most affably by The Major, emerging from what used to be his old office, which surprised him somewhat, until he saw two more chaps with him, who he recognised as architects involved in that development, and had known in the past.

"You have already met these fellows I understand Rogers?" "Yes we've met previously" he confirmed. They nodded to each other and The Major continued,

"Good, shall we walk over to the carwash where we can get down to the detail?" They all trooped behind him, aware that he would enjoy being in charge at the moment, chatting as they went about Jack's new life.

On reaching the machinery, they were approached by Berty Blacksmith, as he had been warned that the boss was coming today. "Morning sir, Morning Mr. Rogers, can I be of any help?" "No thankyou Blacksmith" said The Major, not at the moment. We'll call if we need you." As they walked on Jack grinned at Berty, knowing he was being facetious, and saying quietly I'll be in the pub for lunchtime if you can get away." Berty just turned his thumb up to agree, and went back to his work.

Once they were away from the noise of the machinery, The Major started to talk about the problems of where to locate the carwash without detracting from the aesthetics of the new housing development, but they were unsure of technicalities involved; which was where Jack's knowledge could come into effect.

After wandering around the whole of that proposed development area for some time, one of the architects, (who was fed up with the place, having seen it all many times before), suggested that they go back to the office in order to peruse the plans spread out on a table, (in comfort!).

After another hour of detailed discussion, The Major said "well what do you think Mr. Rogers? Have you a solution for us?" 'Oh no you don't!' thought Jack, 'looking for free advice again', but instead replied, "Not at the moment, but I'll work some ideas out on the computer and talk to the manufacturers if you wish? I'll try to get a feasibility report to you in the next week if that's O.K.?"

Realising that he would not be getting 'something for nothing', he replied, "I suppose it will have to do.

But I must stress the matter is now becoming urgent as we need to put the final plans before the local authority for their consent before we can commence work on site."

'Perhaps you shouldn't have waited so long then!' Jack was thinking, but answered, "I am aware of the urgency and assure you that I shall keep to my side of the arrangement. You will have my report in the next seven days."

Then as an afterthought added, "you have a copy of my consultancy terms, do you not?" Noticing out of the corner of his eye the two other gentlemen grin at each other.

As The Major gave his usual 'Harrumph!' and replied "yes thankyou, I'll see that you are reimbursed for your time, let us hope that you can come up with a solution."

"Then I think that's all we can achieve today, I'll say goodbye for now, and looking at the architects, raised his hand saying, "I'm sure we'll meet again." They both returned his wave, and he walked out of the office.

Heading for the George Hotel nearby, he walked in, and was greeted by the Proprietors **Tommy and Dolly** with, "Haven't seen this gentleman for some time, have we? Perhaps he has been otherwise engaged on much more important business!" Jack laughed saying, "O.K. I take the hint, but believe it or not, I have been very busy in other parts of the City and around the Country." Sitting down at the bar, he said "Anyway, I came into this Hostelry for a drink, am I going to get one or not?" Tommy snorted "Don't fret; Dolly is already pouring your single Malt Whiskey." "That's better, Jack laughed, real service at last." Then as Dolly placed the drink in front of him, he said "I shall be requiring some of your delicious food please."

She smiled and handed him the day's menu, "now he's being over polite Tommy." Then as they were both kept busy with other customers, and he was reading the menu, Berty Blacksmith came bustling into the bar.

"So you got away from The Major then? I thought he might be taking you out to lunch, being the generous chap he is." Jack laughed again, saying "that's something I didn't plan for, I know better. Now then, what would you like to eat? He said passing the menu over. After ordering, and collecting drinks, they moved to a table to talk privately.

Berty had guessed what the meeting with his new boss was about, and he chirped up with "I knew they'd come'n ask you to solve it, they wouldn't ask me of course, I'm much too lowly, I've seen 'em moochin around the site lookin' lost."

They discussed the problem for a while longer, until their food arrived.

Then after they had finished, Jack asked "has your brother moved up from Swindon yet Berty?" "Not yet" he replied, "but it's all set now, he's sold 'is 'Ouse and put a deposit on a flat near our place. All being well, he 'opes to be up here by the end o' next month. Why; you got somethin' in mind then?" "Yes said Jack, I am starting a new business project near where I live now, in Windsor Square, West 11. Do you know it?" "I know the area, nice part o' London," said Berty, "is it in the parkin game then, or car wash?"

Jack smiled to himself; Berty was never 'backward at coming forward' and replied, "It might be both eventually, but mainly secure residential parking. We're just going to start renovating the premises I've found, which will take some time, so it could fit in nicely with your brother's arrival." "Sounds good" said Berty "when he gets settled up 'ere, I'll give you a call shall I?" "Yes that's fine, here's my new phone numbers," he said, passing over his new business card. Berty picked it up and read 'Jack Rogers, Specialist Auto Storage & Parking Consultant' followed by various contact numbers, all in gold embossed print on a Dark Green background.

He chuckled and said, "Blimy! You're a 'CONSULTANT' eh'? No wonder The Major didn't' look too 'appy after you left, if he's goin to have to pay you money"

Jack laughed, saying "he certainly is, much as he tried not to, I shall make sure he pays up too. By the way, you know this is confidential?"

"You can rely on me, you know that." Berty replied. Then, standing up, he said "sorry, I'll 'ave to go, my dinner hour's nearly up, but I'll be se'in you again soon I expect, thanks for the food etc."

"That's O.K. Jack replied, you'll ring me later next month then will you?" Berty nodded, shook hands and left in a hurry, as usual, waving to the landlords as he went. Going over to the counter to settle the bill, Jack thanked them for the food, saying it was as delicious as ever, which he knew would please Dolly as she took pride in her cooking; then as he could see that they were now very busy, left with a cheery wave.

He headed for the underground station to travel home the same way he had arrived earlier in the day; it was quickest and easiest he had found.

Settling back he started to plan his next moves as he always did with time on his hands. He was pleased with his morning's work, not only had he a chance to earn some more money, he would enjoy making The Major pay, after the way that gentleman had screwed others in the past.

Most of the Feasibility Report he would present had been worked out for his previous firm by him prior to its takeover, so that there was little to do to adapt it now. He felt no qualms about this slight deception, as it was a sort of payback for 'trying it on' previously.

Also he had been able to arrange for what he hoped would be a good, reliable manager for the new project at the old school in Windsor Square. He would be busy at home with plenty to do in his room working on the details for the next few days.

Reaching his stop at Knightsbridge Tube Station, he alighted and headed for home, only 15 minutes walk away.

On letting himself into the house, with the new special key, he called out to announce himself to anyone in the house, as they were all much more security conscious these days.

Anne called that they were in the kitchen and as he walked through, found her and Tilly sitting at the table over a cup of tea together.

Tilly immediately went to jump up to get him a cup, but he waved her down with, "don't worry, I'll help myself, I can see you've had a hard day. I suppose you've both been sitting here all morning?"

"No we haven't, Mr. Rogers, I might tell you we've been very busy, haven't we madam?" Anne laughed, saying "don't take any notice of him Tilly; he has probably been sitting in pubs or restaurants all day just talking as usual."

He sat down and poured himself some tea, listening as they explained all that they had been doing in the house and that they had only just finished.

Tilly then stood up to say she must finish up now and get downstairs, as she had to collect young Toby from the Judo class at his school, and then to cook Arthur's meal ready for when he gets home.

Anne told her to just go off home, as she would clear the tea things away. Tilly thanked her, rushing off to see to her home life; Still full of energy, as always.

Jack smiled as she went, saying "I just wish I had half her energy, after a long day's work as she's had working with you. "She is such a willing person," said Anne, "I would be truly lost without her help. Now tell me, if you can, what have you really been doing today, did you achieve anything?"

He described the day to her, and when he got to the part about Berty's brother, she was most pleased.

She told him about the meeting arranged with builders next morning; he agreed it was important to get that sorted out first. He could deal with his other work later.

"Now if you don't mind, I'll go upstairs now and get on with some of it this evening, before dinner. By the way, if possible I would rather just have snack tonight after eating in the pub?"

"That's fine by me", said Anne, "we have not had time to make a big meal today. I'll call you later when it's time." Jack thanked her, picked up his briefcase and headed for his room.

After clearing away the evening snack, Anne settled down in her favourite comfortable chair to read; she was pleased that life was settling down once more. In fact many things had improved.

The house was now in better shape than it had been for years, with the exterior repaired, internal electrics and decorating all completed, and a very good security system in place. Although in her opinion that was a little extreme, but the Director had obviously thought it best, and after all, it was free to her!

She was reminded of Toby, wondering what his duties were these days.

On the following morning, after breakfast, Anne and Jack strolled down to the old school together, unlocking and opening the gates wide, they awaited Mr. Appleton, the builder and his colleague, both of whom arrived on time, able to drive straight into the school yard.

Introductions were completed, when Mr. Appleton presented his colleague as **Peter Wilson**, and explaining that as his firm were committed for some time to work for the Ministry of Works, he thought to suggest 'Wilson & Co', as a replacement building firm, who had been in the business almost as long as himself.

Jack handed each of them a copy of his building requirements and they started to wander around the various buildings, with Jack pointing out his suggestions on the list as they went.

Ending with the exterior grounds where considerable extension to the hard standing was required, for obvious reasons, then the perimeter fence, and gates etc. As they were sitting down together in the assembly room kitchen, Anne produced coffee for them all.

They discussed more detail and costs; until Mr. Appleton excused himself saying, "can I now leave you in Peter's hands, I'm sure he will look after you just as well as I would?"

Shaking hands, he left, but Anne insisted on seeing him out, as he reached his car she said "Thankyou, and don't forget I still owe you money for my house." "Not to worry madam, as soon as I hear from the Ministry, I'll let you know." He then touched his hat, and drove out of the school gates, as Anne returned to the kitchen.

The meeting was braking up, with Mr. Wilson promising to get an estimate to them shortly. After which, they locked up and strolled back home, excited in a way that they were more than ever committed to moving on with the new project, after all the talking and planning previously.

As soon as they were back inside the house, Jack asked to be excused, as he would like to get on with his other work, disappearing upstairs to his room.

He worked all the rest of that day and evening, on the feasibility report for The Major. At the end of which time he had completed a good 90% of it, including use of the work done previously, and various phone calls; so was very satisfied with the day.

Going down early to breakfast, he went to the front door to collect the morning paper, milk and croissants; remembering to disarm the new system first. Heading for the kitchen, he helped himself to a croissant, made some coffee and sat down at the table to enjoy some peace and quiet.

This lasted a full half hour before it was broken by Tilly bustling in, saying "so you brought the milk in! I thought it had been stolen or something and you've made coffee too!"

He smiled at her and said "sorry Tilly, I woke early, hope you don't mind, I'm not trying to take your job away, honest!" Anne now walked in and said "what's this about you taking her job, you could never do it well enough for my liking." Then turning to Tilly said, "Good morning, may I just have some cereal please." She sat down opposite Jack asking "why are you dressed like that then, going to work on your car or something?"

"No, just going to earn my side of our bargain by doing something around the house." To which she laughed, and said, "Have you really looked around the house lately? We told you yesterday what we had done; there is nothing that needs seeing to since the builders left, then Tilly and I finished off." Turning in her chair to say, "there you are, we knew he didn't believe what we had been doing, didn't we Tilly?" To which she smiled and nodded in agreement.

He was somewhat shamed, as he hadn't been around the other parts of the house lately to take in all that had been done. His mind had been elsewhere. "Sorry about that, have they done everything then, all of the decorating etc.?" "Yes, apart from the upstairs, which we had done before John's illness as he needed to spend a lot of time there."

She said "come on I'll show you, I am very pleased by the results, you should have a walk round, inside and out, after all, you do live here now you know!"

As they walked, he was surprised at just how much had been done, and said so. To which Anne replied, "Well apparently Mr. Appleton was under orders to do all that he thought necessary and make good afterwards, including all of the electricity wiring, but I can't find out how much I have to pay towards it all yet." He chuckled, "I shouldn't worry about it Anne, I think you will find your employers have their good reasons."

Then he said, "Shall we go and see what they did outside now? But if this work is anything to go by, you should have no problems for years to come."

After walking all around the house and garden, they made their way back to the kitchen, sitting down at the table once more. Jack laughed and said "Well it seems to me that you'd better put my rent up, what with the house now all up together and the garden Arthur's domain, there's nothing for me to do apart from eating the delicious food I have served up."

Anne bristled at this statement, "Certainly not! I won't hear of it; after all that you have done for me since you got here, plus sorting out my problem with the old school."

"But that was purely for profit, I'm hoping we'll make a lot of money on that business venture" he replied. "You may believe that, but I know how much it has helped me and that's all" said Anne.

A few days later Jack telephoned The Major's office, to let him know that his report was ready. His secretary advised that The Major was away for the day. He told her he was sending the package over by courier as the matter was urgent. She assured him that her boss would get it the moment he came in, and he rang off.

Jack was pleased that job was completed, unless they wanted a further meeting with the architects at some later stage, after absorbing the report.

This would now give him the time to concentrate on Windsor Auto Storage Ltd. and the old school.

He had received an acceptable estimate from the builders, P. Wilson & Co. the good news being that they would be able to commence work within two weeks; he and Anne had asked them to go ahead A.S.A.P. The work would take approximately two months to complete.

It meant that he must start to plan for an opening date, with advertising locally, staffing and general organising of the operation. This held no fears for him; he had done the same thing many times in the past, the difference being that this was now for his own firm. He should now arrange financing from his and Anne's own business account; they had agreed not to use Bank borrowing if possible, to avoid the costs involved.

Sometime later he received the promised phone call from Berty Blacksmith to say that his brother was now settled into his new home and looking for work, if he was still needed.

Jack was very pleased, as it fitted into his planning perfectly saying "I would like to meet him, but I think he should see the location first and decide if the journey over here will be worth it to him."

"That's no problem; will it be alright if I come over with 'im, say, this Saturday, to show 'im the tube stations he needs to use?" "That'll be fine; I look forward to seeing you then." Jack said, replacing the phone.

Berty and his brother duly arrived at the house on the following Saturday morning when Jack introduced them to Mrs. Eden-Smythe, as his co-director in the company. Berty introduced his brother Charley, to them both and they shook hands. Anne asked if they would like a drink, but they refused politely, saying they would like to get on and see the site.

Not to be outdone, she said, "I'll bring some Thermos flasks down there a little later, when you can sit and talk if you wish." Jack smiled, and ushered them out to show the way down to the school.

After wandering around what was little more than a building site at present, with the brothers showing great interest and asking intelligent questions, they retired into the kitchen area which was obviously being used as a canteen by the workmen? Anne had arrived, setting up tea and coffee from the flasks, also snack food made by Tilly.

As they all sat down at the kitchen table, Jack asked "how was your journey over here by the way, did it take long?" Berty replied "not long at all, about half an hour, that's all, just a few stops." Charley chipped in with "it surprised me how quick it was and a lot less hassle than I expected." "So you feel that you could work here on a fulltime basis then do you?" asked Jack. "Yes, I'd be more than happy, if you think I could do the job Mr. Rogers, but I've never done this kind of work before." "That's not a problem; Berty tells me you've been doing a Forman's job at your last firm, which means organising people for working shifts etc. and I have plenty of time to work with you before we open.

I would suggest that you wander around a few of the car parks in your area and central London, just to get some idea of what goes on; Although this will not be a normal operation; more exclusive, and mainly residential customers. One of the main assets would be to be able to talk to them, often to pacify them." Adding, " I think the best way forward would be to go home and consider what has been said and I will phone you in a couple of weeks to take it further if you are happy to; When we can talk about wages and so on."

Charley said this was O.K. by him and he would learn as much as possible in the meantime. They all stood up to say goodbye, and the brothers, thanking Anne for the snacks, went off together.

Meanwhile the two 'Company Directors' cleared the table and walked back to the house, talking over what had been said, and feeling satisfied by the meeting.

Two days later, Jack had a phone call from The Major to say that he had received the report and would like to meet him on site with the architects once more. This was arranged for the following morning.

Leaving the house in plenty of time, he headed for Knightsbridge Underground Station again; arriving at the Vauxhall Bridge development site well on time for his meeting.

On entering the office, he found The Major and his two cohorts sitting around a table with plans for the new development spread out, alongside his own plans within the feasibility report he had produced.

The Major greeted him warmly, (which usually meant he needed help), and the two architects intoned "good morning" in unison. He returned their greetings, and sat down saying, "now how can I be of help to you?"

It appeared that they had not fully grasped his concept, because of the technicalities and finances incurred, as he had suggested an entirely new machine in conjunction with the manufacturers, which would fit into place in the new location he had recommended, much more neatly than the old one.

Here The Major chimed in with, "why should we buy a new machine, the old one seems to be working alright?" Jack had been expecting this and leaning over the table, turned his report to the rear pages, where financial considerations were laid out. He said, "As you will see in these pages, I have outlined the costs of moving and re-installing the old machinery against a discounted cost of the new model, in conjunction with the makers.

I have also found a buyer for the old equipment from the Midlands area, who would be willing to dismantle and remove it, being a haulage company. The figures are all quoted there, showing little extra cost compared to the overall development. You must also bear in mind that it is now almost 5 years old and cannot keep up with the heavy throughput it gets on this site for much longer. I think your manager Berty Blacksmith would confirm it." One of the architects now spoke up, "Yes, I can see the advantages, especially from our point of view; this would be a much more aesthetic solution."

The Major was still unhappy, "if it is so worn out, why do these people want to buy it?" Jack replied

"They have a fleet of vans to wash and have realised how much labour time is being wasted at present, washing them by hand, but it doesn't warrant the cost of a new machine."

So the conversation continued, looking at all aspects of the Rogers report, which the two architects were generally pleased with. The Major finally had to admit to the inevitable and agree to the extra expenditure, obviously against his wishes.

Jack stood up to take his leave, as he had no more to contribute and shaking hands all round, he left the office.

Walking over to the car washing operation, he had a chat to Berty, saying he would be contacting his brother Charley within the next week. "That's good; I know he's really looking forward to the job you offered 'im, he's been out all over the place learnin' about parkin' like you said." Then added sheepishly, wouldn't mind the job myself come to that!" Jack laughed saying, "I couldn't afford your wages now, your too important to your new boss, especially with the new machine going in." Berty looked surprised at that, and Jack realised he'd said too much. "Forget I said that, it slipped out." "Right'o said Berty, I understand. Anyway I'll tell Charley, and see you again sometime."

On his way home, Jack was thinking 'I must remember to get an invoice in the post to The Major, before he conveniently forgets'. He'd enjoyed watching the crafty old codger squirm, knowing how he hated spending money, if he could find any way of avoiding it.

Arriving home, he had a lunchtime snack with Anne, and then worked in his room for the rest of the day, designing leaflets, signs etc. ready for the grand opening in the next few weeks; all being completed as per target date. He would also need to set up a training programme for the new staff, to ensure a proper service for the new customers. He intended to run a very high standard of service, within Windsor Auto Storage Ltd. to encourage the best Clientele for the new company.

CHAPTER18.

Meanwhile back at them M.O.D. decoding dept. The Director was summoned to the Minister's office one morning without prior warning, which was somewhat unusual, this concerned him, wondering what was wrong.

On arrival, he was shown to the inner sanctum immediately, which was also unusual. But his concern left him as he walked in, to see a big smile on the boss's face. Gesturing from his mammoth sized desk, to the chair opposite, he said "I have some very good news for you, direct from the Prime Minister."

"After his meeting with Her Majesty, following that nasty event some days ago, I can tell you that Mrs. Eden-Smythe is to receive a further honour, and don't look so concerned! It is to be awarded 'For Services to the Crown' with no reference to what services; so that her anonymity will be protected.

The Director was most pleased for her, and at the same time relieved, that she would be protected. He said "can you tell me what her title will be Sir?" "Yes, confidentially I can; she will be 'Dame Eden-Smythe C.B.E.' sounds right for her, don't you think? But I know I don't need to stress the secrecy at this stage, until she has been officially informed by post."

"Of course Sir, I do understand, and I am pleased that she is being recognised for all the Sterling work she has done for us over the years; especially during the last few months." The Minister nodded in agreement, replying "The P.M. is well aware that she has been partly instrumental in avoiding several terrorist disasters, including that recent attempt on the Queen and Government."

"That's very true, she provided information to the computer programmers, which was just 'cobledy-gook' previously. This has all been passed on to GCHQ at Cheltenham to assist their International listening also."

Adding as an afterthought, "I am hoping that will be the end of our needing to use her services, so that her anonymity can be preserved."

"Let us hope so," said the minister, "she is now of an age that she should be able to retire quietly, but please don't tell her I said that! She is a formidable lady! By the way, is she alright financially?" The director chuckled, saying "Oh yes Sir! She has a nice little 'nest egg' in the bank and has been paid well for her services by us, and has a very good pension pot. Also would you believe? She is just about to go into a business venture with Corporal Rogers?" "That's alright then, as I said, a ***formidable lady*** indeed, we will leave her be for now; until she gets her new honour of course; I shall try to be invited to the Palace when her presentation comes up. I presume you would like to be there too?"

"I certainly would Sir; it's something I have always wanted for her, without compromising her position."

The Minister nodded to say that would be arranged. Then; "Just one more thing Director, how is the situation with your listening traffic? Is it still busy?"

"No Sir, there has been very little airwave traffic since the explosion, apart from attempts to contact none-existent cells that we have closed down." He then added, "One disturbing aspect is that they are still attempting to trace the source of our ability to break their codes."

"At the moment they are still convinced that it must be a traitor in their own ranks. Let's hope it remains that way."

"Thankyou Director, that sounds most satisfactory, long may it continue, and thankyou for coming."

This brought the meeting to an end and the Director left to return to his own office, wishing he could let his team know the good news, which was of course impossible, as most of them were unaware of Anne's identity and her part in the recent improvements to information gathering.

As he arrived in his office, the chief of security called on the internal phone system. "We have a slightly disturbing development in our personal protection security sir, which I feel is worthy of your attention. Toby has reported sighting a small scooter turning up behind the car on a regular basis."

The Director thought for a minute, and asked "What makes him suspicious? Could it be a co-incidence?" "Toby tells me he has considered all possibilities before reporting, and he's not the type to exaggerate. Apparently the scooter rider's cover is that of Knowledge Trainee, but Toby is concerned that he seems to arrive on roads that he has already covered on previous occasions, too often."

This rather lost the Director, so he asked, "Remind me Commander, what is Knowledge Trainee?" "Sorry sir, I should explain, they are would-be Black Cab drivers who need to go through a period of training before passing an examination to get such a licence. They are seen all over London learning the different routes to take in order to get from 'A to B' efficiently. It makes a very good cover for surveillance. In fact we have used it ourselves from time to time."

Again the Director pondered on why the Chief should call him this time, and then it dawned on him. "Are you concerned because Toby was our special advisor's minder? (Both men knew he was referring to Anne, of course); "Exactly so Sir!" "Thankyou Commander, I understand your concern, and am pleased that you let me know, I take it that you will be keeping it under scrutiny?"

"Certainly we will, I'll keep you informed if anything further develops, goodbye for now Sir."

Replacing the phone, he remembered something else concerning that lady, and reaching for a memo pad, scribbled a note to the Ministry of Works, to say that this memo would authorise him to pay all 'accounts due' from F.W.Appleton & Son, for work recently completed at No.47 Windsor Square, London SW 12.

He then signed it with a flourish and a rare smile to himself, and thinking, 'That should please her! It's the least I can do for that Lady!'

Toby had been in his boss's office when he made the call to the Director, so hearing what had been said. As his boss replaced the phone, he looked up to say, "All I can suggest at present is to keep your eyes open and be even more vigilant than I know you always are Toby." He replied, "Yes, I will Sir, but this chap just didn't seem to be concentrating on his job, as all of the others do. There was just something not quite right about him. Still, my driver Joseph has managed to get a photograph of him when his attention was on me as I escorted my last client into his meeting. It has been sent to the International Recognition database dept. for analysis." "Very good", said his chief, "that was quick thinking on the driver's part. Now let's hope this character is in our records."

Toby stood up to leave, saying "I do hope it is not connected to Madam after keeping her safe for so long, but as I am not required to go anywhere near her for some time, it should not affect her." As he took his leave, the Commander smiled. He was aware that Toby had formed quite an attachment to the Lady in question, mostly out of respect.

His next call was to his counterpart at the Counter Terrorism squad to inform him of the situation, confident that he would know how to counter any possible danger. He was assured that the problem would be dealt with as required and the Commander decided to leave it in their hands; which as things turned out, was the best decision he could have made.

Some days later, as Toby was escorting a senior member of the M.O.D. between the Ministry building and MI5 Head Quarters, to attend a regular monthly meeting, Toby noticed the same moped following well behind. But he also noticed a familiar old van behind the moped, knowing instantly where it was from, and that the 'Squad' were on the job.

He was correct indeed, and it so happened, that it was our old friend, Chief Inspector Theo. Thompson, who had been charged with the surveillance operation. The driver and his companion, in that tailing van were constantly in touch with him back at H.Q. by radio, advising him of the situation in front of them.

Although the scooter rider attempted to look disinterested in the car ahead, it was obvious to a trained observer that he was constantly changing direction, as Toby's driver changed the car's direction as a standard avoidance manoeuvre.

Eventually the car was approaching its destination, then as it stopped at a junction prior to turning into the underground car park beneath the MI5 building; The scooter rider nonchalantly rode up to the back of the car where he considered to be a 'blind spot' to the driver and passengers, reached into a pannier box on the back of his bike, and producing a package, clamped it to the car body just below the fuel tank filler cap, and quickly rode away. Unaware that he had been observed at all times by the van driver and his passenger, who immediately radioed his H.Q. to inform them of the action, before the van driver raced off to catch up with the scooter.

Instantly the message was relayed to Toby in the car, but by this time it had begun to enter the down ramp into the car park.

Calling to the driver to stop and get out, he grabbed his charge by the arm, and opening his side door, dragged him out of the car, bundling him quickly behind a concrete pillar at the side of the ramp; at the same time, glimpsing the driver doing the same thing at the opposite side of the car.

Back at the squad H.Q. Theo Thompson and his team were swinging into action, by dispatching ambulances, the bomb squad and police back-up, simultaneously. While another member of his team was franticly trying to arrange for the mobile phone network in that area to be disrupted; hoping to block a possible mobile phone detonation signal if possible.

Meanwhile, the van driver from Counter Terrorism Squad was swerving through traffic at breakneck pace in an attempt to catch up with the moped, until he eventually saw it pull off the road onto a shopping forecourt where it stopped.

The driver pulled the bike onto its stand and casually produced a mobile phone from the pannier box and started to dial a number, just as the van pulled up and its passenger jumped out to grab the rider in an arm lock intending to put him in handcuffs.

But as he did so, the rider just smirked at him crying out, "you're too late, and ***Allah is great***!" As the agent took the hand phone from his grasp and threw it to the floor. Then he and the van driver hustled the man through the back doors of their van, handcuffing him to the body struts. They then collected the phone, reporting to their H.Q. that the man had been secured, and that they would be bringing him in for interrogation.

At that same moment that the moped rider had pressed the number on his mobile phone, Toby and his driver, having heard cars on the way up from the underground car park, had rushed down towards the sound, after first yelling to the V.I.P. to run to better cover. They were both waving and shouting to stop the cars, when suddenly! There was an almighty **BANG! And WHOOSH**! It was followed by loud **CLATTERING** of debris and a **RUSH of FIRE** emitting from the top of the ramp; sending pieces of concrete and other debris flying through the air towards them, hitting them in the back and legs.

They both crumpled to the ground critically injured, but the car driver was saved from serious injury inside her car coming up the car park ramp; whilst their V.I.P. charge had escaped any injury at all.

It transpired later that because the official car was armoured, the explosive had been unable to penetrate its bodywork, and the power had blown outwards dismantling parts of the building fabric, which had caused those injuries.

Within minutes, help arrived in the form of Ambulances, Bomb Squad, and Police reinforcements, to take control of traffic flow and seal off the area.

Next to arrive was a car full of members of the protection squad, whose first duty was to rush the V.I.P. into the safety of his meeting inside the MI5 building. As others rushed to ensure the welfare of Toby and his driver, Joseph, they were quickly transported by ambulance to Hospital for urgent attention.

Before reporting details back to H.Q. and starting the painstaking scene investigation, with technical help from the bomb squad.

As for the perpetrator of this atrocity, (the moped rider), he was now ensconced in a secure interview room back at the Counter Terrorism H.Q.

Chief Inspector Theo. Thompson was keen to get at him to find out as much as possible, he would need to know more about how it was possible to get through the net of security, before reporting to his bosses.

As it had happened at the MI5 building, he knew they would be aware of the incident by now and asking searching questions.

By talking to individual members of his squad back in the office, and over the radio from the scene, he was able to build up an initial sequence of events and a picture of what had happened.

He prepared a short memo of the details and faxed a copy to all concerned; explaining that it was very much an ongoing investigation and that he would be in a position to supply more details later.

After which, he and a colleague entered the interview room to question the bomber. He was sitting at the small bare table with an arrogant look on his face, attempting to prove that he was not afraid of them, and spouting, “Allah is great!” over and over, with the odd “I am ready to be a Martyr for Allah.” They ignored this, having heard it all many times before.

For a while, they just sat and looked at him, without speaking, which began to unnerve him, and he started to calm down, until he eventually stopped. Now Theo. Said “right! If you’ve finished we’ll get started shall we?”

Sometime later, details began immerge, after the facts were presented to him and he began to realise that there was no one to help him and his family were going to be affected.

It transpired that the car had simply been targeted as belonging to the M.O.D. and used for transporting V.I.Ps. It seems that Mohamed, (as that turned out to be his name), had been chosen from other like-minded, brain washed, young men, by post, from a contact in Pakistan; which he considered an honour of course.

He had been sent money to buy his scooter, and told how to travel around London. Once he had established contact with a target car, he was told where to collect the ready-made bomb, how and when to use it.

He was also told he must be willing to give his life for Allah by being close by to ensure the bomb detonated; but at the last minute had backed away from that sacrifice. He was now afraid that he and his family would be severely punished by his masters for that.

They used this fear to encourage him to reveal the whereabouts of his explosives suppliers.

A squad of armed men was dispatched immediately, before they could discover that Mohamed was still alive, and disappear from sight.

The 'bomb factory' turned out to be no more than a shed at the back of a tenement house, which to the squad's surprise, contained two families with six children between them. But on questioning the ladies of the house, it seemed they were more afraid of the bomb makers than the police, and insisted that it had nothing to do with any member of their families.

They claimed 'the men' just came and went whenever suited them; to bring more 'things' into the shed. Appearing to have no conception of the danger they and their neighbours were in.

All were immediately evacuated, under much protest, with the usual claims of discrimination, unable to understand it was for their own safety.

The Bomb Squad now got to work, completely clearing all explosive materials found there, before allowing the families back in, with a strong warning of what could happen, should the bomb makers return, and that they should contact the police immediately if that should happen. Not that there was any hope of that, these families were much too afraid of the consequences from their own countrymen.

Eventually, all members of the security forces drove away, with a show of a job well done, cleared up, and finished, for the benefit of any watchers up and down the street.

A little later that day, a British Telecom van drove down the Street, containing a pair of uniformed engineers, (both of a similar Ethnic origin to those living in that area, to ease suspicions), and stopped by a BT manhole inspection cover.

Unloading their van, with the usual clutter of equipment, they lifted the cover and set up safety barriers around it. Placing a ladder against the nearest telegraph pole, the female of the pair climbed up, connecting her test handset to the wiring and reported back to the H.Q. of the Counter Intelligence Squad that they were in place, she then descended the ladder, and they both promptly sat down for a smoke before starting work; which all looked very normal to any onlookers.

The two injured men, had been rushed to St.Mary's hospital in central London, protected by members of the squad; who were constantly being pressed for information over the phone by Chief Inspector Theo Thompson leading the squad and Commander Tierney in charge of security at the M.O.D. Although, as they had pointed out, they were unable to give any such news until the injured men's surgery had been completed.

Mohamed, the bomber, was in a holding cell at H.Q. having been questioned for some hours, but it seemed that he knew no more than had already been established. He was obviously a weak tool in the scheme of things and had been used by his mentors as a dupe whose life was unimportant, to see if security could be broken, which had proved to be the case.

The Director at M.O.D. de-coding department was franticly awaiting news of the two men in hospital and more searching information on the bomber and his connections.

He was already under pressure from his Minister and others higher up the chain of command for information, to ascertain if it was an isolated incident, or the beginning of a new threat of violence, using more odd pathetic loners.

It was obvious that a great deal of soul searching and investigation was going to required in the coming days and weeks, by all concerned.

CHAPTER 19.

The great day had arrived at last! Well; it was in the eyes of Anne and Jack; the Grand Opening of **Windsor Auto Storage Ltd.**

Peter Wilson the builder had been as good as his word, completing the required work well on schedule and to a good standard; Charley Blacksmith had now been employed for some three weeks, during which time he had worked with Jack on various jobs, during his training. Designing and erecting signs at the new operation, for direction and information to prospective clients; collecting and distributing leaflets around the area, advertising for, and interviewing further staff etc.

Jack and Anne had been busy working on the financial and legal aspects of running a new company, producing contracts for annual subscription, terms of reference, cash management, wages requirements, tax collection and payment, and general accountancy. Indeed all the requirements of setting up and operating a brand new company.

Luckily, the weather was kind, being more like an 'Indian Summer' as the autumn season was upon them, which made it possible to set up a picnic type reception outside. All organised by Colonel Batseby-Fortesque and his willing team at the request of Anne, who had cleverly turned it into a sort of Resident's Garden Party, making all feel involved; At the same time allowing them to sample the services available to them and their cars.

The whole thing started at midday on a Saturday to allow for all residents and neighbours from surrounding streets to be included, and running into the evening as long as required.

Visitors were impressed by the transformation to the Old School premises, with its new roof, bright paintwork, new security fencing and what seemed like acres of tar macadam surfacing.

Actual start of operations was planned for the following Monday when the new gates would be opened to the public in earnest for the first time.

Several more parking attendants apart from Charley, had been recruited, trained and uniformed in order to handle clients to the best of standards, in consideration for the area in which they were located, (and prices charged); With Harrods and other well known Knightsbridge stores located in the vicinity.

Response from the opening event was most encouraging, with several requests for residents inside and outside the Square for annual contracts, even before they were open for business proper.

This news was received by the two Company Directors with some relief, as they now had many financial outgoings, even before the builder's final account was due to be paid.

Therefore the official opening was deemed to be a roaring success by all. That is apart from one small incident later in the evening?

When all of the visitors had gone and the clearing up done, both owners thanked the Colonel and his team for all their hard work, handing each of the staff a cash bonus, over and above their wage for the day.

But the Colonel now decided to mention that he had been noting the outside interest, and felt that he ought to remind them of their agreement at the Residents meeting, when they had assured those people that they would have first refusal of spaces available. He was correctly thinking in his capacity of leader of the Residents Association, making sure that their interests were protected. They were able to assure him that his charges were well protected and that they would always have priority, which seemed to pacify him. Especially when Jack produced a Magnum of Champagne, which he had been storing on ice for them all to celebrate, since the workers had been unable to drink alcohol all day.

So the day ended, with everyone involved, going home in a happy mood.

Having made sure they were all able to get home safely, Jack locked up all buildings and gates, setting the new alarm system, then he and Anne wandered back to their home, feeling contented with the day; looking forward to a relaxing evening.

For some time they quietly discussed the day's events, and what would be happening in the near future; both looking forward with excitement to the following Monday opening.

They had begun to form a good working relationship together, each being responsible for what their expertise would suit best.

After a while, Anne turned on the television to watch the late news, the main headlines being a story headed:-

'BOMB ATTACK ON THE MI5 BUILDING.'

It gave very few specifics, apart from some sort of explosion at the car park entrance, producing a small amount of damage. Two people had been badly injured in the blast, and a suspect terrorist arrested nearby. But no further information had been forthcoming at this stage.

From this announcement, Anne had no way of knowing that her friend Toby and her driver Joseph, had been involved, and did not give it too much thought at that time. Not realising that she could well have been in the car, had it happened at an earlier time.

CHAPTER 20.

After appearing to work on and off for some hours, the two 'BT. engineers' were instructed by telephone from their H.Q. to pack up and move to another servicing point further up the road, but still in sight of the 'bomb factory' house, at least until daylight began to fade, as the day ended; When they would hand over to a different type of surveillance for the night shift.

There had been very little movement around the house under watch, apart from some of the children at play in the street, running around and laughing; unaware of the danger they had previously been living under.

Several ladies of varying ages had been rushing out to shop quickly, eager to get back home; they were aware that something had been happening in their street, and wanted no part of it.

As the afternoon drew to a close, and street lights began to come on, the 'Telephone Engineers' started to pack up their equipment and load it back onto the van, aware that the 'night shift' would be arriving very soon elsewhere in the street, but still with a view to the target house. They would arrive in the form of 'The British Gas emergency call-out team,, ostensibly to look for a suspected gas leak?

THEN IT BEGAN TO HAPPEN!

The next few minutes seemed like an age to the teams involved, after it was all over, and they tried to recount the sequence of events to their bosses!

It all started as that B.T. van was about pull out of the street; glancing in his rear view mirror, to check if the 'night shift' had arrived, when the driver noticed a medium sized, dark Green van pulling into the other end, confidently heading towards the target house, and pulling to a stop by the curb-side.

Stopping his vehicle to watch through his mirrors, the B.T. driver was amazed to see a lady from that house, (who the police had warned just that morning), come running out to speak to two men in the front seat of that Green van; which immediately started to speed away towards the end of the street where the B.T. van was stationary.

Thinking quickly the driver pulled across the road, blocking it off, while his partner (equally quick to re-act) was radioing her H.Q. for assistance.

At the same instant, the Gas Board truck which was just arriving, had also seen events and quickly pulled across the other end of the street; just as the Green van was attempting the do a three point turn in the road, to get away in that direction. But the driver was by now in a panic, trying too fast to do the turn, he ran hard into the pavement edge, bursting a tyre, so was going nowhere in a hurry.

After several wasted minutes of shouting and screaming from inside the van, as they tried to decide what to do next. Suddenly! Four or five men started to tumble out of all of the van doors, two of them brandishing automatic handguns, and firing them into the air! But if they were hoping to frighten off the opposition with those guns, it was not their lucky day. They would not be expecting a crew from an ordinary BT van or a British Gas truck, to be armed; so that when they let off a warning shot, they had the same warnings in reply. This made them cower down behind their vehicle as best they could, now staying very quiet.

There was no other cover available, to them, as all doors and windows in the street had been quickly and firmly closed.

Meanwhile, members of the armed, elite 'A10 Police Force' (sharp-shooters) had arrived and were getting into position; Taking over that responsibility from the two surveillance crews.

After some five minutes of standoff, a loud screech was heard from behind the van and suddenly one of the gunmen leapt into view brandishing his gun and waving it around his head like a Dervish with a sword about to attack an enemy.

An authoritive voice boomed out over a loud hailer announcing:--

"PUT DOWN YOUR WEAPON AND LIE DOWN ON THE GROUND."

But the man appeared not to hear, ignoring the call he instead, started to run towards the targeted house containing a bomb making factory. Again the voice rang out:--

"STOP! THROW YOUR GUN AWAY AND LIE DOWN".

"THIS IS YOUR LAST WARNING!"

The mad gunman chose not listen, and carried on running. He could not be allowed to reach the house and its inhabitants, who would become hostages. Therefore the order was given; a single shot rang out and he fell to the ground.

After a few more seconds of excited chatter, a handgun was thrown out into the road, and the rest of the van's occupants stood up, walking into the road with their hands above their heads, and no guns in sight.

Again the amplified voice rang out saying with much authority:--

"YOU WILL LIE FACE DOWN, SPREAD EAGLED."

"AWAY FROM EACH OTHER!"

This they all did, with some alacrity; they had witnessed what happened if an order was disobeyed.

Now several of the A10 squad moved forward, armed with automatic weapons at the ready, just in case another 'would be suicide candidate' decided to have a go, with a hidden weapon.

The men were unceremoniously handcuffed behind the back, dragged to their feet and marched off to a waiting secure police transport vehicle. While other members of the group went over to the man who had been shot; on inspection, he was found to be dead. So perhaps he had achieved what he appeared to want, in Paradise?

They next approached the Green van, to inspect it for the explosives they expected it to contain; opening the rear doors tentatively, in case of a booby trap; although the miscreants had not had much time to set one up, as they had not been expecting the reception awaiting them.

At first glance, the van's contents appeared innocent enough, simply boxes of what appeared to be household cleaning products as a house to house salesman might carry; but on closer inspection, under the top layer were other boxes.

These contained all of the ingredients for making up small portable bombs,. Plastic explosive wrapped in greaseproof paper, boxes of nails, ball bearings, and so on, to inflict maximum injury. Plus short pieces of metal pipe, magnets, and most dangerous of all, **DETONATORS!** All in all a sort of delivery system for bomb makers.

The A10 squad immediately radioed for a bomb disposal unit to come and take charge of such a volatile haul, they would know how to make it safe and see to its disposal. Meantime armed men were left to guard it, until their arrival.

Having now made the area as safe as possible, A10 called in waiting police units to start knocking on doors, to re-assure the street's inhabitants.

Also to deal with members of the targeted house, to work out just who was responsible for what had been happening there.

Having given the occupants the 'benefit if the doubt' earlier in the day, and believing that they were working under a cloak of fear; the police were now annoyed that they had been duped and their trust abused, so approached with much more strict caution.

There was much wailing and crying innocence, as would be expected now that they had been found out, but with the help of their colleagues from the B.T. van, who were of that ethnic group, therefore understood the language, and could cut through the excited rhetoric; they eventually isolated house members who had been abetting the terrorists, using threats to keep other members and neighbours quiet.

These people were taken into custody, and driven off to separate police stations for further questioning. It would now be a matter of much drawn out detection work to trace the source of supply for these dangerous materials and any other so far undiscovered networks.

The above was now reported to 'The powers that be?' Who were extremely pleased with the results, including all at the M.O.D. de-coding dept.?

After all! That operation had been derived from of Toby's diligence! Simply doing his job, as usual! Without which, a serious incident would have taken place, and a dangerous group of terrorists would have gone undetected.

Meanwhile, good news had been coming into his office from St.Mary's Hospital, about that gentleman and his driver, as they were both recovering well from surgery.

This gave the Director good reason to phone Anne, to let her know about Toby's injuries, he had not been sure how to approach it previously.

Knowing how concerned she would be about her protector, he picked up the phone, and remembering to press the scramble button, dialled Anne's number.

The phone rang for some time, before it was answered by Tilly, to whom he had spoken previously, so was unconcerned, "good day Mrs. Tilson, may I please speak to Mrs. Eden-Smythe?" Tilly didn't know the voice, but it sounded very 'Upper Crust' so replied, "I'm sorry sir, but she will be out most of today, it's the opening day of the new business and she will be very busy! Can I say who called?"

He was a little surprised, he had forgotten about her new life, but replied, "Thankyou, I'll call her again tomorrow morning. Could you tell her it is rather urgent and I shall need to speak to her then if possible, she will know who it is."

He replaced the phone before she had chance to ask his name again, which Tilly found to be 'quite rude'! But she was not to know the circumstances and security involved.

The Director now decided to inform his staff of the situation with Toby and his driver, by the issue of a memo to all departments; calling his secretary in, he dictated the following, to be sent to all departments involved.

It read :-

It will not have escaped your attention, that a serious incident has taken place over the weekend, involving our security teams. At which time two of our colleagues were unfortunately injured. May I now assure you that they are recovering well, but under no circumstances should anyone attempt to visit them, or discuss the matter outside these offices?

I feel sure you are all aware of the need for discretion, for the safety of others amongst us.

Signed: - 'THE DIRECTOR'

He asked his secretary deal with it 'as a matter of urgency'

His next task was to compile an official report for his superiors and the secret archives, for use in time to come.

But before tackling that, he would need to arrange a conference for all heads of department to glean as much detail as possible.

CHAPTER 21.

That Monday morning, Anne and Jack had been up extra early in readiness for the opening day of the new business. In fact they were already at the re-furbished premises, when Charley and his crew arrived. They had also been up early, in order to beat the rush hour on the tube, they said, yet seemed to be just as excited about their new jobs, and eager to go.

They all set to work organising things ready for the first customers, who soon began to arrive, and continued so to do to do all through the day.

Ending after the daytime parkers finished their day's shopping or work and collected their cars for the journey home.

After which, several of the newly contracted residents began to arrive for their overnight secure parking.

Having worked almost all day, with only the odd break for snack meals, they were all tired, but contented with a very good first day. Although realising there was a lot to learn in organising traffic flows etc. But that would come as experience was gained over time.

Also staffing shift patterns had to be organised by Charley with Jack's help of course, especially overnight cover; but so keen was he, to get it right, Charley offered to stay the first night with his newest employee, so that he would know at first hand, any problems that may occur.

Jack told him that he would keep an eye on things, being just up the road, but when Charley pressed the matter, he didn't wish to take away from the new manager's authority, and simply added that he was always available over the phone, should there be a problem.

With that established, he and Anne now thankfully left the operation to the crew they had employed for that job, and walked back to the house, again feeling that they were most satisfied with the first day's input, especially from a very new and inexperienced workforce.

After consuming another very acceptable meal, left by Tilly, they retired with the remains of a bottle of wine to the sitting room once more, where they both settled into armchairs with some relief after a hard day for them. "This is when I know I'm getting older" said Anne, "thank goodness I won't need to do that every day." "That was enough to tire any age group" Jack replied, "but that's why we've employed younger men of course." From what I've seen today, we seem to have picked a very good crew, they are all enthusiastic for the business to succeed."

"Well if today is anything to go by, it should be a roaring success!" laughed Anne, adding, "Shall we see what is happening in the rest of the world for a change?" and reached across to turn on the television set.

After a little while, the nightly news came on, it seemed there was only one story at the moment. Across the screen was emblazoned the headline;-

SHOOTOUT ON A LONDON STREET! ONE MAN KILLED!

An announcer now came into view and with a grave face, and began his story:-

"Over the weekend, two terrorist incidents have taken, place which appear to be linked. The explosion reported by us, at MI5 headquarters on Friday, led the

Counter Terrorist Squad to a house in Northeast London, where we believe a small bomb factory has been discovered. It appears that a gang were cornered when they arrived in a van containing explosive materials. Shots were fired by them and returned by security forces above their heads. When one of the terrorists ran towards the house, presumably to take hostages, after ignoring warnings to stop and relinquish his gun, was shot dead by marksmen, for the safety of the householders.

Extensive enquiries are ongoing by security forces to trace the source of these explosive materials, we will keep you informed of any further developments as they happen;" He now took a deep breath, then said, "and now to other news."

The TV went blank as Anne turned it off. She said "I can't listen to any more about all this violence if you don't mind Jack? it depresses me after such a pleasant day. I'm off to bed; we can sort out our finances and the company paperwork tomorrow."

Jack suddenly jerked up in his chair; he had been semi-dozing whilst the TV was on and now said guiltily. "Oh! Yes Anne, You go up, you must be tired, I'm afraid I am! I'll just check the house and go up too."

As he went up to his room, he was thinking how he would like to phone the old school to check on things, but knew he could not, for fear of upsetting his new manager, Charley; he would just have to get used to trusting the staff, as he used to in his last job; But then that wasn't his own business after all, it was now quite different?

Both had a good, deep sleep that night, after a busy day; unaware how the events on the news were connected to their lives, how could they?

The following morning while sitting over breakfast, Tilly gave Anne the obscure phone message from the previous day, showing her concern at the abruptness of the caller; but to her surprise Anne seemed to understand who it would be and was not concerned about it. Jack had left a note to say he would be down at the school and not worry about breakfast for him; he would have something with 'the boys'. Anne smiled as she read it, knowing he wouldn't be able to keep away from the new business for long. She decided to get to work in her study to catch up with the company paperwork, which was her new job now.

As she worked, the telephone rang, picking it up, she recognised the Director's voice as he asked, "Is your phone showing secure?" She looked down at the unit to see the red light glowing and answered "Yes; good morning director, I think you upset my housekeeper yesterday, by putting the phone down on her?" with a chuckle in her voice.

But she was somewhat surprised when he did not reply to that, and in a sombre voice said, "I am afraid I have some bad news for you Anne," (he never called her Anne?), "Toby was quite seriously injured the other day", then hurriedly added, "but he is now out of surgery and doing well, as is his driver, Joseph." After an initial gasp! The phone went quiet for a while, so much so that the Director became concerned for her and asked, "Are you there madam?" Anne was attempting to gather her decorum after such a shock, but now said "I'm so sorry director, how on earth did it happen."

Then she suddenly remembered the news bulletins, and added, "Was it to do with these latest incidents on the news?" There was a short pause as he considered how much he could say, he then replied "they were both injured in an incident at the MI5 building on Friday, but no more can be said at present, I'm sure you understand madam."

"I do understand; Will they both recover fully do you know?" "All we know for sure at the moment, is that they will both live, and it is hoped they will be normal, but as their injuries were to the back of the head and spinal area, we cannot be absolutely certain until they are able to get out of bed; which will not be for a while yet. But the doctors are quite hopeful."

All Anne could think was, 'poor Toby, and Joseph's poor wife'? Pulling herself together she said 'matter of factly' "I suppose it is out of the question to visit him?" knowing the implications of this request. "Yes, I'm very sorry Anne, I know how much you think of him, and your driver, as was, but there are many who would like to visit, and I have had to refuse, for their own security. Our only direct contact is with the team of colleagues on watch by his bedside. There could well be undesirables on watch for such connections to our various departments."

He then added, to help her thoughts along; "However, we have allowed for Joseph's wife to visit, as that would be seen as normal. But your good wishes will be passed on to them both." Anne was re-assured to some extent, and knowing how busy he must be, said "Thankyou director, I'm sure you will keep me informed? Goodbye."

He could feel her anguish over the phone, so replied, "You can be sure of that, goodbye to you dear lady." As they both replaced their handsets.

Sitting back in her chair, she pictured Toby as she had known him, always punctual, always beautifully dressed, always polite and correct; ALWAYS THERE when needed! Smiling to herself, she thought, 'even as a builder's labourer in his unlikely overalls! God forbid that he would be crippled, or disfigured in any way'! She then shook herself out of that reverie, it was too negative a thought, and she must get on with her day as best she could.

Jack being unaware of any of this was keeping busy supervising the new business operation. It seemed the first night had passed well, with only a few residents arriving late with their cars, after having an evening out.

Happy to hand over their responsibility for overnight security of the car, and the attendants were happy with the tips handed out by slightly inebriated clients.

Charley had stayed all night as promised, and reported that the night duty man (who had now left for home) would be quite capable without him. Therefore Jack suggested that he should also get off home as soon as possible later in the day, and he would cover for him, which Charley willingly accepted.

So the business had started and flourished, with all of them learning as they went along, sorting out small problems as they got to know their clients little foibles. The crew began to knit into a good understanding of what was required by each of them; all happy with the new job, and eager to please. So much so, that Jack realised he would soon not be needed, as it began to run smoothly. He therefore decided to go home for some lunch, and talk to Anne, intending to return afterwards to relieve his manager, so that he could get off home.

He told Charley what he intended, checking that they had food and drink available, and leaving them to it, walked up the road to No. 47.

Letting himself into the house, he went to the kitchen to let Tilly know that he was home for lunch, but was surprised to find she was not looking her usual happy self. She just said "could you have a word with madam, she's had some bad news? She's in the study."

He then walked into Anne's study to find her working at the desk, but looking unhappy. He said hello and she answered, but obviously had something on her mind. He therefore said "are you alright Anne, you don't look too happy?" "Oh! Jack! "She said, "Toby has been badly injured!" looking tearful, which was not like her at all. He sat down, and let her recount what she had been told, which after a while seemed to relax her. It was as if she had needed to unburden herself to someone, and now felt better.

Jack stood up and going over to Anne, squeezed her hand and kissed her cheek in sympathy, without speaking, he knew how she must be feeling. Indeed he was also concerned to hear the news; he had a great deal of respect for Toby, although he didn't know the driver personally.

At that moment, Tilly called out to say lunch was ready, which was perhaps just what was needed to break the atmosphere. They both went into the kitchen to find Tilly bustling around making a snack for them, and saying, "I know you're not too happy at the moment madam, but you should eat something, it will make you feel better" Caring for her welfare as usual. Sitting down at the kitchen table, Anne said "Thankyou Tilly, I'm sure you are right." Looking over at her fellow company director she said, "Now to get away from that depressing subject, tell me how our new business is going after its first 24hrs."

Jack relayed all that had happened and why he had come home this lunch time. He then added, but I'll stay here with you, if you prefer Anne?" She smiled and reaching over to touch his hand, said "no, I'm fine now, and poor Charley must be out on his feet after being there all night."

Jack was quite relieved really, as he didn't want to let the manager down. Therefore finishing his snack, he set off back to the school, promising to be home early in the evening.

Good to his word he arrived home early to spend the evening with Anne to try to keep her occupied.

To his surprise she was working away at her desk, with the computer on; he said, "Keeping busy then?" she turned to face him smiling and replied "Yes, I'm over my Maudling mood now thankyou, anyway we need to keep up with our company's books now that it seems to be booming?"

He was pleased with that, as it showed that she had recovered her sense of humour. Replying, "I can help now if you like, we have the rest of the evening, is there anything you need help with at this stage?" "Yes please, you can advise me on the charging system and the differing types of parking arrangements, I'm not quite sure about the differences; that would be your expertise."

So they settled down to thrash out how the necessary company book keeping and accountancy system would be organised, in order to produce Profit & Loss figures, to follow how they were doing, and for future use in taxation returns. Also what their future operations should concentrate on to keep the business healthy. They now had employee responsibilities, needing to arrange a payroll system with welfare payments and insurance cover for them. Plus various kinds of insurance cover for the business.

Thankfully in this day and age, there were computer programs designed for just this purpose to make life easier for business operators.

There was much to catch up on, and they got through quite a lot that first evening. Until Anne stood up stiffly, saying, "I will leave you to it and get a meal on the table, thank goodness for Tilly; it will be ready in the oven as usual."

Jack nodded, and carried on for a while longer, until she called him to say it was on the table, when he thankfully closed down the computer for the night.

When dinner was finished, Jack volunteered to clear up, telling her to rest for a while; she gratefully accepted and said, "If you don't mind, I'm going up to bathe and have a read in bed?" "Good idea, it's been a difficult day for you, sleep well!" She stood up from the table and saying "goodnight," headed for the door.

After clearing away, Jack could no longer resist ringing the school parking site, to check on things, but the night duty man reported that all was fine, so locking up the house, he went to bed.

Anne had been trying to concentrate on her novel, but her mind constantly drifted back to the recent events in her 'other life'.

She wondered at the events leading up to Toby's near miss with death; was it anything to do with her work at the Ministry? She hoped not, she could not consider that it might be from her input that people were being injured or dying.

Yet she had always been told to consider what might have happened to many others, had she not helped to break those codes.

Eventually she drifted off to sleep.

So a routine began within the new business and their lives that would hopefully continue for a long time into the future.

That is apart from the occasional 'special event' of course, which they would both be un-aware of until it happened.

CHAPTER 22.

More news had been coming into the Director's office for several days now on an almost hourly basis, as he had asked to be kept continually informed.

First and foremost, news from St.Mary's Hospital was all positive; both men were showing signs of full, if slow, recovery and the long term outlook appeared to be improving.

Next item was in connection with ongoing enquiries from information gained by interrogation of the 'would be bombers' captured while delivering explosives, to the 'bomb factory'.

The story which had emerged in a detailed report to The Director was as follows:-

It seemed that far from being willing to give up their lives for Allah! as their 'brain washers' had drummed into them, they were now happier to save those lives and throw themselves on to the mercy of the British legal system. Consequently, they were being most co-operative, although in truth, they knew very little apart from their immediate contacts.

But from the names gleaned out of them, and the vehicles used, a channel of supply was eventually traced back to an importer of fancy goods and speciality food supplies from the Middle East;

That company had a U.K. office and warehouse in a sleazy area of Tilbury Docks.

This had been raided by the combined forces of Police, Anti-terrorist officers and Customs & Excise, using a search warrant issued under Anti Terrorism laws.

For a long time they could find nothing, apart from some 'shady looking' characters, who claimed they did not know who was in charge, or even what the firm's name was; (although it was on a sign over the doors), constantly proclaiming innocence and racist claims.

Then the big discovery! When trained sniffer dogs found slabs of plastic explosive cleverly wrapped in greaseproof paper, disguised as slabs of Goats Butter, proclaiming 'religious qualities' on the box. Which was to deter prying official eyes, as when a religious connection was made, they tended to become wary of possible repercussions; (So much for the genuine religious beliefs by these fanatics)?

The warehouse was immediately sealed off, the bomb squad called, and all members of staff arrested, still proclaiming that they knew nothing about the materials found; which was nonsense of course, as they had to know which items and who to deliver it up to when collected.

Later in the day, when the place was made safe by explosives experts, who had also discovered other bomb making items, including the dreaded detonators; encased in similar boxes and marked with the same religious connotations; detectives began to search the offices for any documents which could lead to the overseas connection.

This was eventually established, and linked to certain addresses in Three Middle Eastern countries, and by the following day, the relevant security services in those countries were contacted with the evidence gathered. This resulted in searches being made of those premises by local authorities, producing significant finds of sanctioned goods, military munitions, and other explosive materials, waiting to be shipped around the world.

From this, were made many revealing arrests in those countries, including high ranking officials and in one case, a politician.

The whole operation was now being dismantled and many outlets closed down; hopefully saving possible atrocities in the future, in many different countries.

As he read the report, The Director marvelled at what had transpired from just one attempted bombing by a deluded young man; but which could have resulted in the death or serious injury of at least three valuable people, and who knows what else he could done if that had been successful, or given up his life, as his tutors hoped.

Yet through the diligence and co-operation of several U.K. security services and those in other countries, a major terrorist supply chain had been closed down, giving a little more breathing space for the homeland anti-terrorism organisations, and negating planned attacks in the U.K. and elsewhere.

Plus the long term imprisonment of at least six members of a terrorist cell, with several deportations in hand, and more to follow, for their own authorities to deal with, after further investigation by his colleagues.

He was most satisfied with the results and proud of his people in all departments, from the security squads in the field to the listening and de-coding people in his own departments.

Which reminded him of Anne's part in this and previous success's; also that he should telephone her about Toby and Joseph's improvement.

Picking up the secure phone he dialled her number and was pleased when it was she who answered. "Good morning Anne, for once I have some good news for you, I'm sure you will be pleased to know that the hospital tells us Toby and Joseph are both improving considerably, and there is high hope for their long term recovery."

Anne let out a sigh of relief, saying “Oh Director! That is, very good news, I have been so concerned that there may be long term damage to them, could I at least send them a ‘get well’ message do you think?” He chuckled, and said “I suppose you won’t give up, so if you send it to the hospital, addressed;

‘Care of the Sister on Grosvenor Ward’, I’ll see that it is directed to their room. Then, you must wait until he comes home.”

She said “Thank you, now may I ask you a sensitive question Director? Do you know what caused them to pick that particular car?”

There was a pause as he considered his answer, knowing what she had in mind, and then replied,

“I can assure you that it was just unfortunate, they had simply connected the car to our Ministry somehow and waited until it contained what appeared to be a V.I.P. The bomber was just a small time fanatic, looking to ingratiate himself to his handlers, who were using him as an expendable test of security?” Anne was aware that he was putting the best possible face on the whole episode for her sake, but was grateful anyway. She now thanked him for letting her know about ‘the boys’ as she put it, and replaced the phone, feeling somewhat relieved.

As was the Director, as he replaced the phone thinking, ‘that was a close shave, he had put her mind at rest and what he had said was mostly true, but things could have been so very different’. He was adamant in his mind that from now on, he would not use her again, unless absolutely necessary, the risk to her safety was too great and her age was now a factor.

Yet what was now stored in their computer programmes, should decipher pretty well everything thrown at them from now on, thanks to her unique grasp of the worlds languages, and the detailed information recorded.

He needed to find a way of breaking the news to her, without upset, (he certainly wouldn't be mentioning the age part)? That again reminded him that he must check with the Minister about her proposed Honour, and if she was going to the Palace, that of his own invitation?

Now he must start on what would be a very long and detailed report for that Gentleman and the Prime Minister; at least it would be a positive one for a change,

CHAPTER 23.

A few weeks later, Jack received a most unexpected letter addressed to him as Corporal N. Rogers, and carrying the Royal Signals Regimental insignia. It very grandly stated that: -

SDR927680 Corporal Jack Rogers is hereby released from the reserve status register as of this year end, and would no longer be required for current 'Special Duties'. Accordingly your special pay arrangement for those duties will end on that date; After which date a final severance cheque will be sent to you.

The Regiment would like to thank you for carrying out those duties when asked, to the best of your abilities and wish you luck for the future.

Signed; Lieutenant Colonel W. Knightly. M.C.

ROYAL SIGNALS REGIMENT

Jack was amused by the official tone of the letter, but realised that it was their way of breaking his connection with them, without the need of further personal contact. This letter would not mean anything to others who may get to read it, yet a further meeting between them could be scrutinised, if they were aware of Bill's connection with Army intelligence.

But much more importantly, it meant that Anne was no longer in danger, in their opinion. This information would have come from Anne's boss, which was most encouraging.

This was even more so after the recent attack on Toby's car and its passengers. He could not discuss that with Anne, of course, as officially neither knew of the other's connection to security services. He presumed that she had been told she would no longer be required to travel into the Ministry for her advice, due to the possible risk involved.

However, she would now be kept occupied by her work as part of the new company, without the stress of worrying over the results of her previous secret work; as he knew she had been.

It also meant that they could both concentrate on that new enterprise, which was now building rapidly, needing much more attention in order to control the demand, without upsetting residents.

Indeed, one unfortunate aspect of the high throughput of business was an increase in car traffic within the square; although thankfully, access to the old school site was close to the entry into Windsor Square from the main road, so most of the square was not affected.

Jack had considered another Residents Association meeting to discuss this, but didn't think they would be keen, so soon after the last one. Also a general feeling of the majority appeared to be of the opinion that benefits of the new parking arrangements outweighed the disadvantages.

But it was something he must deal with; at least he now had Anne full time to look after the company books, leaving him to concentrate on organisation and best practice to keep clients happy.

He also still had his consultancy work to consider, enquiries were increasing now, as his name seemed to have been handed around London based Architects.

They needed his expertise to offer the best solutions, when building large new commercial developments; being required by planning authorities to provide parking space as part of their proposed plans.

The few jobs he had already completed had proved most lucrative; including the Major's carwash, (he had now paid up)!

So it looked as though his new future was now mapped out, and he was comfortable in his new life; Just as Anne appeared to be.

Thinking, 'It had all come about from that day when he wandered into Windsor Square, looking for accommodation'.

If he had believed in fate, it was certainly smiling on him that day. But helped a great deal by his intelligence bosses of course.

CHAPTER 24.

PROLOGUE.

It was some three months later that Anne's 'Honour' was to be presented by the Queen, and by co-incidence, Toby was to receive a Bravery award on the same day.

As she was driven into the palace in a limousine provided for her, with Jack by her side, she was happy to see The Director, The Minister of Defence and Toby, (who was now walking with the help of sticks) waiting to greet her by the rear palace steps; looking rather like a welcoming committee.

'Thank goodness I shan't need to be alone today' she thought, 'it was going to be enough of an ordeal otherwise'

Alighting from the car, as the door was opened for her by a Palace attendant, and dressed in a 'New Posh Frock' (as her husband John had once said), she was warmly greeted by them, and even gave Toby a little hug, most unlike her, but she was so very pleased to see him after all this time.

As the day went on, they were very well treated by the Royal attendants who were obviously well versed in these occasions, until eventually the dreaded moment came for the investiture itself.

Having been announced grandly as "Mrs. Eden-Smythe C.B.E. and now for Services to The Crown"

She stepped forward to receive the Citation.

On receiving the designated award from Her Majesty; and as they were shaking hands, Anne was most surprised when the Queen said quietly, "May I thank you personally for your part in avoiding a near catastrophe, including my husband and I?" Anne was so taken aback, that all she could manage in reply was, "It was a very small part Your Majesty, but thankyou."

A day to remember for all concerned finally came to an end, and Anne's limousine arrived to transport her and Jack home in regal style.

For safety sake she could not travel with her colleagues by showing any connection with them outside the palace gates.

So Dame Anne Eden-Smythe C.B.E. arrived home in style, she thanked the driver, and Jack let her 'Ladyship' (with a small sardonic bow!), into the secure comfort of her own house.

Relieved that it was all over at last, she could now relax, and kick off her new shoes, telling Jack that she was just going up to change, but would be back down to enjoy some well deserved wine?

Meanwhile Jack was arranging a small celebration with a good bottle of Champagne and Crystal Flute glasses, (all of which he had set to cool, before they left for the Palace,) for just this time!

Thinking; 'I hope this is the right time to put my proposal to her?'

It could be the start of a whole new lifestyle! (**Or not?)**

But it was THE END of a GREAT DAY.

Printed in Great Britain
by Amazon